Catherine Cookson was h[...]
daughter of a poverty-s[...]
believed to be her older si[...]
eventually moved south [...], where she met and
married Tom Cookson, a local grammar-school master. At
the age of forty she began writing about the lives of the
working-class people with whom she had grown up, using the
place of her birth as the background to many of her novels.

Although originally acclaimed as a regional writer – her novel
The Round Tower won the Winifred Holtby award for the
best regional novel of 1968 – her readership soon began to
spread throughout the world. Her novels have been translated
into more than a dozen languages and more than 50,000,000
copies of her books have been sold in Corgi alone. Many of
her novels have been made into successful television dramas,
and more are planned.

Catherine Cookson's many bestselling novels established her
as one of the most popular of contemporary women novelists.
After receiving an OBE in 1985, Catherine Cookson was
created a Dame of the British Empire in 1993. She was
appointed an Honorary Fellow of St Hilda's College, Oxford
in 1997. For many years she lived near Newcastle-upon-Tyne.
She died shortly before her ninety-second birthday in June
1998 having completed 104 works, nine of which are being
published posthumously.

'Catherine Cookson's novels are about hardship, the intract-
ability of life and of individuals, the struggle first to survive
and next to make sense of one's survival. Humour, toughness,
resolution and generosity are Cookson virtues, in a world
which she often depicts as cold and violent. Her novels are
weighted and driven by her own early experiences of
illegitimacy and poverty. This is what gives them power. In
the specialised world of women's popular fiction, Cookson
has created her own territory'
Helen Dunmore, *The Times*

BOOKS BY CATHERINE COOKSON

NOVELS

Kate Hannigan
The Fifteen Streets
Colour Blind
Maggie Rowan
Rooney
The Menagerie
Slinky Jane
Fanny McBride
Fenwick Houses
Heritage of Folly
The Garment
The Fen Tiger
The Blind Miller
House of Men
Hannah Massey
The Long Corridor
The Unbaited Trap
Katie Mulholland
The Round Tower
The Nice Bloke
The Glass Virgin
The Invitation
The Dwelling Place
Feathers in the Fire
Pure as the Lily
The Mallen Streak
The Mallen Girl
The Mallen Litter
The Invisible Cord
The Gambling Man
The Tide of Life
The Slow Awakening
The Iron Façade
The Girl
The Cinder Path
Miss Martha Mary Crawford
The Man Who Cried
Tilly Trotter
Tilly Trotter Wed
Tilly Trotter Widowed

The Whip
Hamilton
The Black Velvet Gown
Goodbye Hamilton
A Dinner of Herbs
Harold
The Moth
Bill Bailey
The Parson's Daughter
Bill Bailey's Lot
The Cultured Handmaiden
Bill Bailey's Daughter
The Harrogate Secret
The Black Candle
The Wingless Bird
The Gillyvors
My Beloved Son
The Rag Nymph
The House of Women
The Maltese Angel
The Year of the Virgins
The Golden Straw
Justice is a Woman
The Tinker's Girl
A Ruthless Need
The Obsession
The Upstart
The Branded Man
The Bonny Dawn
The Bondage of Love
The Desert Crop
The Lady on My Left
The Solace of Sin
Riley
The Blind Years
The Thursday Friend
A House Divided
Kate Hannigan's Girl
Rosie of the River
The Silent Lady

THE MARY ANN STORIES

A Grand Man
The Lord and Mary Ann
The Devil and Mary Ann
Love and Mary Ann

Life and Mary Ann
Marriage and Mary Ann
Mary Ann's Angels
Mary Ann and Bill

FOR CHILDREN

Matty Doolin
Joe and the Gladiator
The Nipper
Rory's Fotune
Our John Willie

Mrs Flannagan's Trumpet
Go Tell It To Mrs Golightly
Lanky Jones
Nancy Nutall and the Mongrel
Bill and the Mary Ann Shaughnessy

AUTOBIOGRAPHY

Our Kate
Catherine Cookson Country
Just a Saying

Let Me Make Myself Plain
Plainer Still

SHORT STORIES

The Simple Soul and other Stories

A Ruthless Need

Catherine Cookson

CORGI BOOKS

A RUTHLESS NEED
A CORGI BOOK : 0 552 14039 2

Originally published in Great Britain by Bantam Press,
a division of Transworld Publishers

PRINTING HISTORY
Bantam Press edition published 1995
Corgi edition published 1996

5 7 9 10 8 6

Set in 10½/12½pt Monotype Bulmer by
Phoenix Typesetting, Ilkley, West Yorkshire.

Corgi Books are published by Transworld Publishers,
61–63 Uxbridge Road, London W5 5SA,
a division of The Random House Group Ltd,
in Australia by Random House Australia (Pty) Ltd,
20 Alfred Street, Milsons Point, Sydney, NSW 2061, Australia,
in New Zealand by Random House New Zealand Ltd,
18 Poland Road, Glenfield, Auckland 10, New Zealand
and in South Africa by Random House (Pty) Ltd,
Endulini, 5a Jubilee Road, Parktown 2193, South Africa.

Printed and bound in Great Britain by
Cox & Wyman Ltd, Reading, Berkshire

Parting is all we know of heaven
and all we need of hell.
Emily Dickinson 1830–1886

PART ONE

On Leave, 1937

1

'Oh, you do look funny, Geoff; like one of those comic spies at the pictures: long black mac and black cap. They don't look like that on your father.'

'They do, but you're used to him.'

'Anyway, why do you want to put them on? It's a dark night and it isn't raining.'

'Well, for your information—' the tall young man leaned down towards his mother whose head just reached his shoulder, and in a confidential whisper, he said, '—it's like this, Mrs Fulton, I've been four years in the army now as you know, but in the first few weeks my dear corporal instilled into me that I had to make all me bits of brass shine, like the good book tells us, as a light before us. That was in the daytime, like. Then what d'you think the silly so-and-so said after that? "The moon shines bright on Tommy Atkins," he said, "so no matter what the silly bugger of a science master might have told you, bullets don't bounce off brass. Therefore, you lot of so-and-so idiots, muck 'em up or cover 'em up before you brave the night." '

'Oh, you!' His mother, who had been leaning on a walking stick, now hung it on the back of a chair, before gripping the lapels of the black mackintosh in an endeavour to shake her son, saying, 'You don't change, do you? Joke, joke, joke. And anyway, now that you're a sergeant, what d'you tell the lads under you?'

Catching hold of her hands, he brought them together, and, using a more serious tone, said, 'I would never dream of telling the boys anything. You don't tell them today, you ask them. Private Reginald Johnson Smith, do you mind if I ask you to keep your kit a little tidier, as an example, you know, to the rest of the boys?'

'Oh, you!' she said again as she pulled her hands away from his; then, grabbing her stick, she turned from him, adding, 'Sometimes I would like you to be serious for five minutes and tell me what really happens.'

As she hobbled up the room he stared after her. From the back she could be taken for a young girl. She had always been slim and bonny, petite was the word. He could remember how she looked when he was twelve. He had always been proud of her, comparing her with the mothers of the other fellows at school. And when, as sometimes occurred, she was out riding and called at the school and pulled him up beside her, he would be transported to an age when knights in armour rescued ladies by yanking them up on to the saddle and galloping off with them. It didn't matter, in his particular case, that it was a lady who had done the pulling; it had still given him a wonderful feeling. Then one day she had ridden too fast and tried too high a jump. The result could have been worse, she could have been on her back for life; as it was, her hip was irrevocably injured, and as time went by arthritis had set in. Yet, she had, outwardly at least, always remained cheerful; what she went through privately he could only guess. However, she had one consolation: besides having a loving husband, she had her music.

As she sat down on the piano stool, she said on a laugh, 'You don't expect to catch Ted Honeysett, do you?'

'What d'you think I'm going out for?' He walked towards her. 'I tell you, there he was yesterday, as brazen as brass, unstrapping a big attaché case from the carrier of his bike and carrying it round the back of the hotel in Durham, as barefaced as you like. And then, back he came, still with the case, looking as smug as a cat that had pinched the cream.'

'I can't imagine Ted Honeysett looking smug. Anyway, what would you do if you were to catch him?'

'Put the fear of God into him.'

'Oh, now,' – she cast her eyes upwards while her pursed lips expressed her derision – 'you've known Ted all your life. Can you imagine anyone putting the fear of God into him?'

'Yes; yes, I can. There's different ways of doing it. For instance, I could threaten to frog-march him up to the Hall.'

'Huh!' She shook her head as she laughed. 'I can see you doing that. What would more likely be in your mind, if I know anything, would be to frog-march Mr Ernest Bradford-Brown down to the river and hold him under.'

'I've been away four years, Mam, don't forget. A lot can happen in that time. I might have changed me tune about that gentleman.'

She smiled, saying, 'Not you. Do you remember what you said to him when you walked out of the Hall yard, and where you told him to put his job? And you only eighteen at the time. And you know something?' Her face lost its smile and she nodded

11

up at him seriously as she went on, 'He would have sent your dad packing if it wasn't that he relies on him so much. Oh, yes, it was touch and go. And another thing I'll tell you, it's a good job this house was not within the boundary of the estate, or like the Rice family we would have been turfed out. He can't stomach the fact that we own it. He's forever on to your dad to sell it. I think that's another reason he kept him on, because after you caused that explosion, and it *was* an explosion, the rest of the men stood out for more pay. They didn't get all they wanted, but they got something, and he gave in only because he didn't want his name to be any blacker than it already was. And look what he did to the Rices. If they hadn't left willingly or, let's say, quietly, he would have sacked the lot: Peter, young Michael, and Sally an' all. And jobs not coming easy, and Bella being poorly as she is, what could they do but go? And all because weekend cottages were bringing in money. He hadn't spent a penny on that place in years, but once he got them out he had water laid on, and electricity, and God knows what. And you know how much he got for it, together with an acre of land and fishing rights?'

'No.'

'Four thousand pounds. A man called Kidderly bought it. He only comes up at weekends. A bit of a queer 'un from what I can gather. Anyway,' – she smiled again – 'if you're going to nab Ted, I think you'd better get moving, or it'll be midnight before you get back.'

She watched him pick up a piece of sheet music and flip over the page, and when he said, 'Oh, it doesn't matter. I could change me mind,' she made no immediate comment, but continued to stare at him for a few seconds, when she asked quietly, 'What is it? Bored?'

He turned towards her. 'Yes, I suppose you could say that . . . a bit.'

'Why don't you go down to The Hare and have a chat with the men?'

'Oh, Mam,' – he jerked his square jaw upwards – 'I've been down twice within the last five days, and what had I to listen to? Ronald Coleman trying to emulate his namesake, and telling of his conquests round about. It seems the further away he goes the more lurid his affairs. And Peter Campbell bragging about laying more bricks in an hour than you could find in the Walls of Jericho. Oh, and May—' his tone changed – 'dear May, behind the bar, pushing the pint pots across the counter with her bust. Eeh!' He shook his head as he solemnly went on, 'I don't know how she does it. She must have 'em stuffed. They couldn't have grown to that size by themselves, now could they? What a pity my lads can't see her; they'd go AWOL just for a peep at them. And then there's her 'Arry aiming to keep the drop off his nose as he pulls a pint . . .'

'Oh, don't! Don't!' Bertha Fulton was now hugging her waist, and the tears of laughter were on her cheeks as she gasped, 'Is that how you see them?'

'That's how they are, Mam; nothing's changed. And there are those who drop in while passing and hoping to see the forelocks being touched. Hobson and Ryebank are the worst. They groan about the responsibility of farming, and the starvation prices they're getting for their crops. Yet Hobson, I notice, has put up a magnificent barn, and Ryebank is getting

13

some new-fangled apparatus into his cow-byres for milking. Poor starving, middle-class buggers.'

After a moment Bertha slowly dried her eyes and, her voice quiet now, she stated flatly, 'You wish your leave was up, don't you? and you were on your way.'

'*No, no,* Mam. No, I don't.' He came quickly to her side now and, dropping down on his hunkers before her, he gripped her hands as he said, 'You and Dad are the only stable things in my life; and every leave I hope to find nothing more has changed. But when I do, I mean outside, roundabout, I become irritated to the point of hitting out . . . bashing. I suppose it's because of what I've seen and learned while I've been away. Life's different out there. This hamlet could be on another planet. Do you know that, Mam?'

Bertha looked down at their joined hands and asked quietly, 'Would it have been different if you hadn't heard that Janis Bradford-Brown was engaged?'

Slowly he relinquished his hold on her and straightened up; and now he pulled at the lapels of his father's coat and buttoned one side under the collar as he said, 'Oh, Mam, what are you talking about? That was a dream.'

'I don't think it was so much of a dream two years ago.'

'Of course it was.' He brought his thick dark brows together until they hooded his deep-set brown eyes as he retorted, 'What chance was there of that? It was a bit of light entertainment for both of us. Secret excitement to break the monotony. It started again when I was sixteen; you know it did. It was the fact that we were hoodwinking her dear papa that kept us both at it, for

14

she had no more love for him than I had, of that I'm sure. And just think what would have happened if he had got an inkling of it then. That kept us on our toes. So rest your mind easy there, Mam.' He nodded down at her, and she, looking up at him now, asked, 'Then why did it go on so long?'

His chin knobbled and he drew the side of his forefinger underneath his large thin nose as he replied, 'Still the same, excitement I suppose, and with me being a soldier, brave and defiant like . . . you remember me little song?' He now sang in a clear tenor voice:

'I'm not afraid of anything,
And some things I know I oughter,
But I'm scared to death to hold me breath,
Ooh! under the wa . . . ater.'

'Go on with you! Get yourself out.'
'You don't mind being alone?'
'Yes, I do. I miss your dad very much. It's the first time he's been away at night for years. Of course Henry would have to die when you were on leave. Henry always did things at inconvenient moments. I bet his last words to your dad were, "Why had you to go and get married?" He's never forgiven him for getting married, you know. Having brought up your dad, he imagined he was his mother and father combined. There's one thing I'm sure of: your dad won't get a penny of his savings and scrapings over the years, for the simple reason I might spend it . . . Look, are you going or are you not? I want to get to bed sometime tonight.'
'There's no need for you to stay up.'

'I'm staying up until you come back. Go on. At least take a walk and blow the cobwebs away. Go on,' she finished softly now.

He nodded at her; then went down the long, narrow room, across an equally long and narrow hall and into the stone-flagged kitchen, out of the back door and into the large, paved yard, bordered by what at one time had been horse-boxes and byres.

He did not take the short drive that led to the road, but crossed the yard and through into a field. Flashing his torch, he made his way across the meadow, all that was left of the once prosperous farm that had belonged to his maternal grandfather.

He leapt the boundary dry-stone wall to land in a narrow lane, bordered on the far side by a rough hedge overgrowing wire fencing.

He paused for a moment, undecided whether to enter the private grounds through one of the gaps in the hedge or just to take a stroll along the road.

If he decided to follow his first thought and managed to nab Ted, that would be something to laugh about. His father had never managed to do it; at least, he said he hadn't; but his mother said his dad had caught the poacher on more than one occasion, but had let him go with a caution because of the squad of young children he had to bring up. But that was some time ago, for Billy, his eldest, was now seventeen, Arthur was sixteen, and Katy fifteen, and they were all in work. There were another three still at school, and younger ones still; yet things were always bleak in the winter. In the spring and summer the farms offered 'the weasel', as he was known locally, plenty of odd jobs, but it was well known that Ted never did anything above board if he could manage it underhand, and trout and salmon poaching was quite a lucrative underhand business, and Ted was an expert at it.

The river had been running high and the bridge at Warren Corner would be the place Ted would likely make for. It was just below Rice's old cottage which, according to his mother, now housed the weekend countryman.

As he got through the fence he naturally asked himself what would happen if, accidentally, he should bump into any of those from the house, even the lord of the manor himself. Well, he could say he was taking his father's place for that evening and seeing all was well. What else?

When he reached the rough path bordering the river, he knew he might as well shine a light on himself, because the dark blur of him would be standing against the night, and if he wished to reach the bridge un-noticed, he would have to skirt the back of the cottage.

He kept well into the tree-covered verge until he came to the railings surrounding the cottage where, thinking he heard someone shout, he stopped for a moment.

There was no wind, not even a susurration in the branches of the trees, and the silence was thick and heavy about him, until he went to step forward, when again he heard the sound; something between a cry and a shout. It occurred to him that perhaps the new owner had brought a female visitor with him and that they weren't seeing eye to eye; or they might even be having a bit of a romp.

He continued to move round by the railings until again he was almost at the river's edge, when once more he was brought to a halt by a cry coming from the cottage, and this time he knew by the sound that whoever was inside certainly wasn't enjoying the weekend.

From where he was standing he could see a light streaming from one of the downstairs windows, but he was too far away to make out anyone inside.

To reach any cover the bridge might afford so that he should not be spotted by Ted meant negotiating the ten yards or so of open ground.

His back was stooped and he was lifting one cautious foot forward when he was startled by a combination of cries, which straightened him up and around to peer over the railings and across the lawn to where the front door of the cottage had been wrenched open and was showing, silhouetted against the light, two struggling figures.

A young voice in a high plea, crying, 'No, no! Let me go. I tell you, no, no! I won't!' came to him, and from where he stood he could see the small figure of a girl struggling in the arms of a man who was trying to drag her back into the cottage.

Instead of running back alongside the fence and to the gate, he leapt the railings, and within a dozen strides reached the struggling pair. He saw immediately that the man was naked to the waist, and it was he who now let out a startled cry as he found his throat wedged in the iron grip of an arm. The next minute he was swung about and a blow caught him in his soft belly, before another under the chin lifted him and sent him sprawling on to his back.

Geoff now turned to the cringing girl who was leaning against the door post, clutching the front of her torn dress with both hands, and when, bending

18

to her, he muttered, 'You all right?' she shivered and gulped in her throat.

Putting his hand gently on her shoulder, he turned her about to face the light streaming from the doorway, and he said, 'You're one of the Gillespies, aren't you?'

She gulped again and slowly nodded.

'What are you doing here at this time of night, eh?'

When she did not answer, he said, 'Come on. Have you a coat?'

At this, she turned from him and stumbled back into the room. Meanwhile, he walked towards the prostrate figure lying sprawled on the rough slabs that fronted the porch. He did not kneel down by the man, nor put an ear to his heart but, bending, he placed his hand on the man's ribs and left it there for a moment before removing it and nodding to himself.

The girl had returned, hugging a coat around her, so he went towards her and, with one helping hand, propelled her towards the gate.

Once outside he said, 'Come on; I'll see you home to your mother.'

Of course he knew that Minnie Gillespie wasn't the girl's mother, but her stepmother, and he also knew that Arthur Gillespie had absconded last year, leaving his second wife with her own three youngsters and one she'd had by him, as well as the two girls he'd had by his first wife.

'Which one of the two are you?' he asked.

'I'm Lizzie,' she said. Then glancing back towards the cottage, she muttered, 'Is he dead?'

'No; he'll survive. Come on now, let's get moving; your mother'll be worrying. What are you doing here at this time of the night, anyway?'

She did not answer but began to walk slowly by his side, and he repeated, 'I asked, what are you doing here at this time of night?'

'She sent me.'

'Sent you? What for?'

'Take . . . take him a pie.'

'Oh!' He looked ahead now as he asked, 'Why couldn't she send you in the daylight?'

When she didn't answer, he added, 'Or your other sister.'

'Midge ran off last month.'

'Oh,' followed by a long pause before he asked, 'Did your mother send Midge with the pies?'

There was another pause, before her voice, small now, answered, 'Yes.'

'How often did Midge go to the cottage?'

'She used to clean it at night-times after she had finished at Bexley's shop in the hamlet.'

'What made her run off?'

And the brief answer was, 'Him. She didn't like being messed about.'

'God!' He muttered the word aloud.

He knew all about Minnie Gillespie, Collier as was. She was a slut, but he hadn't thought she was that kind of a slut. He understood she had married when she was seventeen and that her first man had led her a life, and it was this that had driven her to drink. But then, she was the kind, he judged, that would have taken to drink in any case. Anyway, what she did to herself was her own affair, but to peddle these two lasses was a different kettle of fish.

'How often have you been there?'

' 'Twas me first time.'

20

'Did you expect him to maul you?'

'*No.*' Her voice was high. '*No.*'

'Did your sister not say what happened when she went there . . . with a pie on a Saturday night?'

It was a moment before she answered, 'No. She never told me nothing, except that she didn't like being messed about; but I thought it was about the work, him being finicky, like. He paid her five shillings.'

'My! My! Five shillings.'

There was something in his voice that made her retort, 'Well, she tidied up and all that. She was good at housework.'

I bet she was, he said to himself; then he asked her, 'How old are you?'

'Fourteen.'

'You left school?'

'Yes, just.'

'What are you going to do?'

'She says I've got to go to her sister's in Gateshead and into a factory. You can get fifteen shillings a week.'

'Do you want to go there?'

'*No. No.* It's worse than here. It's mucky round about; and she's awful, worse. I mean, her sister. There's nine of them. But there's no work round here. Mrs Bexley took on somebody else after Midge left. And Mam says she wants half me pay, 'cos I've got to help keep them because of me dad goin' off, and now Midge, and the other half 'll go to her sister.'

They had left the river bank, cut up through a wood and had reached the main road, when he stopped and said, 'You'll be all right now.'

She looked up at him but could not see his face, which seemed lost between the turned-up collar of his coat and the peak of his cap, and she asked, 'Who are you then?'

'Oh,' his voice came lightly; 'I'm a knight in shining armour, only me coat's covering it.'

'You live round here?'

'Yes. Yes, I live round here. I usually ride me horse at this time of night, but he's got a sore foot.'

'You're jokin'.' Her voice sounded flat, and he said, 'Aye, I'm joking.' And now he asked, 'D'you expect to be belted when you get in?'

He saw the faint blur of her face move, and then she said, 'She'll try it on; but I told her if she hits me again, I'd do what Midge did. But then' – she paused – 'I wouldn't, I couldn't; I've got nowhere to go.'

'Had Midge somewhere to go?'

'Aye, in Newcastle. She has friends. She wouldn't tell me about them, but she said she'll write, an' she will. If she says she'll do a thing, she will. Midge is like that. She told me she was goin' to go off weeks ago.'

'But you have no friends?'

'Oh aye, roundabout; but . . . but not that I could go to . . . I mean, that she couldn't get at me, if I went there.'

'So you'll go to work in the factory in Gateshead?'

'. . . Aye, I suppose so.'

'When do you expect to go?'

'She's waiting word from her sister when there's a place open.'

'Then I might see you about?'

'How would I know you?'

22

'That'll be all right, 'cos I'll know you. And anyway, you'll recognise me 'cos I'll have me horse with me, although he'll still be limping.'

'You are funny, aren't you?'

'That's what they say. Go on home now, and stick up for yourself.'

'Ta-ra.'

'Ta-ra.' He stood watching the small figure fade into the darkness before he turned slowly and walked towards home. About half a mile along the road and nearing Grant's Corner, where the telephone kiosk stood, he saw the flickering light of a torch, which was nothing unusual: somebody was coming out of the kiosk after phoning. The figure approached, and presently a torch was flashed in his face and a well-recognised thin voice that matched the body whence it came said, 'Out for a stroll then, Geoff?'

He paused for a moment before answering, 'Yes, you could say that, Mr Honeysett. Like yourself, I've been out for a stroll.'

'Funny things happen on strolls. Guess what I've just been phonin' about?'

'Haven't a clue, Mr Honeysett.'

'Found that weekend countryman in a bad stew outside his place. Jaw broke I would think, an' he could hardly crawl. Just phoned for doctor. Thought it best. Somebody went at him in no small way, I would say, to break his jaw. What d'you say?'

'I would say the same as you, Mr Honeysett. You can't get a broken jaw unless you come in contact with something hard.'

'You're right there. You're right there. I wonder how he came by it?'

'I've no idea. Out for a stroll, just as you said. When I'm not fightin' for me King and country I like peace.'

A throaty laugh filled the night air. It rose into a cackle, then broke off to a splutter. 'If I remember rightly, you weren't much for peace in your young days, not that they're very far behind you. I hear you're a sergeant now an' goin' abroad soon?'

'Yes, that's what they say, Mr Honeysett.'

'I thought for a moment it was your dad comin' along there. He always smothers himself up when doing his rounds. Why? It beats me, 'cos he takes elephant-size boots an' you can hear him comin' a mile off. Well, I must get back and see how that bloke's farin'. Likely a hospital job, 'cos his bottom teeth were almost stuck up his nose. Be seeing you, then.'

'Be seeing you, Mr Honeysett.'

They were going their different ways when Geoffrey's step was checked just the slightest as the poacher's voice came to him, saying softly, 'Goose grease does a power of good rubbed into skinned knuckles.'

Geoffrey lowered his head, bit tightly on his lip to stop his mouth opening to give vent to his laughter, then resumed his walk. You couldn't help but like the old rascal. He must have watched the whole affair. Perhaps he had known what was going on before he himself arrived. Yet, no; having daughters of his own, he wouldn't have stood for that. He now made a derisive sound: there he was, thinking he was clever enough to trail the old codger without being seen, when likely he was spotted soon after he entered the grounds . . .

He heard the music before he opened the gate and went up the drive. He stood for a moment outside the sitting-room window listening to it. She was playing a piece of Grieg; really playing it. Although she had given him lessons since he was six years old and he had practised regularly until he started work up at the house when he was fourteen, he still had little feeling for music, and he knew this had disappointed her. Technically, he played correctly. His playing he often compared to a man in the army. The army could make any man into a soldier if he stuck to the rules and obeyed orders, but to be a good soldier you had to have that something more; your heart had to be in it. His heart, unlike his mother's, was not in music.

When he entered the sitting-room his mother stopped playing and twisted round on the stool as she said, 'Well, did you catch him?'

'I wouldn't say I caught him, but we had a talk.'

'You talked with him?' She pulled herself upwards, grabbed at her stick and hobbled towards him and repeated, 'You talked with him?'

'Yes. What's strange in that? We had quite a long natter.'

'What about?'

'Oh, it's a long story. There I was taking a quiet stroll down by the river . . . By the way, have you any coffee going?'

She nodded. 'It's in the percolator . . . but tell me what happened?'

'Let me get a drink first. On second thoughts, no, I think I'll have something hard.' He walked towards the cabinet at the other side of the room and poured himself out a good measure of whisky; then returning

25

to where she was now seated to the side of the fire, he took the chair opposite and, after a sip at the glass, he asked, 'Know anything about Arthur Gillespie's two lasses? His own two, not hers?'

'Only gossip that the older one, Midge, had run away. She was always a flighty bit, and well developed, I'd say. That's when I last saw her; must be all of a year ago. They rarely come this end. Why do you ask about them?'

'I met the younger one tonight; the one called Lizzie.'

'The young one out and about at this time of night in the dark?'

'Aye, out and about at this time of night in the dark. Disgraceful, isn't it? But it's a further disgrace when she's sent whoring and doesn't know anything about it.'

'*What?*' She sounded shocked and she screwed up her unwrinkled face in protest, saying, 'How do you come by that?'

So he told her all that had transpired, and when he had finished she remained silent for a moment. And then it wasn't about the girl that she spoke, but about himself. 'What would have happened,' she said, 'if you had knocked him out, really knocked him out . . . killed him?'

'I would have likely had to stand the consequences, and I'm sure the judge would have recognised extenuating circumstances, because,' – and now the lightness went out of his voice – 'that lass knew nothing about it. You know what I mean? The way she fought. And how long he had been at her before she managed to open the door I don't know; but I first heard her yelling

26

as I passed along the back way, yet never imagined what it was all about. That woman should be had up.'

'Indeed she should. The authorities should be told.'

'Yes. But what would happen then?'

'Oh,' – Bertha considered a moment – 'if it was proved that she had been used like, I suppose, her sister was, the girl could be put into care.'

'I doubt if she'd like that. She's fourteen.' He drained his glass of the whisky; then placing it on a side table, he said quietly, 'I was doing a bit of thinking coming along the road. Yesterday you were talking about having help. Dad's been at you for years now. You'll need somebody soon to give you a hand. This is no small house: there's still five rooms upstairs and four down, apart from all the offshoots. How would it be if you took the lass on?'

'You mean the Lizzie one?'

'Aye. Aye, I mean the Lizzie one; I wouldn't know where to find the other one. I could look.'

'Oh, be serious. You're asking me to house one of Gillespie's crowd. She's a known slut and the house is like a pigsty.'

'Those two lasses don't belong to her, and I've heard you say Arthur Gillespie was a decent enough fellow. He likely couldn't stand any more and that's why he did a bunk. And what's more, I think she gives the girl a pretty rough time. She said she warned her stepmother that if she was hit again she would run off, like her sister . . . You could do worse; there's not many young lasses round here looking for housework. It's the same now as it was before I left; they want to go into fancy shops or learn to type; housework's beneath them. And anyway,' – he leaned towards her – 'it'll be one less worry on me mind if I know you've got company here when I'm away. And from what I've seen of her, or, at least, heard of her in the dark, she seems a sensible enough little lass.'

'I'll think on it. I'll sleep on it. Anyway, I think your dad should be given a say in this.'

'Oh, don't be silly, Mam.' He got to his feet. 'Dad's been at you for years, as I've told you.'

'Aye, he has, but it's one of the Gillespies, and he knows them better than I do, or you, either; he gets about. And if she's been brought up along of that woman you don't know what she's picked up, I mean, in the way of manners and things.'

'Well, you're the one to alter that, aren't you? Manners and things, not forgetting morals. My! *I'll* say. Sergeant-major-first-class-Fulton.'

'Oh, go on with you.' She flapped her hand at him. 'Get yourself to bed.'

'Aren't you coming up?'

'No, I don't feel tired,' she said, and stood up. 'I'm going to have a little more ding-dong. I'll put you to sleep. Good night.'

He put his arms around her and held her tightly for a moment, and after kissing her on the cheek he went slowly from the room.

Left alone, she did not immediately return to the piano but sat down again in the chair. Her hands joined in her lap, she gazed into the fire. A young lass in the house, someone to direct and train. The thought had been in her mind for a long time, but she had shied from it, asking herself, where, these days, would she get a young lass willing to be trained, and one who might even like to be taught the piano? She

28

had always wanted to teach, but there was no-one interested around these parts. And it was too far out for anyone to come from the town. And with him now going across the seas to a foreign country the hole that he would leave in her heart would widen and there would be nothing to fill it but his letters. Even John, as much as she loved him, would not be able to close the gap. Anyway, he was out at his work for most of the day and often till late in the evening. But if there was somebody else in the house, a young lass that needed to be checked and told and trained, and talked to in a friendly way, the days ahead might not be so long and empty.

John had suggested that they get another dog, because Betsy was so old now that she didn't even bother to bark. She didn't even bother to run when she saw a rabbit, or go for the coalman, as she used to do. She lay out there on her straw bed waiting for her time to come, and John refused to hasten it by taking her to the vet. You could love a dog and talk to it, but unfortunately it couldn't talk to you, except with a lick or a paw.

Yes, she would think about what Geoff had suggested . . . yes, she would.

2

Geoff's nose twitched as he passed the woman to
enter the cottage room. She had been reluctant to let
him in until he said, 'Would you rather I went to the
authorities, those who deal with child welfare?'

Now he was in the room returning the stares of the
children. To his military ordered mind the room was
a shambles, and to his mind that had been trained in
the tidy, scrupulously clean ways of his mother the
place was a dirty disgrace. He saw immediately that
it was used as kitchen, living-room, and bedroom,
for two children were still in a shakedown bed in
the far corner of the room. Two boys were standing
together looking at him. One could have been about
twelve, although he was thin and puny-looking, the
other was a little chap, five or six; he had a bright
round face and a sturdy body. But standing near the
far end of the table was the girl, Lizzie. After one
quick glance at him when he had entered the room,
she hung her head and went on cutting thick slices
of bread from a long loaf. His eyes lingered on her
for a while and he noticed that although her brown
hair hung down the side of her face, it did not cover
a dark bruise on her cheek-bone.

The woman now spoke to the elder boy, nodding
towards the bed as she said, 'Take them into t'other
room.' And after a moment's hesitation, he turned

and beckoned to the two girls in the bed, and they scrambled out and followed him, as did the young boy.

A second after the children had entered the other room, her voice came as a bellow, 'Shut the door!' and then the door banged closed.

'What about her?' He motioned towards Lizzie, and the woman answered, 'What about her?'

'I'd like to speak to you alone.'

'She's no child, she's older than her years. Say what you've got to say.'

For answer he walked up to the table and touched Lizzie on the shoulder, saying quietly, 'Go on outside a minute.'

'Here! Here! Who the hell d'you think you are comin' in my house and orderin'. . .'

'Shut up!' He turned his head towards the woman, and stared her out for a moment; then he looked back at Lizzie, saying, 'Do as I say.' And she did. And when the door had closed on her he said to the woman, 'Perhaps I did the wrong thing in telling her to go, for she might have liked to hear me call you a dirty slut.'

'You! Who the hell d'you think you are?'

'I'll tell you who I think I am. I'm somebody who doesn't like to see young lasses sent along to old men for their pleasure at five bob a time. That's who I am. That's why her sister ran away, didn't she? She'd had enough.'

He watched the woman gulp in her throat, then push her fair hair back behind each ear before she said, 'I could take you to court. Yes, aye, I could. I could take you to court. That's slander.'

31

'Be quiet! Your name's no good. If I remember rightly you had the health people after you years ago for the way your bairns were sent to school. But putting them out as whores is a different kettle of fish and not looked upon kindly. If you're so badly in need of money why don't you keep at the game yourself; you've had the experience, haven't you?'

'*Look you here!* I'm standin' no more of this. And if you've heard about me, I've heard about you an' all, Mr high-and-mighty Fulton. 'Cos you've got a few bloody stripes on your arm you think you're God Almighty. An' what about last night, eh? 'Twas you, and they're lookin' for the man who did it, 'cos he's in hospital, Mr Kidderly is.'

'Well, then, why don't you go along and tell them? I'm quite willing to go into court and explain why I had to hit the bloke: it was just to save a young lass from being raped, with the knowledge of her mother of course. And your two stepdaughters would bear out my story. Oh, I know about the other one going off and nobody knows where she is, but she could easily be found. And the court would take into consideration that you have two more little girls and one, I imagine, not so young as she couldn't be trained by you. Anyway,' he pursed his lips, 'let's forget, or put to one side the recriminations, I'm here to bargain with you.'

His voice had sunk to a quiet and ordinary tone, and she stared at him for a moment, open-mouthed. Then her whole expression changed. The stiff, defiant look left her face, the fear that had been in the back of her eyes disappeared. Her head went back, her full-lipped mouth opened and she let out a high laugh. 'You're here to bargain with me!' she cried. 'My God! 'Cos you've heard I was hard to get by the locals an' I go further afield, you think you've got one on me, and you're missin' it, aren't you? because your fancy piece has gone and got herself . . .'

The fact that she had misunderstood his words brought him bending towards her, his lip curled, his voice a growl saying, 'Shut up! You stinking slut. Want you! I wouldn't touch you with a barge pole. Now listen, woman, and let me tell you why I'm here. My mother wants a young lass in the house to do housework and odd jobs. She wants her living in. She'll be trained and well looked after. I've come to tell you that she's offering the youngster the job. I'm also telling you that if you put up any obstacles, I go tomorrow to the authorities in Durham, come what may of it. Another thing I'll add, you won't get a penny of her pay; that'll be banked. And if you pester her in any way, my father will have instructions as to what to do. Now, take your choice.'

What she said now and through trembling lips that had lost their colour was, 'You'll get your deserts, one day; an' God, I hope I live to see it; in fact, I'll pray I live to see it. I will! I will!'

'That's if you pray.' He took two steps back from her, turned towards the door, opened it, then called, 'Lizzie!'

The girl came slowly into the room and stood to the side of the open fire. Her eyes were wide, her oval face looked pinched, and the dark bruise on her cheek was more evident now that her hair was hanging off her shoulders.

He looked from her to the woman, and when she didn't speak, he turned back to the girl and said, 'Get your things together.'

'*What?*' She stared up at him, then glanced at her stepmother as if expecting an explanation. But when the woman made no response she looked at him again and repeated, 'Get me things together?'

Now bending slightly towards her, he motioned his head sideways towards her stepmother as he said, 'It's been agreed that you will come and work for my mother. She's been looking for someone for a long time. It won't be hard; just housework and odd jobs.' He watched her mouth slowly fall open, then snap closed. Then without another word, she hurried across the room and pushed open the far door, through which there came to him a babble of voices.

During the time he was waiting for her return, which was not more than two minutes, he and the woman stared at each other in bitter hostility.

Lizzie came back into the room wearing a coat, and with a hat stuck on the back of her head. In her arms was a cardboard box that held her belongings. She walked straight towards him and stood by his side and the sight of her thus so happy to make her escape was too much for the woman. She stepped to the table, leaned over it and yelled at the girl, 'You'll be sorry for this! You see if you're not. What am I goin' to do with Joe? Who am I goin' to leave him with? Somebody's got to work for them. Your da wouldn't, the lazy good-for-nothing bugger. And you, and the other one, are like him. No good. Never were and never will be. And here's me that's had to work and bring you up. All my youth spent lookin' after the lot of you. And

34

he's your half-brother, Joe is. What about him? He's not all my responsibility, he's your da's and yours. But I can easily change that; I can put him in a home.'

At this Geoff felt the girl at his side tremble, and he put a hand on her shoulder as he said, 'Don't worry. Let her try. We'll see to that an' all.'

Now turning Lizzie about, he pressed her towards the door. Once outside, he took the cardboard box from her and put it under one arm and with his hand on her shoulder he walked her quietly away from the cottage . . .

They had gone a half mile perhaps in silence, and it was Lizzie who broke it, saying, 'She wouldn't do that to Joe, would she, put him in a home?'

'No, no; don't worry. Joe won't go in a home; I'll see to that.'

'But . . . but you won't be here. You're just on leave, aren't you? You're a soldier.'

'Aye, I'm just on leave, but my dad has some say round about.'

After a moment she spoke again, saying, 'I didn't know it was you at first last night, in that black coat and cap. I've seen you other times about with your uniform clothes on. You looked smart.'

In the ordinary way he would have answered to this, 'You should see me without them on; I look smarter still.' But this wasn't the time or place, and she wasn't old enough to engage in that sort of chit-chat. He said, 'You'll like it staying with my mother. She's a fine woman. She'll train you in lots of ways, good ways.'

'You've got a piano, haven't you?'

'Yes, we have a piano.'

'I've heard it sometimes when I've been passing the gate; not very loud, but I've heard it tinklin'.'

'Oh, you'll hear it tinkling at all times of the day, and sometimes till late at night. Mother's a great player. She loves her piano.'

'Must be wonderful to have a piano.'

He glanced down at her: she was looking ahead, the awe in her voice showing in her face. Her brown hair was pressed into a tangled mass by the pressure of her straw hat that was now pulled down about her ears. Her face was plain and she was no size for fourteen. He expected the first thing his mother would do, besides putting her to work, would be to feed her up.

He was surprised when she stopped suddenly, and turned to confront him, her tone demanding as she said, 'Who put you up to gettin' me this job? What I mean is, did your mother want somebody afore you thought of it? Well now—' she shook her head at herself, then added, 'What I mean to say is, why you doin' it?'

She watched him shut his eyes, press his lips together while his shoulders shook, and then, looking at her, his lids blinking rapidly, he said, 'Lizzie, I know what you mean, although I don't know which of the three parts of your question to answer first, but I'll put it like this. Never look a gift-horse in the mouth, 'cos remember, if it hasn't any teeth, it's still got four legs, and it has iron shoes on its feet into the bargain.'

'What?' Now her face was screwed up, but without laughter.

'Oh, come on.' He strolled ahead, and after a moment she hastened her steps and walked beside him.

They reached a bend in the road and were within a few yards of a bridle path when there emerged from it a young woman on horseback.

On the sight of her, Geoff halted for a second, which altered his stride and caused Lizzie to glance up at him. When they came abreast of the rider, he stopped, touched his cap and said, 'Good morning, Miss Brown.'

The young lady answered briefly, 'Good morning.' She did not add his name.

And now he cast a glance at Lizzie before looking again at the young woman and saying, 'Trespassers will be persecuted.'

And to this enigmatic statement the lady answered briefly, 'No.'

Once more he touched his cap and made to move off, at the same time saying, 'Oh, but yes, they will. Good morning, Miss Brown.'

Lizzie had to walk quickly now to keep up with him. She was puzzled: Miss Brown had been riding on a roadway, not in a field or anything, but he had said 'trespassers will be persecuted'. Shouldn't it have been 'prosecuted'? And that was Miss Bradford-Brown from The Hall; and he had spoken to her like that. She couldn't understand him, nothing about him, least of all why he had got her this job. Nevertheless, she was glad she was going to work in his mother's house because it was a nice place. And the Fultons were quite swanky. Well, they must be to have a piano.

But fancy saying to Miss Bradford-Brown that trespassers will be persecuted, because it had 'prosecuted' on the board along the road. He was a funny fellow.

3

'Well, how is she doing?'

'It's early days yet. It's really early hours to ask such a question.'

'You've had her in the kitchen, though; you should have got her measure there.'

'Yes, I have, and she'll have to be taught to wash up properly, not just dip dishes into the water and take them out again. What's caught her interest seems to be the piano. She keeps talking about it; that is, when she talks.'

'Well, that should please you. Anyway, on the whole, what do you think?'

'Oh.' Bertha shrugged and smiled. 'I'll make something of her. She seems canny enough. Where are you going now?' She looked at him as he did up the top button of his uniform.

'Oh, just for a stroll.'

'Your dad should be here any minute. His train gets in around five and it only takes him twenty minutes on his bike.'

'Twenty minutes now, is it. He used to do it in fifteen. Must be old age.' He pulled a face at her, then added, 'You never know on a Sunday when that train'll get in. I've known it ten or fifteen minutes late, so don't start worrying. Anyway, I thought I'd stretch me legs afore it gets dark.'

38

As he made for the door she called, 'Geoff!' and he turned as she added quietly, 'For the next day or two, stay close to him, will you? I mean, go round with him when you can. He's going to miss you. The Suez Canal isn't Catterick.'

'Don't worry.' He returned to her side and with a doubled fist gently pressed her chin upwards. 'Come on, where's that Fulton gumption? Anyway, I might meet an Egyptian lass out there and bring her home. What would you say to that?'

'I'd say, if you picked her, she must be right for you.'

They stared at each other for a moment, before he, turning from her, picked up his cap from the hallstand and went out. And she remained standing, one hand patting her lips. That wasn't true what she had said, if he picked her she would be right for him.

When he had first taken to following his dad round the estate, she had thought it so nice that he wanted to be with him, until one day John had laughingly said, 'I'm not the attraction, so much as the young miss on her pony.' She remembered she had said, 'Do you think *he* wants a pony?' And to this he had replied, 'Not at this stage. I think he's in love for the first time. It's like measles, we all get them, but it wears off.'

And it had seemed to wear off when he was fifteen, when not Janis Brown but Janis Bradford-Brown had come back from her boarding school on holiday all hoity-toity. But it had started again when he was sixteen. He had been working in the stables at Low Tarn Hall then, and had seen more of her. Oh indeed, he had seen more of her. His dad had said, 'Don't worry, it's calf-love. Anyway, nothing can come of that, and he knows it. He's sensible.'

Sensible. Had John himself been sensible when he came after *her*? Camping outside in the fields with that bossy brother of his from when he was a young lad, then trundling out here on his bike nearly every weekend, though knowing she might marry Andrew Cole to help her dad through his bad times. Even though Andrew was twenty years older than her and with a son and a daughter almost her age, she had been willing to do it . . . well, not really willing. If her dad hadn't been such a caring and thoughtful man she would have gone through with it, and he would have kept his land. But he knew where her heart lay, and so, as he said, instead of selling her, he sold nearly all the land to Cole, and she had married John, and he had come to live in this house, and Mr Conway at The Hall had taken him on as an estate worker.

At that time, there was a strange situation up there at The Hall too, almost like it was with her dad, because Mr Conway's affairs were also in a bad way; but his only daughter Miss Alicia hadn't been so lucky as she was, because she married Ernest Bradford-Brown, and he came to live at The Hall, bringing his new-found wealth with him. If ever there was chalk and cheese, it was he and Miss Alicia. And if ever there was an upstart in this world, it was Mr Ernest Bradford-Brown; and being made as he was, as time went on, he developed big ideas for his own daughter.

So when at sixteen he found her walking in the dark with Geoff, he made short work of him; but not before Geoff had told him what he thought of him too. He had voiced what everybody thought but no-one dared to say, because jobs were hard to come by.

The fact was that Ernest Brown had had a very poor start in life; and there should have been all credit due to him for rising to the position he now held, so why didn't he receive that credit?

His career had begun when, at fifteen, he obtained a position at the firm of Lee & Paddock, Estate Agents, in Newcastle as an odd job and messenger boy, which position eventually led to his becoming a clerk. Ten years later, however, Ernest Brown was no longer a clerk but a member of the board. Then, following on the deaths, in quick succession, of two partners he became head of the firm . . . No-one quite knew how he had managed it.

Now, in 1937, he not only owned Lee & Paddock but streets of property as well, mostly in the lower ends of the towns round about. And not everybody could be telling lies when they maintained that the houses were a disgrace, some of them not fit for animals to live in; and he wouldn't spend a penny on them.

It was also said that his father was still alive and living in one of his son's houses, and he in his eighties, but that Mr Bradford-Brown did not recognise him any more. Well, he couldn't be expected to, could he? having married into the Conway family.

Bertha knew that Ernest Bradford-Brown would have sacked John at the same time he had dismissed Geoff, if he hadn't depended on him to see to the estate while he was about his money-making business.

As she watched her son walk down the path the submerged worry in her mind rushed to the surface: the girl was engaged; so what was he thinking about? Oh, what was *she* thinking about to ask such a question, especially about her own son, who took after his father, except that John's deeply passionate nature was covered by a quiet and seemingly placid demeanour, whereas her son covered his with a jocular façade.

For the first time in her life she had a very disturbing thought with regard to her son; she wished him away from her, miles away across the sea.

The old barn was situated at the far end of the estate. It had long since gone out of use and hadn't been considered worth repairing. Having once housed the winter hay when part of the estate had been run as a farm, there were still old farm implements lying in one corner and memories of the diabolical in the form of rusty man-traps hanging on equally rusty brackets high up near the roof timbers.

The first time he set eyes on these relics, Geoff asked his father why they had been left there. And he was told that the old master, Mr Conway, had given the order that they were not to be touched, but were to remain as a reminder of man's inhumanity to both himself and animals.

Geoff sometimes wondered why Mr Ernest Bradford-Brown hadn't countermanded that order; but then there was his wife, and it was a known fact that, although he lorded it over almost everyone with whom he came in contact, he had to watch his step with her. Delicate she might look, quiet she was, but it was known too that there was a firmness and disdain in her that he was wary of treading on, for, in a way, she was an insignia for him.

Geoff had first become aware of Janis Bradford-Brown when he was nine years old and she seven. They had met on several occasions before when he was out walking with his father. But on this particular day he had been filling his cap with blackberries from some low bushes near the barn when he heard a voice behind him call, 'What are you doing there, boy?' And he had turned to see the pert face of a small girl. And even knowing who she was did not smooth his tongue when he answered, 'If you use your eyes, you'll see what I'm doing!' This had apparently nonplussed her, but after a moment she had said, 'I know you. You are the Fulton boy.'

And he had answered in the same tone: 'An' I know you an' all, and that's not gona make the sun shine.' Again she was puzzled by his reply, and as if searching for an answer she had moved her head from side to side, and in doing so caught sight of an old notice board lying askew in the grass. But the writing was still legible and, pointing to it, she said loudly but slowly, 'That says trespassers . . . will . . . be . . . persecuted.'

At this he, too, had looked at the board, but had then remarked with an annoying calmness, 'It says nothing of the sort.'

'Yes, it does.'

'It doesn't. You can't read. It says trespassers will be *prosecuted*.'

'You're being forward. I shall tell my father. And . . . and you're stealing our blackberries.'

This last caused him to forget all the advice his mother had given him about watching a tongue that had become too sharp at times and too frivolous at others. But of course she had been referring to his attitude towards his elders; this *thing* standing in front of him wasn't an elder, she was a cheeky monkey. Forgetting his position and that of his father with regard to his attitude towards the daughter of the house, he scooped up a handful of ripe blackberries from his cap and, stepping towards her, he demanded, 'Hold out your hands.' And when she obeyed, out of real fright now, he squashed the blackberries into her palms, then said, 'Take them back to your father. An' you know what you are? You're nothin' but a swanky little bitch!' With that he marched away, fully expecting to hear loud sobs and running footsteps. But when he had gone some yards beyond the barn, simply out of curiosity he had glanced back to see her bending down and wiping her hands on the grass, an unusually feminine reaction which brought him fully round. Slowly he had walked back towards her, and when a yard from her he had stopped and said, 'Why didn't you run home and tell your father?'

'How old are you?' she said.

'I'm nine,' he said.

'I'm seven.'

Then she had looked towards the notice-board lying in the grass, and asked quietly, 'Is it really pros-e-cuted?'

And he had nodded and said, 'Aye, it is.'

To this she had remarked, 'Oh, well, I'll have to tell Mrs Bassett; Nancy, you know; she's our washer-woman and every time I go near the wash-house when she is there she orders me away, and always says "trespassers will be persecuted".'

He had laughed and she had laughed. It was a funny laugh, he thought: it went high into a squeak, and the tears came into her round blue eyes and ran down her face.

That's how it had begun . . .

He had been waiting in the barn for over half an hour. She knew the time they used to meet, and she hadn't come. She would know too that he was being posted abroad; such news was carried on the wind on the estate; it didn't need a carrier pigeon.

What if she didn't come? Perhaps it would be better, because it was the end, anyway. He had faced up to that over the past few days. He'd even told himself it would be wiser to let it remain there, the end unspoken. Yet with the feeling that raged in him he couldn't bear to leave without seeing her once more and this time telling her what he thought. But hadn't he told her before what he thought? She knew all he thought, all he felt; and he knew what she thought and felt . . . Yet did he? He had had to recognise over the past months that he wasn't as clever as he had imagined regarding her feelings towards him.

Here he was a sergeant, known as a real tough-'un when dealing with those under him; tough yet fair. Oh yes, begrudgingly, the lads said he was fair. And then, in the sergeants' mess, he was the life and soul of the party, a real he-man. But how deep did these two guys go? Hardly under the skin, for at this moment the real man was feeling physically sick, exactly as he had been at sixteen, when he would wait for her return from boarding school, very much the young miss.

Then came the day during her vacation when he had kissed her, and during the following year he had never

45

felt sick while waiting for her; that is until the day her father got wind of it and all hell was let loose.

She had been sent to a finishing school down south, and they had apparently done a good job with her, for now she had an air about her not unlike that of her mother. They had met once on the open road, the daughter of the house and he, a private in the Durham Light Infantry. He had felt gauche and clumsy in his uniform, and it had impregnated his manner.

The next time they met he was twenty years old and she eighteen. He was then a corporal and she had completed her education. She had been home for more than a month when he came on leave and it was she who had sought him out. She must have made herself aware of his movements, because he had been passing the old barn when he saw her walking towards him from the direction of the river. Their meeting had been awkward, polite and strained, until he had remarked, 'You're finished schooling now?' And to his surprise she had answered, 'Yes, thank God.'

'You . . . you didn't like it?'

'Like it!' She had put her head back and laughed, that strange, high laugh of hers, saying, 'Have you any idea what a girls' boarding-school is like?'

And to this he had answered freely, 'Well, not so far. But in the army they are getting up all kinds of schemes for educating and enlightening us soldiers, so I might get a chance yet.'

She had grunted, 'Huh!' But then said, 'I've thought a lot about you, you know, over the past years.'

'Flattered, I'm sure,' he had answered inanely.

46

'Did you think of me?'

He had stared at her for a long moment before saying bluntly, 'Are you out to play games, Janis? Because if you are, I'd better tell you I'm past that stage.'

'I don't know what you mean.'

'You know what I mean right enough.' He had moved his head slowly up and down, in reply to which she had bowed hers and in a low voice, had said, 'We could be friends.'

'What kind of friends?' he had asked her.

And at this she had amazed him by looking him straight in the face and saying, 'Any kind you like.'

He had heard people say that their hearts had jumped with fright, and those of others had jumped with joy. Well, at that moment, his heart had jumped with joy. He had put his hand out to her and quietly they had walked back to the barn and, after staring at each other for a long moment in the dimness, he had kissed her; and she had responded with a fervour matching his own.

For a full year he had lived only for leaves. Thirty-six hours, forty-eight hours, some of them wasted because he wasn't able to see her. They had arranged a signal. If the old broken signpost was erect and leaning against the railing, he was to come to the barn later that day. If she couldn't make it, it would be leaning to one side. If it was still lying in the grass, she was away.

When had he stopped finding it erect or leaning to the side? Eight months . . . ten months ago? It had been shortly after his being made a sergeant. And on that occasion, when they met, he had said, 'Next step, officer-type.' And to this she had answered flatly, 'Some hope.'

'Come a war,' he had said, 'you are jumped up on the field of battle, acting this, acting that, and then comes the real thing.'

'Come a war,' she had answered flatly, 'fits adequately with that saying of yours, "Live horse and you'll get grass".'

And was that the time Richard Boneford's name was mentioned? His mother, with intentional tact, had remarked that Miss Janis's picture was in the county magazine: she was dancing with a Mr Dickie Boneford who, apparently, had an estate in Scotland and went steeplechasing.

So he had said to her, 'What's this I hear about you and the Boneford fella, the well-known so-and-so, and so-and-so and so-and-so?'

To this she had answered, 'What do you hear? That we danced together at the Hunt Ball? I also danced with ten other men, four of them eligible. What do you make of that?'

He made nothing of it until his next leave, when the notice was lying in the grass. Two weeks later he received a letter from her, addressed to him at the barracks. It was the first letter she had ever written to him. It was of the kind you might read about in a novel, one that could have been written at the end of the last century. It stated simply that she had enjoyed his friendship and companionship over the years, but now she must look to her future. Her parents were anxious that she should settle down. So she had to tell him that she was planning to become engaged to Richard Boneford. She knew he would understand and that he had understood the situation from the beginning. She would always think of him most warmly. She signed herself simply 'Janis'.

He had not been able to take it in, not only the fact that she was to become engaged, but that she could write this kind of letter. It was as if she had been trained never to commit herself in writing. He had sat on the side of his iron bed and stared down at the words that became jumbled on the page. Theirs had not been a friendship as such. Two years ago he had taken her and she had been more than willing. Oh, yes, more than willing. To use her own words, she just lived for the time when he was on leave.

The letter should have stung his pride and killed what feeling he had for her. He should have said that she was a cold-blooded bitch, no better than a whore, but he said none of these things, even to himself: what he did was repeat her name over and over again, 'Janis! Oh, Janis!' And yet, at the same time, part of him sneered at the softness within himself. He was Sergeant Geoffrey Fulton, he was in the army, and, by God, he would rise. Who the hell was she anyway? Only the upstart daughter of an upstart father. But the sneer had no power to penetrate the skin; it lay outside in the trappings of the soldier, the duties, the parades, the drills, the playing at warfare, the pride in the battalion, the respect of the men, for, as any soldier would tell you, officers were ten a penny; it was the sergeants who ran the army.

He tried to lose himself in bawling his men into shape for the Coronation parade in May.

And then on 3 July came the order: embarkation for the Canal in October. And he welcomed it, for it would make it impossible for him to go home on every leave.

Yet, here he was on leave prior to embarkation, and he was back in the torment that followed his last one. Yet not quite, because now the bitterness had seeped through his skin and it was having a hardening effect on all that lay below. However, he wouldn't feel vindicated until he had told her exactly what he thought of her.

He glanced at his watch. He'd wait another ten minutes. When that was up there'd be no hesitation; he'd go. But he'd write her a letter, not one made up of platitudes, but of his definition of friendship. And he would not mince his words . . .

Suddenly, she stood there in the doorway, silhouetted against the twilight, and she said softly, 'This is very unfair of you, Geoff.'

'Unfair? I can't see it's unfair.' His voice had an airy note. 'As I suppose you know, I'm on embarkation leave. I just wanted to say goodbye, for it isn't likely we'll meet again. Is it, now?'

'No; I don't suppose it is . . . well, at least, not for some time. So, that being so, I can't see the point of this.'

'Why did you come then?'

'Because I knew you wanted to hurt me and wouldn't be satisfied until you had.'

Her voice still held that soft, plaintive note, so unlike her usual tone. Indeed, her whole manner was unlike that which he had come to know so well: breezy, sharp, aiming to cap everything he said, even his jokes. Knowing this, his own voice was almost a bawl as he cried, 'Come off it! Surely being engaged hasn't softened you up all that much. Drop your little Orphan Annie pose and be yourself!'

Instantly, she did, by responding, 'Oh, that's you! That's why it was impossible. You could never change. Raw, always raw. You were bad enough before you went into the army, what with your constant wisecracking, but then you became uncouth. What chance was there for us ever to get together? Really, I mean. You must have known it from the first.'

The word 'uncouth' had stung him, and he was about to take it up, but instead, he said, and quietly, but through clenched teeth, 'No, Miss Bradford-Brown, ˉI didn't know from the first, because you could say I was led up the garden path: I imagined you had sufficient character to stand on your own feet and become a real woman, one who could see through your money-grabbing father and your social-conscious mother who, as sweet as she appears, won't, for a moment, let anyone forget she is county. And, of course, I overlooked the fact that you've got them both in you, the snobbery of your mother and the avarice of your father who, for all his money, remains an abysmally ignorant slob of a man who won't open his eyes to the fact he is tolerated merely because of his wife. No; you see, I didn't understand, now I do. But tell me one thing before we part' – he made a dramatic movement with his arm – 'does Mr Richard Boneford know about us? I mean . . . well, you know what I mean, don't you?'

She stared at him, her mouth a tight line now. 'You wouldn't dare!'

'Oh, I would, and I could; I'm that kind of uncouth yokel. It's something I'd like to brag about in the pub, the conquest of the Lord of the Manor's daughter.'

He saw her blue eyes mist over and the colour drain from her cream-skin cheeks. She was actually afraid that he would do what he threatened; she really thought he was capable of it . . . But was he?

When her whole expression changed, and, while moving a step towards him, her hand came out to touch his arm, he knew it was the first step in a softening-up process and he was amazed, saddened, and disgusted at the same time. The moment he felt her touch he brought his hand with a sharp cutting movement across her wrist, causing her to cry out.

As he watched her rubbing her wrist, he said, with a sneer, 'You know something? You're not worth a spit, and that's straight from my uncouth mouth. You'd be willing to roll in the grass with me again to keep my mouth shut, wouldn't you?'

Thrusting her aside, he strode out of the barn, and he had gone some distance along the path when her voice came to him, calling, 'Wait! Geoff, wait!'

He paused, turned, and his face white with the intensity of his feelings, he cried, 'You go to hell, Janis!'

He walked on, his back straight, his head erect, his arms swinging, until he came to the thicket. Here he stopped and gripped a young sapling with both hands and shook it until its roots moved in the earth.

Well, it was over, finished.

His step slowed as he walked along the road towards home. The stiffness had seeped from his body, his ramrod back was slightly bent, his head drooped forward. Uncouth she had said. Uncouth.

He entered the house by the back door. The kitchen still retained the appearance of the farmhouse: a long, white-wood table down the middle of the room, an open fire with ovens to the side, black beams across the ceiling, and an oak dresser laden with crockery. And, standing before it now, was Lizzie. She had been hanging cups by their handles on the hooks attached to the bottom shelf. She turned towards him, and when he didn't speak, she said, 'Hello.'

Then he answered, 'Hello. You all right?'

'Yes, fine . . . lovely. I'm . . . I'm goin' to like it here.'

'Good.'

'Will . . . will I make you somethin', a cup of tea? Your mam's playin' the piano.' The last was very evident.

He said, 'Is my father home yet?' And she nodded, 'Aye, yes; and he's spoken to me. He . . . he says I'm welcome.' She smiled widely.

'That's good,' he said. 'That's good. You're settled then.'

He knew he should go in and greet his father, but at the moment he felt he would be unable to put a face on things.

He nodded at her, then walked to the far door, out into the corridor and up the back staircase to his bedroom.

He took off his coat and loosened his tie, then stood for a moment thinking: uncouth. It was strange, but to be thought of in that way was, at the moment, troubling him more than her wholesale rejection of him.

He had always prided himself that he was as good as the next man in holding a conversation. He had the knack of remembering quotes, which at times could be very impressive. Old Pybus, the English master at school, also had a penchant for ancient history which he endeavoured to ram into the blockheads. Funnily enough, he himself had taken to it, and the knowledge of which now supplied him with impressive quotes.

He went to the far end of the room and opened a cupboard door, in which his mother had stored all the regalia of his schooldays; and on the top shelf were his books: *Treasure Island*, *Kidnapped*, *David Copperfield*, *Kim*, *The Riddle of The Sands*, *The Last of the Mohicans*, piles of *Magnets*, and there, standing out, *The Legends of Ancient Greece and Rome*.

He picked it up, thumbed through it, then replaced it on the shelf with a confident thump, and muttered aloud: 'Uncouth!'

He picked up a dictionary and read the definition of the word: *strange, awkward, clumsy, uncultured*.

Uncultured. Yes, that summed up his own interpretation of it; uncultured; and added to this he put the words, drunken bore. He was now thinking of Bill Titon, who almost lived at The Hare. And there were some of the fellows round about; not all, no, not all, but some to whom he could attach the tag of awkward and clumsy. Strange? No; he would have considered one had to be a bit mental to be strange, or at least eccentric. But he knew what she meant when she had called him uncouth . . . Uncultured. Yes, that's what she had indicated.

But had she thought him uncultured as she lay with him in the long, tangled grass near the barn? No, by God! she hadn't. She had told him he was marvellous and that he took her out of this world. Not once, but many times she had told him that; and she had kissed him with a frenzy that matched his own. At these times he knew they were made for each other and felt that nothing or no-one could part them. And she had told him that he stood above all the people she knew: the menfolk, the hunting, shooting, and fishing crowd. Of course, that was after she had been satisfied and lay curled up like a kitten within his hold. He knew every part of her and she of him and they had both been beautiful to each other. But now he was uncouth . . . and she was a bitch. So much for love everlasting.

There was a pain between his ribs, sharp, searing, just like a bayonet thrust.

His mother's voice came to him, calling, 'You up there, Geoff? Dad's home.'

He opened the door and called to her, 'Won't be a minute . . .'

Five minutes later he entered the sitting-room, his face drawn, although his head was up and his back straight.

His father was sitting by the side of the fire and he said to him, 'Well, you've got it over then?'

'Yes, lad, I've got it over, and I'm not sorry. My goodness! it would drive me mad to live in the town. I don't know how our Henry stuck it.'

'Oh, you know how he stuck it, John, because he liked it. He hated the country,' said Bertha.

'Aye, I suppose you're right.'

Bertha now turned to Geoff adding, 'He's feeling guilty, Geoff, because Henry's left him his money.'

'No!' He looked at his father, a smile on his face now. 'Was it much?'

'Was it much?' Again his mother was interrupting. 'You wouldn't believe it, living on the poverty line as he did, bread and scrape most of his life, and a good job like he had. We could never understand it. Yet all that money in the bank.'

'All that money?' Geoff turned to his father again, and his mother piped in, 'Tell him. Tell him, man.'

'Two thousand, seven hundred pounds.'

'What! He's left you that?' For a moment the main event of the night was blotted out and, sitting down by his father's side, he put his hand on his shoulder and pressed it, saying, 'Why! that is something, two thousand seven hundred. Now you can throw that bike in the river and get yourself a car.'

'A car?' His father slanted his eyes towards him, saying, 'You can see me driving a car, can't you?'

'Yes, I can. And look,' – he cast a glance towards his mother – 'don't stick it in the bank and hoard it up; enjoy it. Get yourselves out and about, go places.'

'I don't know.' His father shook his head. 'I can't help feeling guilty. You know I've never bothered with him much of late; he got on my nerves. Yet, I always knew I owed him a debt for looking after me when I was young. He brought me up, you know. You can't get away from that; he brought me up. And if it hadn't been for him and his mania for camping, I wouldn't be here the day, nor have found this lass.' He put out a hand and gripped Bertha's where it lay on the top of her stick, then went on. 'He's been off me for years . . .'

'No, not off you, off me,' Bertha interrupted him now, 'and all women for that matter. He didn't like women of any kind. He wouldn't have one in the house to do his cleaning. Yet, he had all that money.'

She sighed, then smiled, saying, 'It's been an eventful weekend.'

'Aye, so I heard from Phil Connor. Met him on the road coming back. He tells me there was a do yesterday at the cottage. Somebody tried to break in, and Mr Kidderly fought him off and got a broken jaw into the bargain; landed in hospital. Fancy that happening round here. Now what did he expect to find in the cottage?'

Geoff looked at his mother now, saying, 'You haven't told him?'

'Not that part.'

'What part? Keeping something back? What should I know? Come on.'

Bertha, pursing her lips before pointing her thumb towards Geoff, said, 'This soldier here was the intruder. The Kidderly man was handling the girl, and she was screaming the place down.'

John looked at his son for a moment; then he asked quietly, 'Did he recognise you?'

'No.'

'He would see your uniform.'

'I was wearing your old coat and hat.'

'Believe it or not,' Bertha laughed, 'he had gone out to catch Ted Honeysett.'

'No! What did you want to catch Ted for?'

'Couldn't tell you now, Dad. I must have been feeling bored. Missing army manoeuvres, I think. Truth is, I just wanted to see if I could do it. You've always said that he was as sly as ten weasels.'

'Well, did you catch him then?'

There was a smile on his father's face now and Geoff shook his head, saying, 'No. He caught me. He must

57

have had me in view all the time, because it was he who phoned for the doctor. For my part I would have left the fellow there and let him get on with it. He wasn't dead, so he would have come round. But Ted went to the telephone box and did the Samaritan trick.'

'He's all right, is Ted. A scamp where fish and fowl are concerned; he takes the fish at the wrong time and the pheasants afore they fly. But he's all right underneath. We understand each other. And I'd like to bet he knew it wasn't me underneath that coat and hat. Were you standing still?'

'Yes; yes, for a time.'

'So would he be, laughing at you . . . my! the things that happen when I leave you for five minutes. Well, as it says on the Lyle's golden syrup tin, "Out of the strong comes forth sweetness", so out of bad comes good, 'cos I like the little lass. And she'll fit in. She looks the type.' He shrugged his shoulders now. 'But I don't know how she'll stand it when she finds she's under a female sergeant an' all.'

'Oh, you!' Bertha lifted her stick and tapped his leg with it, while saying, 'I've never bossed anybody in my life; trained them, yes, but never bossed them, so I don't know who your son takes after.' Then looking fully at Geoff, she added, 'It's a funny thing, you know, but I cannot imagine you bawling your head off and ordering people about, fully-grown men, I mean, and some of them tough guys at that.'

'Wait till he's made sergeant-major.' John nodded towards his son, and Geoff, raising his eyebrows as if in derision, said, 'Aye, wait; and that'll be the day.' And as he turned about, he added, 'I'm going to see what's eatable in the kitchen. Sit where you are' – he pushed out his hand towards his mother as she made to follow him – 'I'm a big lad now; I can see to meself.'

Once outside the door he paused and said to himself, 'Aye, that'll be the day; sergeant-major . . . but it will come. Yes, if I know anything, it'll come. God! I'm sure. And after that? pips? If it's the last thing I do, I'll show her . . . Uncouth!'

Now, as if on parade, he marched across the hall, thrust open the kitchen door and almost knocked Lizzie on to her back. His arms reaching out quickly, he caught her before she fell and held her suspended for a moment as he looked down into her face, saying, 'This is the second time I've saved you in two nights. You're gettin' to make it a habit.'

When she was standing straight again she stroked her hair back from her forehead as she looked up into his face, and she said, 'Yes, I will, won't I? 'cos third time's catchy time.'

It was a childish saying, an unexplained childish saying, for what had one to do in the first and second place in order to be caught in the third? And what happened when you were caught? Her childish mind had never probed this far, so she left him with a smile as she went through into the hall, and he went down the kitchen repeating, 'Third time's catchy time.'

PART TWO

Low Tarn Hall

1

'I'm not having any squalling kids billeted in this house. You can go down and tell them.'

Alicia Bradford-Brown looked at her husband's reflection in the mirror and, her voice irritatingly quiet as always, she said, '*You* can go and tell them that, but I won't.'

'You bloody well will!'

'Don't swear at me, Ernest.' She turned from the mirror, a comb in her hand and her arm extended, and she wagged the comb towards him, saying, 'I have warned you before about that. You can rage and chatter at me in your imbecilic way, as always, but I will not tolerate your swearing at me.'

'Look!' He took two quick steps towards her and, thrusting out a hand, he knocked the comb flying from her fingers, saying, 'This is my house, and that's what you seem to forget. It is my house now, and I'll swear . . . I'll bloody well swear whenever I like, and in which part of it I like. Now get that into your head.'

The shiver that ran through her slim body did not show in her face as she said, 'You do, Ernest, and I will do what I have threatened more than once in the past: I shall leave you. And should I do so, you know only too well that most of the doors in the county will be closed to you. We are at war, yes, and there is now a camaraderie between landowners and their workers;

63

but beneath all that, there is a distinction made for people such as you, Ernest, because you have never let anyone forget that you are a man of means, while at the same time trying to hide how you came by those means, and from where you originated. Strangely, had you owned up to your parentage from the beginning, you would have been accepted for yourself. I tried to tell you that so, so many years ago. But no, you are a very small man inside a large frame, Ernest, but it is a transparent frame . . .'

'My God! woman, you're going too far. I've stood enough; enough, I tell you.'

'Not as much as I have, Ernest.'

'Don't keep repeating my name in that fashion, as if it was something sticking on your tongue, woman, you've . . . And don't turn your back on me!'

She turned fully to him again, saying, 'Would you rather have me continue to look at you, my face expressing my feelings?'

His large pale face was now engulfed in a purple hue and the beads of sweat were running from each side of his thick grey hair down his temples.

At one time when his anger turned him into this sweating, purple-faced lump of quivering flesh, she had felt sorry for him, she'd even pitied him for being such as he was, but not now, and not for many years. She had married him to save her father and this house. Her father had not long survived her sacrifice, and this house, she knew, hadn't been worth the torment she'd had to pay for it. The only thing that had brought her any happiness during her married life was her children. She had him to thank for them, yet whoever she had married, there was always the possibility that she would have had children.

At the present moment she was missing them both, Andrew more than Janis, because she did not know yet if he were dead or alive, or still on the French beaches, or a prisoner of the Germans. Her son-in-law Richard had survived, yet in what condition was not yet known. Janis had gone down to Dover, where he was in hospital. All Janis knew was that he had been wounded, yet she had the consolation of knowing he was alive, whereas Andrew, her dear Andrew . . . The tears were in her throat as she turned now, her voice unusually loud as she said, 'You create a scene in case we might have one or two children in the house and yet you give no thought to your son and what might have befallen him . . .'

'How do you know I haven't given a thought to my son? You always imagine you know so much about people and what goes on in their heads. How would it be if he turned up now, and they brought Richard home too, and him needing quiet and nursing, with hordes of unknown youngsters running round the house? You know what happens when children come here. It's the space; it goes to their heads, they go mad. Look at those three we had last year.'

'These are not children as such, they are fourteen-year-olds, two boys and two girls, and they would help about the place. You're crying out because Tom Midgely and Michael Rice have left, but do you give a thought to the house? All I have now is Cook and Florrie Rice and Nancy Bassett, when she is sober enough to come.'

It was odd, he thought as he stared at her: sometimes, as now, she talked like a housewife. He could understand her then, he could meet her half-way. But the other half of her so maddened him it made him feel insane. At times he wanted to throttle her for her calmness, and in doing so ease the torment that her presence created in him. Why he had to love a woman who scorned every inch of his body and ridiculed and demeaned every thought in his mind, he didn't know. All right, all right; he knew what he was, nobody better, and he wasn't going to change; it was too late. He couldn't change. Anyway, why should he? He had fought his way up into this stiff-necked bloody set, the goal of which at first had appeared as a lodestar; but what had happened when he reached it? He had found it to be a dead, cold star. But there was no going back to the warmth of his beginnings, for he had rejected them entirely, as in turn he had been rejected. There was only one person who was any comfort to him, and that was his daughter, because in Janis he saw something of himself. She, through her marriage, had ensured her position in the magic circle and that had brought him satisfaction, coupled with relief, for after she returned from finishing school he'd had his suspicions she might be seeing the Fulton fellow again, and this he had thought he had nipped in the bud years before, and he knew that if he had caught them at it, he would have used a gun on him. But all such suspicions were swept away on the day she came and told him that Dickie Boneford had proposed. And that day he had shown her his delight, for the Bonefords were a family to be reckoned with. They were from over the border. Their estate wasn't large, and they weren't all that wealthy, but they had a name that went back a long way down the line, and a manor house that stood proof to it.

Things had gone well for Janis. She had played the lady almost as well as her mother; then the bloody war had to break out, and now her husband was lying in some hospital at Dover, shot to pieces, as far as he could gather. What if he died and she hadn't given him an heir? She had been stubborn that way.

He turned about slowly and had reached the door when his wife's voice came at him, saying, 'Are you going to tell them?'

He paused but did not glance back towards her, then left, banging the door behind him.

His answer had been his silence, she thought. She would have to deal with the matter. Truth to tell, she didn't want children running round the house any more than he did, but if they didn't take them, they could be landed with a family, or members of the forces. As Clara Johnson at The Towers had found, when she made a stand against taking evacuees, she'd had to billet six soldiers, and these had turned out to be a thousand times worse than any children.

But that was an idea. *She* wouldn't mind having one or two officers billeted; in fact, that would be rather nice. And Janis wouldn't get so bored if there were young company in the house. But then, why she should be bored at all with all the voluntary work she was doing, she just couldn't understand. Likely she was missing Richard. Of course, she'd be missing Richard. She wondered at times why she had preferred to come home rather than stay with his parents, because they were charming people. A little quaint, perhaps, but charming. But then Janis wasn't a quiet type herself; she had too much energy. She was too much like . . . She cut off her thoughts abruptly,

67

for she would not even acknowledge to herself that her daughter took after her father.

When there came a tap on the door, she called, 'Come in,' and Florrie Rice entered, saying, 'The lady from the billeting office says she's got to get the bus in fifteen minutes from the corner or it means waiting another hour and a half, ma'am.'

'I'm coming down immediately, Florrie.'

Florrie had a cast in one of her eyes, very likely the reason why she was still working in the house and not in one of the forces. And now the eye seemed to bob up and down under her flickering eyelids as she said, 'I should tell you, ma'am, she's got a person with her, common-like. She's been raising her voice. She's elderly, sort of. I thought I had better tell you.'

'Thank you, Florrie. Thank you.'

'Ma'am.' Florrie jerked her head, then went out, and a few minutes later Alicia, drawing in a long breath, followed her across the broad landing, down the shallow oak stairs into the hall, and across it to the far end and into the back study, where all . . . persons were shown.

She heard the person's voice before she opened the door. 'Not on your life. I worked in one of these from a bairn. Oh no; ta very much. I don't mind work, but I can't stand them kind.'

Alicia opened the door and saw 'the person'. She was small, fattish, and what she termed, frowzy-looking. She was wearing a blue serge coat and a grey straw hat, and the face under it seemed to be made up of a pattern of wrinkles, out of which two coal-black eyes stared at her.

'Good afternoon, Mrs Bradford-Brown.' There was a definite nervous tremor in Miss Taggart's voice.

'Good afternoon, Miss Taggart. How can I help you?'

'Well,' – Miss Taggart glanced at her companion – 'it . . . it was about the children. I . . . I phoned you, you remember.'

'Yes, yes, of course.'

'Well, I got the two boys settled but . . . but it's still the girls, and . . . well, they're of an age, fourteen and . . . and . . .' When she paused, 'the person' put in while staring unblinking at the mistress of the house, 'What she's trying to tell you is that they're two young rips, man-mad, an' they'll take lookin' after, an' she thought that she'd dump me here to help see to them. But I've said no. Thank you all the same, missis, no. Whether you say you'll take me or not, I have me reasons for not wantin' to be housed in a place like this, very good reasons at that. So, as I told Miss Taggart here, she was wastin' bus fare on me and I'd as soon as not go back to Shields. I'm not afraid of bombs; rather have bombs than some people.'

'Mrs Price, please!'

'Please what?'

'Be quiet!'

'Nobody's tellin' me to be quiet if I want to talk. I told you afore I come. And look, I can find me own way back.'

'Be quiet! will you?' Miss Taggart turned to Alicia, saying, 'I'm sorry. But if you could take the girls.'

'Just a moment.' Alicia held out her hand in a gentle gesture. 'If as this . . . er . . .'

'Me name's Meg Price, Mrs Meg Price.'

'Yes, yes, of course. If, as Mrs Price says, they are girls who need some attention, I'm afraid I haven't got the staff to see to them. Anyway, I've been informed . . . at least, I understand through the Ministry, that I might have to put up some military personnel.' It was quite easy to lie with conviction. She was quite used to it; over the years she had made an art of it.

'Oh. Oh, I see. Well, in that case I'll just have to look elsewhere.' Miss Taggart turned her gaze towards the window, adding in a conciliatory tone, 'It's such a pity, isn't it, that your beautiful flower garden has had to be turned into a vegetable patch? Well' – she made a little hee'ing sound, 'not exactly a patch, but you know what I mean. It must be distressing for you.'

'No, not at all; you can't eat flowers, and we're so glad to do anything that's going to help the war effort.'

'Yes, yes, of course. Well, I must get away. You see, the bus . . . well, it passes the end of the road at two-forty-five.'

'I understand. Good day, Miss Taggart.'

A minute later Alicia stood at the drawing-room window and watched the two visitors walking towards the drive, and as she thought, what a dreadful person, she was also congratulating herself on how neatly she had got out of that situation. If only it hadn't been preceded by that exchange in the bedroom. Whether she liked to admit it or not, such incidents always upset her.

Turning from the window, she glanced at the French clock on the mantelpiece. A quarter to three. She smiled to herself; they would have missed the bus.

*　　*　　*

70

Miss Taggart leaned against the farm gate while her companion sat on the grass verge, her feet in a shallow ditch, her back to the road. They hadn't spoken for the past five minutes. They were both tired, thirsty, and in their own individual ways, angry. Miss Taggart was angry with Mrs Bradford-Brown, who had kept her waiting for nearly twenty minutes, and for once she agreed with her companion's opinion of the gentry: they could be very inconsiderate.

Mrs Meg Price was angry for letting herself be persuaded to come all this way for protection against only what *might* happen. It wasn't that she disliked the country, it was the people who lived there she didn't like. Well, not all of them; but it should happen that the nice, kindly ones were all full up. This last place Miss Taggart had wanted to park her was even worse than the parsonage. Parson Drinkwater had seemed a jolly enough bloke, but his wife was another madam, just like the one they had just left. She had preferred the two scamps of lads to her. Good luck to her. She hoped she had her silver locked up.

She gazed along the road. They hadn't seen a soul during the last half hour. Everybody could be dead.

Suddenly, Miss Taggart pulled herself from the gate, saying flatly, 'Here is someone coming.' One was a young girl of seventeen or eighteen, the other, an older woman walking with the aid of a stick. They both stopped when they came abreast of Meg, and the woman with the stick looked from one to the other and said, 'Don't tell me you've missed the bus?'

'Yes. Yes.' Miss Taggart nodded.

71

'How long have you been waiting?'

'Oh' – Miss Taggart looked at her watch – 'gone twenty minutes.'

'My! My! You have nearly another hour to go. Would you like a cup of tea?'

Both Miss Taggart and Meg Price exchanged glances and they both smiled and answered almost as one, 'Yes, we would. Yes, indeed we would.'

'Well, if you can walk for another five minutes you'll find the kettle boiling.' As Bertha spoke, the young girl helped the old woman up from the grass verge, and they exchanged glances and smiled. ''Tis hot, isn't it?' Meg said.

Lizzie nodded, saying, 'Yes, it is. I like it, but' – her smile widened – 'I can see you don't.'

'You're right there, lass. You're right there. Give me a good east wind an' I'm happy.'

Lizzie walked alongside the old woman and Bertha accompanied Miss Taggart.

Ten minutes later, the four of them were sitting round the kitchen table drinking tea, and one of them, forgetting, or at least not knowing, that politeness should stop at two scones in these meagre days, was biting into a fourth as she looked across at Bertha, saying, 'By! I've never tasted anythin' like them for a long time. You make them?'

'No. Lizzie here does the cooking, and well at that, as she does everything else.' Bertha smiled proudly as if she were speaking of a daughter; and Lizzie's answering smile could have been that she was looking lovingly at a mother. And there was silence at the table for a few seconds until Bertha said, 'Are you going back to Shields, then?'

'Aye. There's nothin' for it; but I don't mind. Although I'm a bit worried that they might have taken over me room. I locked it up with me bits and pieces. But any one of the others left in that street could be a dab hand with a hairpin, or a bit of wire. And I shouldn't be surprised that, thinkin' I've gone for good, they've stripped me place already. Mrs Ridley opposite, she's all right, she said she would look after it, but she's out most of the day workin'. So I ask you.'

Bertha stared at the older woman; then glancing towards the window, she saw John passing as he made his way to the garden shed, likely to get a hoe to do a bit of weeding in between times, as the ground was bone dry. She bit on her lip; then pulling herself to her feet and, taking up her stick, she said, 'Would you excuse me for a minute?' and with that she left the room.

After the door had closed behind her, Meg looked at Lizzie and asked, 'How old are you, lass?'

'Seventeen.'

'You look older; you could be eighteen or nineteen.'

'I wish the authorities could think that way. I . . . I would like to join the ATS. But then it would mean leaving Mam alone.'

'What d'you do with yourself around here?'

'Oh, I've got a lot to do. I go to a typing school in Durham; have done for the past year. I'm also studying music under Mam.' She jerked her head towards the door. 'She's a wonderful pianist and a marvellous teacher.'

'She said you were her companion. She's not your mam then?'

'No, but she's as good as, even better. I . . . I've been very fortunate.'

'Well, all I can say is she's done a good job on you. She mightn't have borne you, but she's bred you all right.'

'Tut! Tut!' When Miss Taggart's tongue clicked the old woman rounded on her. 'What's that for? What have I said out of place?' She didn't wait for an explanation, but leaned across the table and added, 'You know what's wrong with you, miss? You're too stiff for a plumber's pipe; you need a blow lamp through you.'

Lizzie had to make a firm effort not to splutter. This certainly was a funny old woman, but she liked her; yet at the same time she felt sorry for Miss Taggart, and as that offended lady went to rise abruptly from the table, she put her hand out towards her arm, staying it; and, looking up into her face, she said, 'Have another cup of tea.'

Miss Taggart swallowed deeply, then slowly sat down again, to be surprised when the awful old woman leant towards her once again, and said, ''Tis sorry I am if I've upset you. 'Tis me tongue; it runs away with me. And I'm not used to polite society. 'Tis ignorant, I am. Me own dad used to say that: "'Tis ignorant you are, Meg," he would say. "You've got no more sense in your head than them what allowed themsels to be packed into holds instead of ballast when comin' over from Ireland."' She nodded and turned to Lizzie, saying, 'Now wasn't that terrible? But it's true. It was the time of the tatie famine, an' the poor devils were starvin'.'

'Oh, Mrs Price.' Lizzie was laughing aloud now and her face was alight as she turned to the door to see John and Bertha come into the room.

Bertha, turning to Miss Taggart, said, 'This is my husband, Miss Taggart.'

'Pleased to meet you.' John held out his hand.

'And this is Mrs Price.'

John looked down into the wizened face and Mrs Price looked up into his, and they surveyed each other for a moment; then John, holding out his hand, said, 'How d'you do, Mrs Price?'

'I do fairly well, thank you. An' yourself?'

'Oh, I'm fine, fine.'

'That's all right then. 'Tis a nice house you've got here . . . homely. I like homely houses.'

'I'm glad of that, because my wife here,' he inclined his head towards Bertha, 'says that she'd like you to stay for a while, if that would suit you.'

He watched the lined mouth open to disclose a gap in the upper set of teeth and two gaps in the lower; then the lips closed again. He watched her turn her astonished gaze on Bertha, to whom she now said quietly, 'Is he right?'

'Yes. Yes, he's right.' There was a chuckle in Bertha's voice.

Now Meg cast her glance on Miss Taggart and what she said was, 'How d'you see that?'

'I . . . I think you're very fortunate to be offered a home here.'

It wasn't the right thing to say, and certainly not to this perky old girl, and at least two other people in the room realised this and expected a lively retort. But what Meg said was, and quietly, 'Aye, perhaps you're right for once.' Then looking again from John to Bertha, she said, 'I promise you I'll be no trouble to you, an' there's a lot of work left in me yet.

I'll do all I can, an' more. You'll see. Aye, you'll see.'

Now John spoke, saying, 'Have you any things with you?'

'Aye, a bit of baggage. It's in the schoolroom, back in Durham.'

'Well, we'll have to pick it up, won't we? I've still enough petrol left to take you there and back. And you, Miss Taggart, will get back quicker than waiting for the bus. How about it?'

'Oh, thank you. Thank you, Mr Fulton—' Whatever she was going to say next she shortened to, 'And grateful.' It wasn't until she was saying goodbye to Bertha, that she finished the sentence, adding now, 'I hope everything turns out all right. You must let me know if you are worried or anything.'

'I will. I will,' said Bertha. 'But I'm sure everything will be fine. There's another thing, too: I don't think we'll be lost for a laugh.'

Miss Taggart would have liked to answer, 'You're easily pleased then,' but she refrained. She had got the person off her hands, and at the moment, that was all that mattered.

Bertha knew to some extent what Miss Taggart was thinking, and she could have explained her actions to her, by saying, 'You see, Lizzie's out all day at the school, and John is out at work, and then there's the LDV, and so, because of my handicap, I'm mostly tied to the house, which leaves me too much time to think, for nearly every waking minute is taken up with thoughts of my son: I haven't heard from him for nearly five weeks now. So you see, someone like Mrs Price would take my mind off things; and she can

76

always help with the housework because, as she said, she's handy, and that will save Lizzie having to bustle about at night doing all the things I'm unable to do. And it makes a long day for her.'

And if she had said this to Miss Taggart, she also felt her reply would have been in the nature of, 'Well, Mrs Fulton, I know how you are feeling, but you must remember that you're not the only mother that's worrying at the present moment.'

And she was well aware of that, too, but it didn't lessen the anxiety. She had always thought that was a silly thing for people to say: they knew just how you were feeling. Nobody really knew how the other person was feeling because some folk had a deep resistance to pain and were silent about it, while others cried out if their little finger ached, and thereby gained sympathy: there was no measurement to pain and no detector to determine the depth of it, be it mental or physical.

2

Dusk was falling as Lizzie bicycled home from Durham. She always dismounted half-way up Brook Hill. She could have made it to the top but she didn't consider it worth the push. Reaching the summit, she was about to mount again and freewheel down between the two stretches of woodland that separated the Bradford-Brown estate from that of Nine Stint Farm, when she stopped, one foot on the pedal, for a few yards in front of her, just visible in the dimness of the overhanging trees, she saw a figure emerging from the right-hand side wood. For a moment her heart gave a little leap and her mind said 'Andrew'. Then when the figure jumped a ditch and stopped in the middle of the road, she let out a short breath, and her heart was still affected, but in a different way.

She recognised Captain Boneford even from this distance, and in the dimness his scarred face seemed to make him stand out.

She pushed the bike quickly forward, saying, 'Hello Captain. You're back again, then?'

'Oh, hello. Hello, Lizzie. Yes, yes, I'm back in the old corral.' The voice sounded high and cheerful. It always did. It was all part of the brave show.

'How long are you home for now?'

'Oh, three weeks, this time. Ticket-of-leave, you know. Good conduct and all that. How are you?'

'Oh, I'm fine, except, if I see another ration card before Monday morning I'll scream.'

'Boring, eh?'

'Yes, a bit.'

'Pity you couldn't have joined up. But then, you've got to ask yourself, who needs you most? The WAAFS, the ATS, the WRENS, or Mrs Fulton?'

'Yes.' She nodded at him, smiling, as she forced herself to look straight into his face.

That was another part of the game he played: he looked straight at you; and he didn't reveal the side where his eye was round and brown and quite long-lashed, and his skin, although pale, was smooth – at least his cheek was – down to the left corner of his mouth. From there, across his chin and up to his right hairline, was a contortion of sickly-pink patches of skin, pulling down the corner of his right eye and leaving the mouth a mere shapeless slit, above which both nostrils looked pinched.

Lizzie was quick to notice that the mouth no longer dropped at the corner, and that the thin lines, although still not shaped, appeared a little fuller. But he still wore the glove on his left hand. Three months ago, he had indicated in his assumed casual manner that they were giving him a new paw, but apparently nothing had happened yet. Anyway, his face, she considered, was much more important. Poor, poor, fellow.

She had first encountered him early in 1941. It was late in the evening, as now, and he had tried to turn away as she had come on him unexpectedly. She too had wanted to turn away; in fact, to run, but she had made herself stand and force a smile to her face, while saying, 'I'm trespassing, as usual. I'm . . . I'm Lizzie Gillespie, you know, at Mrs Fulton's.'

'Oh, yes, yes, of course. I'm . . . I'm sorry if I startled you,' he had said; and straightaway she had thought, what a pleasing voice.

'No, no.' She had answered, shaking her head. Then they had stood peering at each other for a moment before she forced herself to say, 'I'm . . . I'm glad to see you back home, sir.'

And to this he had answered, briefly, 'Yes. Yes, glad to be back. Just taking a stroll.'

When she reached home that night she had sat down at the kitchen table and cried. And Bertha had put her arms about her and comforted her, saying, 'You shouldn't let it affect you like that. He's lucky to be alive,' to which she replied, 'Oh, Mam, he'd rather be dead. I'm sure he'd rather be dead.'

Here, a full year later, she held much the same opinion.

Richard Boneford said to her now, 'May I walk with you?' and she answered, 'Of course. I'll be glad of the company. I don't usually like this stretch, not between the woods.'

'Soldiers?'

'No, strangely enough,' – she laughed – 'civilians. The older they get the worse they are.'

'Have . . . have you a boyfriend?'

'No. No, I haven't.'

'Well, I would say somebody's missing out on something.'

She laughed now and turned her face towards him as she said, 'I don't think so.'

'You don't?'

'No, I don't.' Her voice had a serious note to it.

'How old are you now, Lizzie?'

'Almost *nineteen*.'

'Wonderful age. Oh, by the way, I met up with Andrew. I say I met up with him. He came to the hospital and met up with me, and he spoke of you.'

'Yes?' Her tone was noncommittal.

'It was only last week I saw him: he's hoping for some leave.'

'That'll be nice for him.'

He put his hand on the handlebar and pulled the machine and her to a stop. They were out in the clearing now, and he stared across at her, his good eye in evidence as he asked quietly, 'And don't you think it'll be nice for you, too, Lizzie?'

'Aw, Captain.' She moved her head impatiently. 'What could come of it?'

'Anything you wish, Lizzie, I'd say. If the war's done nothing else, it's brought down a lot of barriers, and will likely bring down more before it ends.'

'Not where Mr Bradford-Brown's concerned, Captain.'

'Mr Bradford-Brown's power is declining, Lizzie. It's a pity it didn't before and then things might have been different all round.' His voice had lost its high jocular air, and it remained so when next he said, 'How is the sergeant-major?'

She gulped slightly before answering: 'Very well, judging by his last letter. But he's no longer a sergeant-major, Captain; he's been given his commission. He's now a second lieutenant.'

'Second lieutenant? My! My! We do go up, don't

we? Well, well! That's war for you . . . His leave is well overdue, I should say.'

'Yes. Yes it is; and . . . and his mother worries. Of course, that's natural. She won't know any peace until she sees him back home.' Her voice had trailed away. She felt that had been a silly thing to say because, if this man knew of his wife's association with Geoff, and from the way he had spoken of him, she imagined he did, then his peace of mind would be further shattered were Geoff to return now.

From what she had heard from Meg, who got it from Florrie Rice, Mrs Boneford had thoroughly enjoyed herself with Geoff before her marriage, and with others too during the long periods her husband was in hospital; even when he was first home, she hadn't been backward in making a name for herself.

As Meg, in her forthright way, had remarked only last night, 'She wants her lugs scudded, that one; a bit of a madam, I'd say, and in more ways than one. Good job I didn't park meself on them, else I'd have let me tongue loose.'

As if he had picked up her thoughts, he said, 'Have you still got your evacuee?'

'Meg? Oh yes.' She laughed. 'She's a marler.'

'A marler?'

'Haven't you heard that before? Apparently it's something to do with glass-making, and means an experienced hand. So anyone who is exceptional in some way we call a marler. Meg applies it to good or bad, especially to jokers.'

'She's a character . . . but kindly, I'd say.'

'Yes, she's very kind and thoughtful, much more than a casual observer would give her credit for.

82

Mrs Fulton's been very glad of her company, because, as you know, I'm out all day.'

'Well' – he paused – 'you're nearly home, which you could have reached ten minutes ago if I hadn't chattered.'

'Oh,' she turned fully towards him, saying quietly, 'it was nice seeing you. And you may waylay me any time you like.'

He did not come back with any facetious quip, but the lid of his good eye blinked rapidly, and he said softly, 'Thank you, Lizzie. I'll remember that. Good night.'

'Good night, Captain.'

On reaching the house, she put her bike in the shed, then hurried towards the kitchen door, and when she opened it, there, as nearly always, were Bertha and Meg waiting to greet her. The tea was set on the long kitchen table; the fire was burning brightly; the kettle was hissing on the hob. It was all so homely. She loved this kitchen. She loved the atmosphere that always met her. It was her habit to take off her outdoor things and lay them on the wooden settle that fitted into the alcove to the side of the fireplace; and then while listening to their chatting and answering both Bertha's and Meg's questions concerning the happenings of the day, she would wash her hands at the sink before sitting down to the table. But tonight, on entering the room, she immediately looked from one to the other and muttered, 'I . . . I won't be long. I'm just going upstairs.'

Bertha and Meg exchanged glances; then Bertha hobbled to the far door of the kitchen and looked across the hall to where Lizzie was running up the stairs; then turning, she said to Meg, 'Go up and see what's wrong with her. It takes me all my time to make those damn stairs last thing.'

When Meg tapped on Lizzie's door she received no answer. Nevertheless, she pushed it open to see, across the darkened room, Lizzie drawing the blackout curtains. And she said to her, 'Anythin' wrong, lass?'

'No; no, Meg . . . Switch on the light, will you?'

Meg switched on the light; then, crossing the room to where Lizzie was now opening the wardrobe door, she said, 'Somethin's upset you, lass.'

Lizzie bowed her head; then drooped it forward and pressed it against the edge of the wardrobe door before she said, ''Tis nothing,' only as quickly to contradict herself by adding, 'Yes, it *is* something. I've just been talking to the captain. I'm so heart-sorry for him. He seems lost. He had been walking in the wood again by himself. When he's at home he seems to spend most of his time walking in the grounds.'

'Lass! Lass!' Meg put her arms around her. 'We're all sorry for him; but it's no good takin' on like that. There're thousands like him, so I understand. The hospitals are full of them, poor beggars, some of them not fit to be seen. At least, it's only part of his face that's gone, and they're patchin' him up real fine, I think.'

'They can't patch up everything, Meg; and what's more, I've an idea he's got things on his mind.'

'What things?'

'Oh, I just don't know.' She thought it best not to confide her thoughts in Meg with regard to Geoff and Mrs Boneford, because, although quite unintentionally, the old woman might let something slip one day, forgetting that Mam was Geoff's mother.

Her hesitation caused Meg to say, 'Well, you know more than you're goin' to say. But I'll say this, lass, there's no good gettin' too het up about the captain. He could go up to his own folks and spend time there. But naturally, I suppose he wants to be near his wife. His wife, huh! Anyway, lass, come on downstairs, 'cos Bertha's worried about you. And then the mister will be in in a minute, and if he sees you upset he'll have the doctor to you afore you can say Jack Robinson.'

Lizzie smiled, saying, 'All right, Meg. I'll be down in a minute.' And impulsively now she leaned forward and kissed the old woman on the cheek; and just as impulsively, Meg put her plump arms about her and hugged her, muttering, 'I'll bless Miss Taggart till the day I die for bringin' me here, lass; I've never been so happy or so comfortable in me life. You don't know. You don't know.' She pulled herself away and went hastily from the room, leaving Lizzie, standing thinking, Yes, I do, Meg, I do know how some of the other half lives. I was brought up among some, and was only enlightened when I came here. Just as you have been. Not a mile and a half along the road is the cottage in which I was brought up and in which my stepmother still lives with three of her children, and another man.

During the first year she was at this house her step-mother persisted in sending the eldest boy here. His message was always the same: his mother wanted some of her pay. Her demands had stopped only when Dad, as she called John, had forced himself to go to the cottage and quietly threaten her with the police by stating why he had taken her stepdaughter under his care.

Since that time, she had come face to face with

her stepmother only half a dozen times and they had not exchanged a word. But as Lizzie had grown older and her prettiness had turned to beauty, the woman's venomous glances had spoken volumes to her.

Over the years too she had seen little of her sister Midge, who had married shortly after she had left home; but like her father, the man had walked out on her after the birth of her first child. She was now living with a man who had given her two more children, but was kind to them all. She had visited them a few times and had been made very welcome, yet it had been embarrassing for both Midge and herself, for they had nothing in common. Midge had remained stationary: her old, bold effort in leaving home had apparently sapped her initiative. She was quite content with her life as a none-too-spruce housewife with a man who turned over his pay to her every Friday night.

She now stared at her reflection in the mirror as she combed her hair. The captain had asked her if she had a boyfriend. And she had answered 'no'. Well, she hadn't, had she? Well, not one that anyone knew about . . .

When she entered the room John was in the kitchen, and Bertha cast a quick glance towards her, then turned her attention to her husband, saying, 'Well, he can't hold you responsible for that.'

'But he does. That's what I'm paid for. He says we've lost a hundred birds since the grouse season started in August, but that's pure exaggeration. Thirty would be more like it. But then, thirty is thirty. And pheasants are going too, and that's before the season starts.'

'Did you tell him you can't be in two places or

three places at once? You've got Home Guard duty two nights a week. Why doesn't he engage somebody to prowl on those nights?'

With a sigh John sat down at the table, saying, 'You can't keep watch from twilight to dawn; it's impossible. I used to look upon it as a bit of a game when I had just old Ted Honeysett to watch and an occasional pirate now and then. Eeh my!' He shook his head as he turned to Meg. 'Life was simple in those days, Meg. We didn't know we were born.'

'Well, we do now.' Bertha put in. 'And come on, let's get the tea over because you, me girl' – she turned and looked at Lizzie – 'have a night's practice before you. You're not going on that stage tomorrow night and not know your five-finger exercises.'

'That reminds me,' put in John. 'I'll have to try and scrounge some petrol. I have enough to get us there, but as things are we'll have to walk back.'

They had been eating for a few minutes when Bertha, turning to John, said, 'Well, what's the other news from round about? We haven't had one caller, have we, Meg?' But before Meg could answer, John, looking down on his plate, said, 'Bill Titon's George has been reported missing. His ship went down. So I don't suppose Bill will be in The Hare tonight letting off steam. But I'm sorry for him. Aye, I am; but more so for her, even though she's got the other two.'

No-one spoke, but it was in all their minds, even Meg's, that the same news could come any time, and about the son of this house, the only son of this house.

3

The concert had been a success. Featured were a singing trio, two solo singers, a conjurer, three sketches, one of which was booed because the soldiers thought it was putting over a sergeant's point of view, and two piano solos played by Miss Elizabeth Gillespie.

The piano was set below the schoolroom stage and Lizzie had just finished leading the players and the audience in combined singing of a number of old-time songs, from 'Pack Up Your Troubles' to 'Down By The Old Bull and Bush'. And now the audience was dispersing, except for a group of soldiers and some civilians who remained standing around the piano urging Lizzie to carry on with the sing-song. And this she did.

As she played, John pushed his way to her side, saying, 'We are off. Will you get home all right?'

And one of the soldiers, standing by, shouted, 'It'll be all right, Dad. We'll see she gets home, and accompanied by full regimental turnout.' And he saluted with a quivering hand, which caused laughter, until John gave him a cool look, before saying to Lizzie, 'I'll meet the last bus at the corner. All right?'

'Fine.' She nodded at him, the while continuing the sing-song.

Half an hour later, when the singers were in the pathetic throes of, 'If those eyes could only see and those lips could only speak', the caretaker, somewhat irate, shouted above the din, 'It's ten o'clock! I've got to close up and get this place ready for the morrow. Finish now, will you?' and he carried on down the hall, switching off the lights, apart from the one near the stage, and when this brought a chorus of protest, Lizzie, with a trace of relief in her voice, said 'He's right. He's got the place to tidy up. Anyway, I've got to get that bus.'

'We promised your dad we'll see you home and we'll see you home; or at least I will.' The soldier now grabbed her music case from the top of the piano and caught hold of her arm, and at this she put one hand against his shoulder and pressed him off, saying, 'Thanks all the same, but I'm getting the bus.'

'Well, I can see you to it, can't I?'

'Me an' all,' put in one of the other soldiers; but at this the first man said, 'In this case, one's enough, two's a battalion.'

Forcing herself to laugh, Lizzie was about to remonstrate again with her persistent escort, when a figure moved out of the shadows and a voice said, 'There you are, then. Sorry I'm late. Couldn't make it earlier.'

The soldier slowly loosened his hold on Lizzie's arm and the rest of the group moved back, their bodies automatically stiffening as they did so, their eyes on the newcomer's sleeve. And when he asked brightly, 'Had a good night, lads?' they answered one after the other, 'Yes, sir. Yes, sir. Fine.'

'Good.' The officer nodded his head towards Lizzie, saying, 'She plays well, doesn't she?'

There was laughter now as some of the men answered, one saying, 'She does that, sir. She swings it. Could go on all night.'

'Well, that wouldn't be fair. She's a working girl; not like you lot, nothing to do all day but walk.'

There was a chorus of laughter, boos, and jeers. The men had all relaxed. Their opinion of the newcomer was evident. He was all right, was this one, even though he *was* in the navy.

'Well, good-night, good-night all,' he said, as he took Lizzie's arm.

'Good-night, sir. Good-night, sir.'

Smiling at the group, Lizzie said, 'Good-night, boys. I've enjoyed it.'

'So have we, miss. Good-night. Good-night.'

Outside, Andrew flashed his dimmed torch into her face and said, 'Aren't you going to thank me for rescuing you?'

'I don't think I was in much danger,' she said; 'at least, no more than I am now.'

'I wouldn't be too sure of that, if I were you.'

He now directed the flashlight on to the ground, and taking her arm firmly in his hold, he led her out of the school gate; and there he pulled her to a stop, and they stood facing each other but unable to make out any feature, other than a pale outline blur, and quietly he said, 'Are you going to take that bus? It'll go in ten minutes; otherwise we could walk it; we could take the short cut. Before you decide, let me say, I have forty-eight hours' leave. We are on the move the day after tomorrow, destination not generally known. Anyway, I may not be home for some time; and what is more to the point, I want to talk to you. And I

90

have wanted to for a long time, but you've always managed to make yourself elusive.'

She said quietly, 'We'll walk.'

And so they walked, although without speaking, until they were out of the town and on a stretch of the country road.

The sky was high and star-filled and it seemed lighter here than in the town, where the buildings emphasised and helped distribute the blackness of the night. Of a sudden he began talking, and rapidly, his words clipped. 'Lizzie,' he said, 'I'm twenty-five. This war isn't just being fought abroad, it's right on our doorsteps and either one of us could be dead tomorrow. More likely, it could be me, in which case I want you to know something. I love you, Lizzie. I think I've loved you since the first time I saw you. You were fifteen, scraggy, weedy, with no promise of the beauty you are today. But there was something. Now, no!' His voice had risen almost to a command as he cried, 'Don't pull away from me.' His hand tightened on her arm and he hugged it into his side. 'I know what you're going to say: there's Father. Well, Father, or no Father, he's not going to rule my life. I'll tell you something, Lizzie, something I have even been afraid to face telling myself. I dislike my father, dislike him intensely. When I meet other older men whom I like and admire I hate to think I was born of him. He is common, in the real meaning of the word . . . Don't get me wrong. I said, in the real meaning of the word he is common. All he thinks about is money and trying to force himself into a level of society that from the very beginning rejected him. I should thank him for educating me, yet, in doing so, he has done himself a

91

disservice because away from him I've been taught to think and learn the true meaning of values. Well, that disposes of Father; now what about me?' He pulled her abruptly to a stop and, placing his hands on her shoulders, he repeated quietly now, 'What about me, Lizzie? Do you care for me?'

Her voice had a break in it as she said, 'Yes, Andrew, I care for you. I . . . I more than care for you.'

'Oh, Lizzie, Lizzie, you mean that . . . that you love me?'

'Yes, just that. But I wish I didn't.'

'Oh! Lizzie.' He pulled her fiercely to him, and for the first time they kissed and clung together. And when at last he released her, he put his head back and laughed and shouted into the night, 'The war's over!'

'Andrew. Andrew. Be quiet. You don't know who's lurking.'

'Well, it's true, it's true; *my* war's over. I have won. Oh! Lizzie.' Again he kissed her; then asked quietly, 'Will you marry me?'

'Oh, Andrew, Andrew, I don't know; for no matter what you say, there's your father. He could make life unbearable for Dad.'

'Oh, don't worry about that. He knows he wouldn't be able to find anyone to run that place as well as John does. It would drop to bits if it wasn't for him.'

'What about Mrs Boneford?'

'Ah; Janis. Well, I don't think she'll give us any trouble. She has enough on her plate as it is. If she would only look down on it and tackle it, but she won't.

92

Poor Dickie. There's a tragedy if ever there was one. Lizzie—' he pulled her into his arms again, but went on talking, 'if we were married and that happened to me, would you turn from me?'

'No. No, Never! Never! because you would be the same man under the skin.'

'Do you know she won't even look at him? She avoids looking at him. At the table, he sits with his good side to her, but still she won't look at him. God knows what goes on when they're alone together. But then, they aren't any more; he has a separate room. I feel heart-sorry for him. But as for my sister, there're times when I want to knock her flat on her back. She's very like Father, you know. She would hate to think that, but she is. Anyway, back to the main question. When will you marry me? But first of all, Miss Gillespie, you'll have to take into consideration that I will likely be cut off without a penny. If I survive the war, I'll have to find a job. But Richard and I were talking. He says I could go in with him; he has ideas about breeding cattle. I was supposed to follow in my father's footsteps, although that never appealed to me; but he thought accountancy would come in handy. Yet even there I would have to re-start and finish the course again. So if nothing comes of Richard's business you'll have to work for me until I get on my feet. How do you like that prospect?'

'Not at all, Mr Bradford-Brown, not at all. I've always dreamed of marrying a man with money and possessions and a title. Oh yes, I'd like a title.'

They fell together and swayed, before walking on, their arms about each other now, and she saying, 'You haven't mentioned your mother. How will she take it?'

'Very politely. One never knows what my mother is thinking.'

'You'll know all right when you break this news to her. It will act like a bombshell. It would be bad enough if I was really John and Bertha's daughter, but considering where I was brought up . . .'

'Don't be silly. Anyway, we'll cross that bridge when we come to it. But no matter what she thinks or says, it will make no difference.'

'I wish I could think the same.'

They were brought to a halt suddenly by a voice coming out of the darkness, saying, 'Is that you, Lizzie?'

'Yes. Yes, it's me, Dad.'

She drew herself away from Andrew's arm, but he caught her hand and together they walked quickly forward towards John, who flashed his torchlight on Andrew's face, saying, 'Oh, it's you, sir. I was getting worried. I didn't manage to meet the bus and I began to wonder if she was still fighting off that horde of soldiery.'

'I rescued her from them, John; and by the way, I've made good use of the walk. I'll leave her to tell you about it. But I'll be over to have a talk with you tomorrow, John. All right?'

There was a moment's hesitation before John replied, 'You're welcome any time, Mr Andrew,' then he added rather sharply, 'Come along, dear. Bertha's had to go to bed; she's not very well.'

At this Lizzie said quickly, 'Good-night, Andrew.' And he replied, 'Good-night, my dear.' Then added, 'Good-night, John. Good-night.'

'Good-night, Mr Andrew.' John was walking quickly away now, his hand on Lizzie's elbow, and they had gone some distance before he said, 'And what was all that about, may I ask?'

'I'll . . . I'll tell you when we get inside. But . . . but what's the matter with Mam? Is it that pain again?'

'Yes, yes; although she won't admit it – I'm calling in the doctor tomorrow morning – and the fact that you weren't in wasn't helping.'

'I'm . . . I'm sorry.'

When they entered the kitchen Meg said, 'Ah, there you are, lass. I was beginning to think you were lost.' She turned from the stove, bringing the teapot with her, adding, 'But it was a grand concert and you played lovely. By aye, you did that. I was for joining in that sing-song at the end an' all and . . .'

'How is she?'

'Oh, fast asleep, John. The pill did the trick. Don't worry, she'll be all right. D'you want tea or cocoa?'

'Tea.'

'And you, lass?'

'Yes, tea, thank you, Meg.'

John pulled out his chair and sat down by the table and looked to where Lizzie was smoothing her hair down after taking off her hat, and he said quietly, 'Well now, let's have it.'

She then stood by his side and looked down into his eyes as she said, 'Andrew's asked me to marry him.'

He turned from her, joined his hands together, and thumped them a number of times on the table before he said, 'It won't work. That won't work.'

'Why not?'

'Oh, Lizzie' – he shook his head – 'do you have to be told? Does it have to be put into words? His father will never stand for it, nor will his mother; she less likely than he in this case, for underneath that quiet manner of hers she's more county conscious than most, and the war hasn't done anything to alter it. And then there's him; all these years trying to break down barriers and squeeze in alongside her, which he's never been able to do. But you wouldn't be able to get your business into his thick head. So you see . . .'

'No, I don't see.' Lizzie's voice was harsh. 'I don't agree with you. Things are different. People are different. When this war's over it'll be as different again.'

At this John screwed round on the chair and came back at her, his voice as harsh as hers, saying, 'When this war's over, Mr Andrew will be out on his backside if what you want takes place, 'cos he's dependent on his father, not being qualified.'

'He's got hands, hasn't he?'

'Don't be silly, girl; you don't take hands into account with that class of man. You wouldn't expect him to go navvying, would you? No. He'd have to use his head. And as I said, he's not qualified for anything.'

'He . . . he's an accountant.'

'He started at it, lass, and didn't finish; and just think, after this war's over, there'll be thousands of them grabbing for work, just like it was last time. Officers selling encyclopedias. Oh, you don't know anything about it.'

'I know this much, Dad.' Her voice was low and her tone sad. 'I love him. I've always loved him from when I first saw him, and . . . and he loves me. We'll take our chance on things.'

He turned from her again and, bowing his head, he said, 'Likely you will, lass. I'm sorry I went on so. But you know' – he now glanced at her sidewards – 'you're like one of me own. And as for Bertha, well, it would be hard to convince her that you're not.'

'I'm sorry. I'm sorry.' The tears were now flowing down Lizzie's face, and John rose quickly from the chair, saying, 'Aw, don't; don't do that, lass. It'll likely work out. I'm sorry I've opened me mouth so wide. Look, I'll go and see how she is.' He turned quickly from her and went from the room.

As Lizzie's hands went to her face, Meg led her to the settle, saying, 'Don't take on, lass, it'll work out. You do what your heart tells you. As for after the war an' findin' a job, well, you'll do what I did: work for him till he gets hissel' fixed. My Jimmy didn't do a stroke for three years after he came out. They had stopped buildin' ships, an' when he did get a job, he couldn't hold it for long because of the gas. He wasn't bad enough to get a pension, yet not fit enough to work, but nevertheless, we survived and we were happy. An' it'll be the same with you. Anyway' – she patted Lizzie's shoulder – 'God knows where we'll all be afore this is over. So, live and love when you can, lass. Aye, live and love when you can, because in the long run, life's short, and you don't really find that out until you're old, an' ready for your box. Well' – her voice rose – 'come on now, drink your tea and show your old spunk: stick to your guns. And as for John an' his class, my God! As I see it there'll be such a levellin' out after this war is over that they'll scrub that word out of the dictionary. Come on now, drink this tea.'

She handed Lizzie the cup of tea and Lizzie, looking up at her, nodded by way of acceptance, but did not reply. She was a comfort was Meg; so uncomplicated. Class held no barriers for her: she remained Mrs Meg Price on whatever level she found herself. Yet, of the two of them, she knew that her adoptive father was right. But even so, she'd marry Andrew. Oh yes, she'd marry Andrew, and after the war put up with whatever life presented them.

4

'Lizzie Gillespie!' Alicia screwed up her eyes and peered at her son, and the expression on her face seemed to imply that even the name on her tongue was most distasteful, and she repeated it, 'Lizzie Gillespie. You can't mean it, Andrew.'

'I mean it, Mother. Oh yes, I mean it.'

'Since when? I mean, how long has this . . . ?'

'Been going on? Seems years to me. I first really noticed her when she was about sixteen at the beginning of the war.'

'*You've actually asked her?*'

'Yes, Mother, I've asked her; and she's accepted.'

'Of course she has!' Her voice unusually high, she went on, 'She's no fool. But do you know where she comes from?'

'Yes, Mother, I know where she comes from. Who doesn't around here?' His voice matched her own now. 'But that woman was her stepmother and she's had no connection with them for years, and she's really been brought up by the Fultons.'

'I know by whom she's been brought up; and after all, what are the Fultons? He's a worker on this estate. You can't do this. *I forbid it, Andrew. I forbid it.*'

He looked at her sadly now as he said quietly, 'You can forbid me nothing, Mother. You seem to forget I'm twenty-five years old. I've been in the navy since the war started. My views might have remained the same if we hadn't been at Dunkirk. Get it into your head, Mother, I am no longer a boy, and you can't forbid me anything.'

He watched her thin neck swell as she gulped in her throat, and her voice was small as she replied, 'Your . . . your father, he'll . . . he'll . . .'

'Yes, I know, he'll go mad and go into his usual rage act, and he'll likely tell me he'll cut me off without the proverbial shilling. Well, that being so, I'll know where I stand, won't I?'

'You're hurting me, Andrew, you know that?'

'I cannot really see why, Mother. Would I have hurt you if I had been standing here telling you I had proposed to Irene Pringle? She's fat, hasn't a constructive idea in her head, but is the only daughter of the wealthiest man around. Would that have made you happy, Mother? Or even Kitty Bewick? Now what about her? She would be married on her horse, the one horse, because she never gets off it. But nevertheless, since her father died, she's quite wealthy, isn't she?'

There was a moment's silence between them, before Alicia said, 'Yes, Andrew; I would have welcomed either of them and without their estates.'

'It's to hell with happiness then, Mother, to hell with personal feelings, to hell with contentment so long as the face is saved, so long as you don't breach the county code. That's it, isn't it?'

'I would put it another way, Andrew: the more usual phraseology would be, not letting yourself down; however, I would say, not forgetting that you have a duty to your class, especially at a time when it is in more danger of being destroyed by the common people. You see, Andrew, I myself conveniently forgot it, and so now, unfortunately, I know what I'm talking about.'

As he stared at her it came to him that the real reason for the unhappiness that existed in the family was caused not so much by his father's dual nature, that of a bully and a social crawler, as by his mother's indomitable will to imbue and maintain what she had: the status quo, the only state in which her family should exist.

Quietly, he said, 'I'll go and pack.'

As he turned from her she said, 'You know your father won't give you a penny?'

'Oh, I'm well aware of that. Still, I suppose I'll survive.'

'You won't take to life in a cottage, Andrew. You've always had expensive tastes. It takes a great deal to keep a hunter, let alone a wife.'

He paused for a moment and looked at her over his shoulder, then left the room. And she remained staring at the door for a moment before swinging about and walking through into the library; and there she picked up the telephone and got through to her husband's office.

'I wish to speak to Mr Bradford-Brown, Miss Perkins.'

'He's in a meeting at the moment, Mrs Bradford-Brown.'

'Tell him to come to the phone, please!'

There was a pause before Miss Perkins said, 'He . . . he doesn't like to be disturbed when he's at . . . at a board meeting.'

'Will you please get word to him, Miss Perkins, that I wish to speak to him! It is important.'

'Yes, Mrs Bradford-Brown.'

Alicia waited, one hand tapping the inlaid table on which the telephone stood; and then she found a piece of inlay that had come loose. Instead of pressing it down, she placed her nail under it and began picking at it as if to lever it from its base.

The picking became more rapid as she waited; then the fingers became still when she heard her husband's voice. 'What is it, in the name of God! You know I have a board meeting and it's important. I told you before I left . . .'

'Listen to me, please. I'm sure you will welcome *this* news. Andrew has just told me he is going to marry Lizzie Gill . . . es . . . pie.' She spaced out the name then repeated, 'I hope you heard what I said. He proposes to marry Lizzie Gillespie.'

'*What!*'

'I've said it twice, Ernest. He is bent on it and if you don't do something it will likely take place under our noses. He's leaving on the one o'clock train.'

'My God! That girl Lizzie Gillespie?'

'That girl Lizzie Gillespie.'

'Has he gone mad? How long has this been going on? Did you know about it? Why didn't you . . .?'

'One thing at a time. I knew nothing about it. I don't know how long it's been going on, I only know that he admits having been interested in her since the beginning of the war.'

'Well, leave this to me. I'll soon put a stop to his gallop. If he thinks I'll support him after that he's mistaken. Leave this to me.'

'That was my intention when I phoned you, Ernest.'

She could picture him gritting his teeth not only at the news that she had imparted, but also at the tone of her voice. She repeated, 'He is catching the one o'clock train, remember. Goodbye.'

As she put down the phone Richard entered the room, saying immediately, 'Oh, I'm sorry. I . . . I didn't know you were talking.'

'It is all right, Richard, I'm finished.' Unlike her daughter, she *could* bear to look at Richard. He had always had impeccable manners and his voice remained the same. When she could get him talking he was a good conversationalist and well-versed in music and the arts. Last night, after dinner, they discussed Stravinsky and the Firebird suite, and the composer's connection with Rimsky-Korsakov. She had been surprised that he liked Dylan Thomas, but was not so fond of T.S. Eliot. And when she herself explained her doubts about her feelings concerning Picasso's art, he said something very strange. 'Picasso,' he said, 'started a war before this one, and in a way it was just as important because, through his paintings, he was expressing the need for freedom in all ways and all walks of life.' Although she couldn't agree with him, she listened to him. She only wished that Janis would listen to him; even look at him. Janis had been wayward since she was a child. In her own mind she had held her up against Andrew, wishing she was more like her brother. But now, here was Andrew stepping out of line as Janis never would have, because, give her her due, she had a sense of the fitness of things, as she had demonstrated by discarding that loud-mouthed Fulton fellow and taking Richard.

But had she really taken Richard? In his great need she had turned her back on him; and her affairs now were causing much comment.

She watched Richard walk towards her: his back was slightly stooped, his chin drawn in. He had once been so straight of carriage. She said, 'Have you seen Andrew?'

'Yes, Alicia. Yes, I had a quick word with him. He was getting his things together.'

'Did he tell you anything?'

'Yes.' He nodded at her. 'He wants to marry Lizzie, Lizzie Gillespie.'

'What do you think of that?'

Richard turned to the side and she could not see the expression on his face, because the stretched scarred skin hid all emotion. And she waited for his answer to her question, and she stiffened visibly when it came, for he said, 'I know you're not going to like it, Alicia, but I think it's a good thing. She's a charming girl; intelligent, and very beautiful.'

'Oh, Richard!'

He turned to her again: 'I knew you wouldn't like it, but there it is.'

'You didn't . . . well, you didn't tell him that you agreed with his choice?'

'I'm afraid I did.'

'How could you? You know who she is? I mean, where she was brought up?'

'Yes; yes, I've learned all about her since coming to this part of the world.' And now, his voice seeming to be wrenched from deep within him and becoming almost a stammer, he said 'She's the kind of g-g-girl, Alicia, who would stick by the m-m-man she married

104

and once professed to love, whatever happened to him. And I can't imagine Lizzie Gillespie closing her eyes when he looked at her.' And with this, he swung about and left her leaning back against the table for support, her hands gripping the top of her dress, and saying to herself, 'Good gracious! Good gracious!'

The girls in the Food Office were most intrigued by the good-looking, very smart naval officer who would pass the window every now and again, and between times they laughingly whispered among themselves and gave a guess as to whom he was waiting for: likely, one of the clerks from the first floor; perhaps the latest toffee-nosed recruit, the one who referred to her parents as Mama and Papa.

Lizzie said nothing. She kept her head down and attended to the customers. But on the dot of twelve o'clock she whipped her coat off the peg in the ante-room, and, as she left the room that had once been a shop, she knew that tongues would soon be wagging.

Her first greeting to Andrew was: 'You shouldn't have waited. They're all wondering.'

'Yes, I guessed that.' He smiled at her, turned her about and, taking her by the arm, walked her along the street.

Nearing the bridge, he said, 'Do you want something to eat?' And she shook her head saying, 'No. Let's go down by the river.'

So they sat on a seat still showing rimes of frost.

Taking her hand, he said, 'You're cold, icy cold.'

'No. My hands are always cold. I'm all right. What's . . . what's happened?'

He turned from her to gaze across the river to where the houses rose steeply up the opposite bank, and after a moment he said, 'It doesn't matter. Nothing matters, only you and me. What happened with you?'

She too looked across the river as she answered, 'Dad's response, I should imagine, was much the same as your parents'. He thinks it's madness and that they'll never stand for it. Mam's, I don't know yet. She was in bed when I got home last night and asleep when I left this morning. What exactly did your father say?'

'I don't know; I haven't seen him yet.'

'So, it was your mother's reaction, then?'

'Yes. But, Lizzie' – he gathered her hands within his and gripped them tightly – 'let's get this clear between us. It doesn't matter a damn what anybody says, we are going to be married, and we'll make it as soon as possible. I should get another leave shortly: we're on the move, but as I said, I think it's to the south coast, where the boys sometimes decide to drop from the air into the Channel. Anyway, I'll write to you every day. Will you write to me?'

'Of course, of course. Oh, Andrew, I . . . I'm so happy; yet even when saying that, I'm afraid: it doesn't seem quite true; and . . . and I know that if the war hadn't come about, it would not have happened. Strange, until now I didn't have anybody of my own in this war. You see, Geoff . . . well, I only saw him for a couple of days before he left for overseas and it seems a lifetime away. I was fourteen then. In my mind I'm always so grateful to him, but now I can't even picture his face. He doesn't seem to be like the various photos that Mam has around the house. He has been away so long that I feel she is going to get a shock when he returns. But anyway, he has never seemed to belong to me, not as you do. From when you first joined up, I started to worry over you.'

'Oh, my dear. My dear.'

She laughed gently now saying, 'I have a picture of you. It was taken by the *Journal*, but it doesn't show your face; mostly your behind.' She giggled now. 'You were disappearing over a gate after your horse had thrown you at the hunt.'

'Oh! Lizzie.' He too was shaking now. 'And you kept that?'

'Yes; and the caption, obviously written by someone with a sense of humour, said, "Master Andrew Bradford-Brown climbing over a field gate".'

'Oh, I remember that one. Yes; yes, indeed.'

Holding her hands, he felt her shiver, and he said, 'Come on, we must walk. You're cold.'

When they stood up, he looked first one way then the other before taking her into his arms and kissing her hard, after which he held her face gently between his hands, and said softly, 'It's got to be soon, our wedding,' and she nodded and fell against him, and whispered, 'Yes, yes, Andrew, soon, soon . . .'

As the train puffed into the station, Ernest Bradford-Brown rushed on to the platform, looked up and down, then espying his son at the far end, he pushed his way through the crowd of passengers towards him and his companion.

Andrew, about to give Lizzie a farewell kiss, saw him first, and he muttered, 'Oh, dear dear! The enraged parent . . . Hello, Father. I'm sorry I missed . . .'

'What the hell do you think you're up to? I . . . I'm putting a stop to this. I'm . . .'

His teeth gritted now, Andrew said, 'Who do you think you're talking to, Father? You can put a stop to nothing I intend to do. Get that into your head, and the sooner you accept it the better.'

The train had come to a stop and people were pushing into the compartments. Andrew picked up his case, took Lizzie's arm and pulled her towards a carriage door. As he thrust his case on to the floor, eager hands gripped it and put it on the rack, and then he turned and confronted his father again, who now growled out in an undertone, 'You'll have nothing. I won't give you a penny. You'll be on your own. What about that?'

'That's how I want it. Now goodbye, Father.' With that he turned to Lizzie and, putting his arms about her, kissed her stiff white face. And when she did not return his kiss, he said, 'Don't worry, my dear, I'll write, I'll see you soon.' He touched her face gently with his fingers, then jumped into the carriage, slammed the door and pulled down the window.

The train was beginning to move now and Lizzie moved with it, her hand extended and gripping his until she reached the end of the platform; and there she stood until his face was hidden by a cloud of steam.

Mr Bradford-Brown was waiting for Lizzie outside the station, and his first words, 'Think you've made a catch, miss, don't you?' loosened the anger within her, and, in no small voice, she cried at him 'Yes! Mr Bradford-Brown, but not in the way you are inferring. And who do you imagine yourself to be, anyway? Let me tell you something, Mr Bradford-Brown. I've always wanted to say this to you. The

108

opinion you hold of yourself is not shared by others. I could imagine your wife objecting to your son's choice, but not you, because just as you can make comparisons, which you are doing now, I can make them too, and tell you I was born and bred in a better class than you ever were. Poor, maybe, but respectable. And if I had my mother or father here today I wouldn't disown them. So, don't you take the high hand with me, Mr Bradford-Brown.'

To say that he was astonished at this tirade was putting it mildly: he was amazed and made blazing mad. And now he spluttered at her, 'You! You! How dare you! You'll suffer for this. You've stepped out of your place, miss, but I'll see that you're knocked back into it. And . . . and let me tell you this; I'd rather see my son dead than linked up with you.'

The last words silenced them both. They stared at each other. Then, as if only now realising what he had said, he nodded at her, adding, 'Yes; yes, I would. That's how strongly I feel about you, miss. I would.' And at this he turned from her and left her standing trembling, an object of curiosity to a small group of people gathered further along the kerb.

As she turned about she had to pass by them and one of the women touched her arm and said, 'Stick to your guns, lass. Stick to your guns.' She sounded just like Meg. And of a sudden, Lizzie wanted to rush home and lay her head on Meg's shoulder and cry out her fears. She did not in this moment think of Bertha, because Bertha would be like John: she would say that one should know one's place in the scheme of things and that nothing good ever came of stepping over boundaries.

Her thoughts recalled the picture of Andrew being tossed over the farm gate and about to land on his head, which could have killed him; and she heard again the words, 'I'd rather see my son dead than linked up with you.' For a moment she imagined she was actually going to be sick on the pavement.

5

When Lizzie arrived home that evening, Bertha wasn't in the kitchen; nor was she playing the piano; she was sitting by the fire in the sitting-room. And as she opened the door, Bertha turned her head towards her and said, 'Hello, there,' and Lizzie knew by the look on her face and the tone of her voice that she was in for what was termed 'a talking to'. And it soon became evident, for she had hardly taken her seat at the other side of the fireplace than Bertha was shaking her head and saying, 'Well, what are we going to do about this, lass?'

'You mean, what am *I* going to do about it?'

For answer Bertha said, 'He's been here, Mr Bradford-Brown, raging. He's threatened that if you persist in seeing Mr Andrew, he'll not let him into the house, that the door will be closed on him.'

'Did he now? Well, I'm sure that that won't worry Andrew over much.'

'Lizzie' – Bertha leaned towards her now, her hands outstretched in plea – 'I've treated you as though you were my own. You know I have. We both care for you very much and I don't want to see you hurt or upset, but . . . but you will be if this goes on, because you know the saying well' – she drew in a deep breath before she ended – '"Never the twain can meet." They are county folks. At least, she is; his mother. I don't hold much for the father, but she is. And . . . and you'd be like a fish out of water . . .'

'I'd be like no fish out of water.' Lizzie was on her feet now. 'Think what you're saying, Mam. It doesn't say much for how you've brought me up over the past five years.'

'Oh, lass, I don't mean you can't pass yourself off in ordinary company, but they're a different kettle of fish. They're a sort of law unto themselves. They have their ways. They're not our ways.'

'Mam! Mam!' She bent over Bertha now. 'You surprise me. You're kowtowing to them. I couldn't imagine you kowtowing to anybody. What are they anyway? Just ordinary people. Let me tell you this. I'm going to marry Andrew, in spite of his father, his mother, or—' She closed her eyes tightly and swung away as Bertha said, 'Me or John or anyone else? That's it, isn't it? And John's in a state, I can tell you.'

There was a long pause before Lizzie said, 'Yes, Mam, I'm afraid that's it.'

'Well, lass, there's nothing more to be said then. I've done what I thought I should do: try to make you see sense. But since I can't, then . . . well, I can't. But I know one thing: if you go through with this it's going to make everything very awkward for John, very awkward indeed. Although Mr Bradford-Brown won't get rid of him, he'll drive him to the last ounce of his strength.'

Bertha rose to her feet and, sighing heavily, she muttered, 'Well, that having been said, let's have some tea. And by the way, I've had a letter from Geoff. He's safe and sound, but as usual, he can't say much about where he is or what he's doing, only that . . . well, he would like to be home. And I must

112

tell you he asked after you and said he didn't expect he'd know you when he saw you.'

Lizzie turned about, the tears in her eyes now, and, going hastily towards Bertha, she put her arms about her as she said, 'Oh, Mam, Mam. I'd do anything rather than upset you, but I . . . I must tell you now I've . . . I've been in love with Andrew for years. That's why I haven't taken up with anyone else. And I've had plenty of chances.'

'There, there! girl. There, there! Yes, as for chances, I know all about them, and I wondered why, many a time. Still—' She pressed Lizzie away from her and smiled at her now, saying, 'I was young once too. I'll have to remember that. And look! Give me my stick, where you've knocked it onto the floor.'

As they made their way towards the kitchen, Lizzie said, 'Where's Meg?' And Bertha answered, 'She went into Shields to see if her home's still standing. She should be getting off the bus about now. I thought John would be in to go and pick her up because she'll likely come back laden with more of her bits and pieces.'

Lizzie glanced at her wrist-watch. 'It's due in five minutes; that's if it's on time,' she said. 'I'll slip along and meet her.' And with that she hurried across the hall, picked up her hat and coat from the cloakroom and left the house glad to escape from the feeling of thinly veiled censure still emanating from Bertha.

The twilight was drooping like a mist over the far hills; the sky was low, threatening rain again. They'd had two dry days, but previously it had rained almost incessantly for a week and the river was swollen and had overrun the banks along many stretches.

The bus stop was on a part of the road that skirted

the river. At one spot the bank dropped steeply to the swirling waters, and she was surprised to see a pile of debris lodged in a large bush half-way up the bank. She had never known the river to have risen so high.

As the bus approached, it slowed down and the driver waved to her. She could see it held only three passengers, none of them Meg, and she continued to watch it until it disappeared beyond the bend in the road.

This was the first time Meg had missed the bus. Had something happened to her? Oh, she hoped not. She had become fond of Meg; there was something comforting about her.

Slowly now she began to retrace her steps towards home, only to turn and look back towards the hill in the distance, the while thinking: having missed that bus, surely Meg would take the one to Fuller's crossroads, even though it would mean a longer walk home. Yes, that's what she would have done.

Should she go and get her bike? No; she would walk. But again she paused, undecided; an indecision she was to remember in time to come for, had she been riding or pushing her bike, her gaze, in all probability, would have been directed straight ahead. And it was now as, with the strong wind behind her, she set off for the crossroads.

In a very short time, added to the noise of the wind was that of the river flowing strongly nearby and to her right. Normally an unfamiliar noise, but the recent heavy and prolonged rain had transformed the river into a wider, much deeper and fast-flowing torrent, with the wind blowing downstream, determined to urge it on.

She was on the hill now, a gradual incline rising to the small bridge which, at one time, had been the only line of communication between two villages and was still much used by farm and light traffic.

Any excitement that might have stirred in Lizzie on hearing the unusual sound of the nearby fast-flowing river was suddenly turned into fear. She had sighted the bridge and the mass of debris built up on this side, and the obvious cause of the build-up: a tree, uprooted further upstream, had been constrained by the stone-work and was stretching well across the opening of the arch.

The restriction of the flow of water had caused the faster flow through the free part of the arch opening and the obvious, but previously unfelt, power of the river in spate created a fear, which was increased when she saw a man moving down the bank towards the water; and her fear turned to horror when she realised the identity of the man now wading into the water.

My God! What was he up to? No! No! And the denial drove her, too, into the water, screaming, 'Captain! Captain!'

The water was up to her shivering waist when she saw his arm go out and grab a branch of the tree and shake it vigorously. And his attempt to free the tree must have been partly successful, for it suddenly swung him round, leaving him facing towards her.

And now it was he who was screaming: 'Oh my God! Lizzie! Lizzie!'

He was aiming to make his way towards her when the shuddering of the debris caused him to look upwards.

Suddenly he was swung round and struggling to clutch the branch again for support, and she almost threw herself towards him.

It was as their outstretched hands touched that there came a thundering, tearing sound, as if the bridge itself were being uprooted, for under her clutching hand the timber heaved, wrenching her away and flinging her on to her back.

When the water swirled over her head she realised that she might drown. Then she had surfaced and was being bombarded from all sides with wood and wool. She knew it was wool when her fingers clawed at it. And then again she was drawn under; but now she knew she was holding on to something, not just with her hand, but with her arms too, and it wasn't the shape but another kind of weight. First, it was on top of her; then under her.

As if she were seeing it happen, she felt herself rolling on to hard ground and she imagined she let out a long, long sigh of relief and became content to just lie where she was. And this she did for some time before she endeavoured to open her eyes.

She had to force her lids up a number of times before she could take in that she was lying in shallow water and that she wasn't alone, for she was embracing that weight and the weight was embracing her.

She turned her head to the side, coughed and spewed up the river water; but he didn't move nor, for a time, did she. Then, as if coming out of sleep, she brought her arms from around him and patted his face, gasping, 'Are . . . are you all right?'

The patched side of his face and across his jaw was covered with scum from the river. It seemed to have more easily clung to the skin and he looked like a wild man.

His good eye opened and the pain in it silenced the question she was about to put to him, for it was a silly question, 'Why? Why?'

He drew in a shuddering breath, spat out some water, wiped his mouth with the fingers of one hand, then gasped, 'Oh! Lizzie, Lizzie, I'm sorry.'

'It's all right.'

'It . . . it was the last straw.'

She didn't ask what the last straw was; then he said, 'You . . . you could have died. I . . . I'll never forgive myself.'

'Don't be silly. Look! Let's get up out of this.' She went to rise but fell on to her knees, her whole body shivering. And when he went to move he gave a groan, and she turned to him quickly, saying, 'What is it?'

'My leg. My foot. I . . . I must have twisted it.'

'Can you stand?'

When he tried, he winced. Then, using his elbow, he pulled himself further up the sloping river bank. Once there he fell on to his side and his body went into a paroxysm as if with the ague. Quickly she knelt beside him and put her arms about him, saying, 'There, there; you'll be all right. You'll be all right. But listen: I . . . I'll have to go and get help. You understand?'

He now stammered, 'Li . . . Li . . . Lizzie. Oh, Li . . . Lizzie, don't leave me. Please don't leave me.'

She looked about her helplessly. She had imagined they must have been driven some distance down the river by the debris. But there was the bridge not fifty feet away. Fortunately they must have been thrown to the side.

Then she couldn't believe her ears when a raucous voice came from the road yelling, 'Is that you, Lizzie? In the name of God! what you doin'?'

She twisted round and looked upwards, her face bright with relief as she cried, 'Oh, Meg! Meg! Am I glad to see you!'

She noticed that Meg wasn't alone, but she couldn't make out who was with her. She called, 'Can you come down here a minute?' Then taking her arms from around Richard, she pulled herself to her feet and shouted, 'No! Meg. It'll be too steep for you. Go back to the house and get Dad. Tell him Mr Boneford's hurt his leg.'

'I can make the bank; and Mr Honeysett's here.'

In a few minutes Meg and Ted Honeysett were gazing at the pair of them. And Meg cried, 'You're wet! You're both wet! What's happened?'

'He . . . he fell in the river. He . . . he's in a bad way: I don't think we can manage him on our own.'

'We could if we could get him up the bank.' Ted Honeysett leaned over Richard now, saying, 'I've got me flat cart up there, sir. I was trundling some wood, but I can tip that off. Can you stand, Mr Boneford?'

Richard made the effort and, with Ted's help, Lizzie got him on his feet, and with Meg supporting him at the back, slowly they negotiated the bank, all of them gasping by the time they reached the road.

There, they laid him on the verge, while Ted tipped out the wood from the flat cart.

Richard was still shivering as if with the ague when, at last, they had him lying crosswise on the flat hand-cart. To Ted's enquiry, 'Is he for the house?' Lizzie answered, 'No; our place.' And at this, Ted nodded, and began to push the cart, saying, 'Aye, I suppose that'll be better.' Then, looking at Lizzie with concern, he said, 'I think you're in almost as bad a state as him, lass. What happened?'

'He . . . he fell in the river.'

'Oh, aye, aye. Well, I've heard of such things. Anyway, lass, an' you, missis, you might have to put your weight on to this side of the cart to act as a brake when we're goin' down the hill . . .'

'In the name of God!' was what both Bertha and John said almost together when they were confronted by the spectacle at the kitchen door.

What Lizzie said was, 'I'll explain later, Mam . . . Dad. Can he be put in Geoffrey's room? He's in a bad way.'

'Yes, yes, of course.' And John helped to get Richard into the kitchen. Then he and Ted Honeysett together almost carried him up the stairs.

But it was Meg and Bertha who undressed him and put him to bed, John having been given orders to run a bath for Lizzie and see that she got into it, and quickly.

Downstairs, John asked Ted Honeysett, 'What happened?'

'It's no use askin' me, Mr Fulton; that's what I'd like to know an' all. I'd met up with Mrs Price; she was trudging along the road. She had got off the bus at Fuller's Crossroads, a daft bus to take, I think, to get here, but then she had missed t'other one. I'd been gathering some wood . . . not from your place!' And he dug a finger towards John. 'Robank had a tree down in the wind. He told me I could have the odds and ends if I swept up round about. You have to pay for everythin' these days; you don't get owt for nowt. Anyway, there we were at the top of the hill and she was chattering away, Mrs Price, tellin' me about Shields and the mess they've made of some places there. She was making me laugh. She's a star, that one. Anyway, I happened to look down the bank and I see these two figures. I thought they were courting, but it was a funny place to do courting, lying on the water's edge, their arms around each other! Then Mrs Price let out a squeal, and well, there they were, Mr Boneford and your Lizzie, like drowned rats, clinging together. That's . . . that's all I know, except she said he had fallen in the river. What I did notice, mind, was the muck that had mounted up by the bridge.' He nodded again at John. 'Funny business, I say, him falling in the river; but why should she fall in the river an' all? And all with their clothes on. Now what d'you make of it, Mr Fulton? Eh?'

His voice very quiet now, John said, 'I don't know what I make of it, Ted; but I'll ask you this: don't spread it around until we find out what's behind it. You understand?'

'Oh, I understand, I understand. I can keep me mouth shut when I like; I've had plenty of practice.' He grinned now, then as he made for the door he said, 'It's understandable, isn't it, wanting to do away with yourself when you look like that? She's a brave lass, is your Lizzie. A good lass. Aye, a good lass. Good night to you.'

'Good night, Ted; and thank you. Call in when you're passing sometime; I might have something for you.'

Ted Honeysett turned from the darkness of the door

and, his face beaming, he said, 'That's right civil of you, Mr Fulton. I'll do that. I'll do that.'

Meg came into the kitchen now, saying, 'I'll have to get a hot-water bottle or two, but I can't see it's gona do much good. I think you'd better get the doctor; that fellow's bad. And what about tellin' them up there?'

'Yes,' John sighed. 'Yes, they'll have to be told up there, all right. Is he still shivering?'

'Aye, as much as ever; and he's a bit light-headed an' all. Lizzie's not too bright, either. Have you got any whisky left?'

'Yes; there's a drop in the bottle.'

'Well, I'd give her a strong dose in some boiling water and take it up to her. But I'd phone the doctor first.'

As he went to the phone in the hall, he was thinking how odd it was that Meg seemed to take charge in a crisis. It was good to have her about . . .

The doctor said he would be unable to come for another hour or so; he still had one or two patients to see to in the surgery; but that he'd be along as soon as he could.

A few minutes later John told Lizzie this as he handed her the steaming mug; and as she sipped at it and shivered, he said, 'He'll have to look in on you an' all.'

'Oh, I'm all right. Is this whisky? You know I don't like whisky.'

She put the mug on the side table, then pulled the bedclothes around her shoulders and watched John lower himself on to the side of the bed before he said, 'What happened?'

She looked down the length of the eiderdown before

121

she replied, 'I . . . I think he was trying to commit suicide. He . . . he's a good swimmer – he told me so once – but there would have been no chance of swimming if he had been hit by the full force of the debris, and he in full uniform as he was. I . . . I feel he was sort of making sure.'

'He could have made sure of you an' all, then.'

'Oh, I . . . I was some way back.'

'Then how did you manage to get hold of him?'

'I . . . I didn't; I think he got hold of me. I don't know really; it all happened so quickly. I only know I was petrified for a time. I thought it was my end.'

'And it could have been, damn fool that he is!'

'Oh, Dad, just think . . .'

'Aye. Aye.' And he nodded. 'I'm sorry for him, heart-sorry, but I'm thinkin' of you. You could have been down the river an' all.'

'No, no, I wouldn't. I know he made an attempt to come back when he saw me, but it was too late.'

'What d'you mean, too late?'

'Well, he had loosened the branch, or whatever it was, that was blocking the debris across the arch. Have you phoned the house?'

'No. I won't do anything until the doctor comes.'

'They needn't know, Dad, need they? I mean, *she* needn't know. It'll make him feel awful.'

'Look, lass, that's for him to sort out. Anyway, how are we going to explain to Doctor McNeil that he's in this house and you're not in very good trim, either? And Meg says he's jabbering, so you don't know what he might come out with. Anyway, don't you worry your head about that. You've done more than you should. My God! I'd say, yes. But as it is, I don't suppose he'll be grateful to you.'

'He's a nice man, Dad. He's . . . he's still the same underneath, you know.'

'Aye, aye, I know that. But you can't get people to think like that when they look at him; you've got to know him first. In my opinion, I think they should stay in hospital until they are right.'

'Oh, Dad.' She jerked herself up on the pillow. 'That could be years. I think he's had six operations already. What he was like to begin with, God only knows; and he's still human. They're all still human; they want to get back into ordinary life.'

'All right, all right. Don't excite yourself. What's the matter with you? To my mind you've had more than enough the night without doing any more championing. Now lie still. Bertha'll be in in a minute.'

It was odd that at this moment she noted he didn't refer to Bertha as 'your mam', although she herself called them Mam and Dad. And Bertha always referred to him as John. Over the years this had irked her and had caused her to wonder why, on her sixteenth birthday, Bertha had said, 'You always call me Ma'am, like for "mistress", but it could be Mam for mother, too, and I'm sure my John wouldn't mind being called Dad. Would you like that?' She had answered that she would like it very much. It had taken her a little time to get used to the idea and she'd never felt actually sure that Mr Fulton, as she had previously addressed him, agreed with his new title.

When the door had closed on him she let her body sink into the bed. She was feeling tired, exhausted. Her head was aching, and she was still feeling cold. She reached out and, pulling a face, finished the rest of the whisky, and in a short while she became drowsy; but as sleep was about to overtake her she felt herself once again under the water, and then she was gasping and rolling over and over, still held in a fierce grip. Now his face was above hers, and he was crying, 'Lizzie! Lizzie!' and she cried back, 'It's all right, Richard. It's all right.' From then a calmness came upon her. Somebody was stroking the hair back from her brow and a voice was saying, 'There, there, me dear, go to sleep. You're all right. Go to sleep.' And she knew it was Meg, and she said to her, 'I've never called him Richard before.'

'There, there, lass. Go on, go to sleep. You'll feel better in the morning. Go to sleep.'

6

As Meg said, things always happened in threes. There was that poor fellow lying upstairs for the past four days not knowing where he was. Concussion, the doctor had said. And there was Lizzie with a cold on her that was tearing her chest out. Then there was that madam and him, the big noise from the house: they had been here twice and each time had gone upstairs as if there was a smell under their noses. And this morning *she* had come, his wife. They'd had a job to find her. She had gone off without telling her parents or her husband where she was going. They had only located her last night. She had been civil enough, she'd say that for her, and subdued like. She herself had been washing him down when the door opened and John said, 'Here's Mrs Boneford, Meg.'

He had come round this morning, and thankfully was right in the head. He had spoken to her quite sensibly, apologising all the time for the trouble he had caused, and saying he was all right, that he had better get home. Then the door had opened, and when he saw his wife, he had closed up like a clam. And she hadn't had much to say either, at least not while she was in the room. She hadn't acted like a wife who was concerned: she had spoken polite like, and had remained at the foot of the bed, not gone up to him; and what she had said was, 'How are you?' He hadn't

125

answered her; he had just stared at her with that good eye of his, the one that could do a lot of speaking for itself if you took notice of it.

She herself had felt embarrassed, which was a new sensation for her, and she had jabbered and said, silly like, 'I'll come back and powder you down in a minute or so,' as she had gone out, leaving them together; but she had hardly got down the stairs when the wife came down into the hall, saying, 'Is Mrs Fulton about?' And she had answered, 'She's upstairs in her room. She's had some disturbing news.'

'Oh, I'm sorry,' she had said. 'Nothing too bad, I hope.'

'Well, she doesn't really know how bad it is. But she's had word that her son Geoffrey has been wounded.'

'Geoff . . . rey wounded?'

'Yes. That's the latest; and it's no time since she had a letter from him. Of course, it wasn't dated. So you can reckon she's a bit upset. John's with her.'

'Yes, yes, of course. I'm sorry,' she had said, that was all, and had walked towards the door.

'Perhaps, when you come back this afternoon, you can have a word with her,' Meg had ventured to say, and the woman turned at the door, saying, 'I . . . I may not be back this . . . this afternoon, but tell Mrs Fulton I'm very sorry to hear about . . . her son. Very sorry.'

'Aye, I'll tell her.'

Standing in the kitchen, Meg nodded to herself as she mashed a pot of tea and spoke aloud saying, 'Something fishy atween those two. Likely as not he didn't open his mouth to her. He looked as if he wouldn't. Poor fella, I'm heart-sorry for him. Why

126

can't they put brown skin on them transplants, instead of that baby pink stuff? Where do they get it from anyway? It wouldn't matter so much about the skin being stretched tight over the bones, but that colour! As pink as a baby's backside.'

It was a week later when almost the same thought ran through Lizzie's mind as she sat opposite Richard in the sitting-room.

His uniform had been cleaned and pressed. His sprained ankle was almost mended, although his stick was leaning against his chair, which had caused a little merriment between him and Bertha, albeit, forced on both sides.

They had been sitting by themselves for over fifteen minutes, their conversation ranging around the weather which was showing the first signs of snow, and it was still touching on the weather when she asked, 'How long will it take you to get home; that's if you don't run into heavy snow?'

'Oh, remembering how Matty drives, and now with the wheel of an army vehicle under his hand, I think we should do it in four hours.'

They stared at each other across the space of the fireplace. Then Lizzie, bending forward, picked up the poker and pushed a smouldering log into the red heart of the fire as she said quietly, 'Why aren't you going back to the house?'

He turned the good side of his face fully towards her, the eye blinking; then he said quietly, 'To answer that I'd have to tell you why I tried to do away with myself,' but then, patting his disfigured cheek, he went on, 'It wasn't only because of this, because, believe it or not, there are worse than me back there . . . in the hospital, much worse. Nor was it only the fact that she can't bear to look at me, although at first that did nearly break me; it was—' and he exhaled a deep breath, then wetted his lips before going on, 'because I found her with one of my friends. I'd had my suspicions for some time, knowing there was someone, but when it turned out to be him . . .' He stopped abruptly, stood up, and, turning to the fire, held his hands out towards it, and remained thus for some seconds before swinging about again to grab his stick and to look down at her and say, 'I'd been in his company the day before. We'd had a drink, and a long talk. Then there he was, there both of them were. It . . . it was just by chance I found them. You see, we had talked about getting together, he and I, and doing a bit of shooting; and all of a sudden I felt so low that I decided to go home . . . to my own home, and knowing that he had a leave due, I thought I'd ask him to come with me. I . . . I went over to Durham, where I knew he was billeted. I had been there a few times before; in fact, it was there that I introduced him to Janis. When I knocked on the door and the landlady opened it she stared at me, her mouth agape, then said, "Oh, my God!" Then she gabbled, "He's not in. He's not in." I stopped her closing the door with my foot and as I did so I glimpsed, draped across the hall chair, a green mac with a hood hanging from it. The hood was lined with fur. It was a very smart affair. I had bought it for Janis when we were first married.'

He paused again, and she could see sweat running in rugged rivulets over the patched skin, and then he went on, 'In pushing open the door I almost knocked

128

the poor woman on to her back. But I rushed up the stairs, and I opened two doors before I saw them. If I'd had a gun with me, I'd have shot them both; if I'd felt fit enough, or able enough, I'd have throttled, not him, but her. But since getting this,' – he tapped his chin gently with his finger – 'I seem not to have any guts in me, no strength: energy and I have parted company. So what did I do? I just turned about and walked out. Well, the rest you know.' He turned from her again and, reaching out, he placed a hand on the mantelpiece as he said finally, 'I felt humiliated to the very core of me; I felt less than a man in all ways. I looked less, I was less. I told myself I shouldn't blame her because all I wanted from her was comfort, understanding, enough to get me through until the miracle happened and I could look like a human being again, even though I knew it never really would in my case.'

'Oh! Mr Richard.' She rose, and taking his hand from where it was resting on the mantelpiece, she held it, saying, 'You'll come through. I know you will. I feel you will after this. You'll come through; just hang on. When do you have to go back to hospital?'

'In a fortnight's time.'

'Well, that'll be another step.'

'I don't want to go. I've made up my mind I've had enough.'

'Oh, please! Please! They're working wonders. Keep at it. You said last week you owed me something, your life. Well, I want paying for it: your promise that you'll keep up the treatment . . . well?'

He stared at her in silence for some seconds; then smiling his twisted wry smile, he said, 'All right, Lizzie, yes, all right. One thing I'd like to ask of you. Would you and Mrs Fulton and Meg take a trip to my home sometime? My parents would love to meet you all, especially you. By the way, they know nothing of this business, but I'll tell them when I get back, and also that I'm filing for a divorce.'

'Divorce?'

'Yes. I've told her. She's not averse, but they are, her parents.' He smiled grimly now. 'The scandal, you see, the scandal. You know what her mother asked me yesterday? She asked if I would take the blame. And when I said I wouldn't, she was astounded. "You're not behaving like a gentleman," she said. Huh!' he grunted. 'If you had trained your daughter to behave like a lady it might have rubbed off on me, I said. As for him, her father, well, Meg will tell you, he raised the roof. I had to remind him where he was.'

'So you mean to go through with it?'

'Oh yes, yes. You see, Bernard wasn't the first, not as far as I can gather, or the second, or the third, for that matter. I've even heard rumours, although I don't know how much of it is true, that she had a longstanding affair with the son of this house.'

In the silence that followed as they looked at each other, Lizzie blinked, and as she did so, she thought, Trespassers will be persecuted.

As she withdrew the hand that had been holding his all this while, he put his head to one side and said softly, 'I hope you and Andrew will be very happy. He's a good fellow, is Andrew. He doesn't seem to belong to that family. Anyway, I couldn't imagine anyone not being happy with you.'

The colour flooded her face and she said on a laugh, 'I'm no ministering angel. I've a temper. You haven't experienced it. Ask Mam.'

He smiled; then on a solemn note he said, 'I'm going to put this to you, Lizzie. It seems silly at the moment and of no worth, but this war could go on for a long time and things could happen. I want you to promise me that if you ever need a friend, you'll call on me. Will you do that?'

She stared at him, her mind telling her that she couldn't see any situation arising when she'd be so badly in need of a friend that she would have to seek him out. Yet, he would be a good friend, a wonderful friend; he was such a nice man. She said quietly, 'I promise you that, Richard.'

It was such an easy promise to make, because once he returned to his estate in Scotland, she couldn't see them meeting again: now that he was divorcing his wife, there would be no reason for him to come here again. But, of course, he had asked her, together with Mam and Meg, to visit his home. But that could have been out of politeness and in return for the hospitality he had received here. She felt sorry at the thought for, in some way, she imagined she could have been of some help to him: he had himself said he could talk to her; and as Meg was wont to say of her, she was like a tin opener when she was in company. It would seem that she could not only chatter, she could also listen.

Of a sudden he said, 'There's the car. Goodbye, Lizzie. And thank you. I'll . . . I'll go and say goodbye to the others,' and when she made to walk with him, he added, 'Don't come to the door, please. Just stay where you are,' and turned somewhat abruptly from her.

After the door had closed on him she remained where she was staring towards it. She decided she was sorry he was going.

132

PART THREE

1943

1

It was the end of May, 1943. So much had happened in the country and abroad, and also at the house. During March, so many ships had been sunk. The whole country was gasping for breath. The only hope seemed to be that the Americans would inject some miracle drug into the affairs of state and turn the war about.

On this day, Thursday 27 May, Meg was seated at the kitchen table, which was set for tea, and gazing at the four other people seated there: Bertha and John, Lizzie and Geoffrey, and as Lizzie put her hand out and touched Meg, saying, 'Oh, don't cry, Meg,' Bertha said, 'Have a strong cup of tea. There! There!'

Meg roughly wiped her face with a large handkerchief before saying, 'Thanks, all the same, Bertha, but it seems I've been drinkin' tea all day. Everybody was kind. Eeh! You never saw anythin' like it. I've thought I'd never see anythin' worse than the market place that Thursday in '41. But today, our street is a shambles. Me house is no more. All me bits and pieces gone. But then, what does that matter? All those poor folks killed, and I don't know how many hurt. Eeh! I just stood there and cried. I've never cried so much in me life. When I lost the twins after the boat capsized, I cried. And when I lost him, me man, I cried. But it was a different cryin' the day. It's a good job I brought me photos with me. That's all I've got left of them.'

John rose from the table and placed a hand on Meg's shoulder, saying, 'You've lost your home, Meg, but let me tell you, you've got one here as long as you've got a mind to stay. Isn't that so, Bertha?' He looked across the table and Bertha nodded her head, saying, 'Definitely. Definitely, Meg. And you know it, don't you?'

Again Meg wiped her face with the large handkerchief, then said, ''Tis kind of you. 'Tis kind of you, John, and you too, Bertha, but . . . but I'm gettin' on an' I wouldn't be a burden to anybody. Anyway, one of the officials said the day that they'll see me well-housed when I go . . . back.' She forced a smile to her face now as she said, 'I'll take badly livin' in a town again after bein' out in the wilds. I've got to kind of like it. And when you think of it, people say nothin' happens in the country. Eeh! I've seen more how'd y'do since I came here than I did in years back there.'

'Oh, we've plenty of how'd y'do, Meg. We can always supply you with that.' John had taken his seat again and grinned across at his son, saying, 'Oh, there's plenty of how'd y'do here. What do you say, Geoff?'

Geoff turned his head to the side and gave a tight smile as he answered, 'Yes, of all varieties: "Bumps-a-Daisy", "Knees Up Mother Brown", not forgetting "Roll Out The Barrel", the lot,' and as John watched him pushing his chair back to get to his feet, an anxious thought struck him: his son had changed. He had imagined that with his new rank and status he would have returned . . . well, sort of polished. But most of the time now he was morose, whereas he had always been one for a joke or a jest. Now there was neither wit nor humour in his replies; in fact, as

136

inane as the bit he had just come out with. Perhaps it was his wounds that had upset his mind; even though he had been lucky to get off as lightly as he had. Of course he would limp for the rest of his life, and his left forearm was now little more than useless. Still, he was alive; he should be grateful.

He had been at home now well over two months but he hadn't settled. It was as if he had been injured more in his mind than in his body.

John watched him walk towards the back door and lift his cap off the wooden peg. Although he was finished with the army, he still wore his lieutenant's uniform, and even if he was just going for a walk through the woods he would spruce himself up before going out. He had longed for his son's return, but he had to admit to himself there had been a tenseness pervading the house since he had returned. He wasn't the same fellow who had gone into the army. Whatever he had been through had changed him entirely . . .

Geoff walked along the road between the two woods. His pace was controlled by the fact that he had to lift his left foot well off the ground before he could bring it forward and put his weight on it. It would have been easier if he'd had the aid of a walking stick, but since he had been home he had discarded it. It was enough, he thought, that his mother had to use one. His shoulders were slightly slumped and his head bent forward. Walking like this it appeared he had lost inches.

For the countless time during the last few weeks he asked himself what he was going to do. Look for a sitting-down job? Learn to be a clerk? He glanced towards his left arm. It wasn't swinging in the same way as his right. He supposed he should be thankful it was still there and he hadn't been given a tin tube fixed at his elbow with a hook on the end. There were lots of things he should be thankful for, but he couldn't feel thankful for anything. It had all been so different out there, where he had felt himself to be somebody. He had got his promotion; he would have gone further: he had been accepted, and he was known to be a first-class leader. His surface skin had thickened, but any sensitivity left in him, he had imagined, had been smothered and died. Its burial place had been in Sidi Barrani, Christmas 1940, when they had chased the Italians through Bardia, Tobruk, Derna, and Benghazi, and as far as Agheila. Of course the bloody Germans then had to come in and they had to leave Tobruk at the double. Yet they came back again near the end of 1941 and got as far as Agheila again. God! It had been a see-saw, but he had come through whole, with not a scratch. He had seen men drop all around him, a bullet had even dented his helmet; and so he believed that there was no number on him; that is, until the see-saw swung back the other way, when the German and Italian counterthrust forced them back to the Ghaza line outside Tobruk. And it was there that his skin thinned again. It wasn't only that he copped it right down one side, because for a time he wouldn't believe it, for he had carried on, at least, crawled on, yelling his bloody head off. Then the shell had burst, and they'd all gone in one fell swoop. His sergeant, Jim Rolston, and young Hal Fairbanks, too. He had got him made corporal only a few weeks before. And Bodger Ripton, who was never out of the cooler but who had been the best scrounger in the battalion. You mentioned it, Bodger got it; and nearly always got it in the neck for getting it. And Spud Winter, who told the hair-raising tales about his Irish mother, and if you summed them all up, she must have been the biggest whore in Dublin. Spud had come through all the way with him and he had missed him when he got his buttons up. Yet, given the opportunity, and there he was, saying, 'Sarge, I mean, sir, I mean . . . well it was like this, sir. You see, me mother . . .'

Aw, Spud! Spud! And then there was Harry. Harry Cole, Captain Harry Cole. He had been good to him, had Harry. That was the only word he could put to him: 'good'. He had welcomed him into the club. There was no 'risen from the ranks' attitude with Harry as there was with some of the others. Harry had been out of the top drawer. His father was a big noise, and he was the only son of his father. Then there he was with no face, no shoulder, no arm; just a bloody mess. His legs were still there, and they were lying across Spud.

He himself had lain on his side, his mind dizzying away from him, although before it went completely he had grabbed what remained of both Spud and Harry, which was all he remembered, until a voice said, 'Hello, there! How are you?' and he had gazed up into the face above the white coat, and instead of saying, 'All right, sir,' he had yelled, and swore, and cursed, and when his voice had reached a scream in his head, all had gone quiet again. And that's how it had been since. The only difference now was that the shouting happened in his dreams and he would wake up whimpering their names.

He turned abruptly about to return to the house, and as he neared it he saw Lizzie coming out. She

139

was wearing a blue print dress with a three-quarter white woollen coat over it, her feet in putty-coloured open-toed sandals, and on her head a cream leghorn straw hat.

They both stopped. She was the first to speak. 'Enjoyed your walk?' she said.

'Yes. Yes,' and he nodded at her, but became silent again. It was some seconds before he said, 'You know, I still can't get over you. I'm still seeing you as that scraggy, plain-looking thing I brought to the house. How many years ago is it?' He bent his head towards her, enquiry in his eyes.

'Well, you should know; you left in 1937 and it's now 1943.'

'You are nineteen?' He shook his head.

'Coming on twenty.'

Again he was silent. She was beautiful. She had a freshness about her such as he could not find words to explain. It wasn't only her skin or her eyes, but somehow the whole of her. And she was going to marry Andrew Bradford-Brown.

As he had found of late, he didn't want to talk much, but when he did, he didn't think twice or couldn't think twice, so now he said what was in the forefront of his mind: 'You're sure you want to marry Andrew?'

She stared at him for a moment: it was the first time he had brought up the matter of her marrying. He seemed to have pointedly ignored it: even when Andrew had come and stayed, as he had done recently, sleeping on the sitting-room couch, he hadn't spoken of it to him, either. When, later, she had remarked on this to Andrew and added that the image of the man she had earlier known for such a short time did not fit the man who was now in the house, Andrew had, in his way, reasoned with her, suggesting it need not be wondered at, because he must have gone through the mill out there, and that such experiences were bound to change a man. Look at Richard, for instance. To his mind Richard was in a much worse state for, as he himself said, 'You could face up to things if you had a face left to do it with.'

Her voice was slightly curt now as she answered the forthright question, 'Yes, of course I'm going to marry Andrew; you know I am. Why do you ask such an obvious question?'

'Just because he's a Bradford-Brown. They're not reliable, you know, any of them. Look how his people have shut the door on him; yet he's still part of them, he's still one of them. You can't get away from what your parents put inside you.'

'Andrew is nothing like them, mother, father, or' – she now brought out the last two words with a bounce of her head – 'his sister!'

His skin should have been a nut-brown colour, for it still held a kind of tan, but this seemed to fade away at times, and leave it a washy grey, as it was doing now. She knew all about his association with Richard's wife before she had married; a detailed knowledge that hadn't come from either Bertha or John; nor had she heard it through Meg, but through Nancy Basset, a one-time washer-up woman at the house. Nancy now helped in a canteen in Durham and loved to gossip. She supposed she should have shut her up when she started on about the occupants of The Hall, but she didn't.

It was from Nancy that she had heard of the rows between the master and the mistress, and that Mrs

Boneford could not bear to look at her husband, and of her 'carrying on' for years with this man standing before her.

When he had first come home she had felt sorry for him: it had been a feeling similar to that which she had for Richard. Yet, as the weeks had passed and he had shown himself to be a morose and difficult person, the feeling had passed, and she found that she even came to dislike him, and it showed in her tone as she added, 'Of course, you know more about them than I do; but one speaks as one finds, and I've always found Andrew to be good and kind, and . . . and' – she paused – 'a . . . a gentleman.'

For a moment they stared at each other in hostility; then, his face relaxing, he gave a small laugh as he said, 'That's making a comparison, isn't it? You mean I'm not. Oh! Oh!' He held up his hand as a warning signal, saying, 'I know what I am, all right, I know what I am, and I'm sorry you see me as you do, but' – his voice dropped – 'I've been away a long time, things have happened, as you say, and I know the Bradford-Browns better than you do. But yes, I must admit I had very little to do with Andrew, and . . . and I'm glad for you if you think you'll be happy.'

He had taken the wind out of her sails, and the feeling of dislike vanished: 'I know I will, Geoff,' she said. Then putting her hand out to him, she added, 'Why not come in with me to the concert. You mightn't enjoy it, I mean the turns, but you'll get a laugh.'

'Thanks. Thanks all the same; I will some other time. Mam tells me that you've made quite a name for yourself in the town. What is it tonight, a sing-song?'

'Oh no, nothing so common.' She shook her head. 'I'm one of twelve turns. Anyway, I open the first half, and I open the second half. As a certain lady soprano who happens to be on the concert committee said to me at the last do, "We always keep the stars till last."'

He laughed more freely now as he said, 'And what did you say to that?'

'I said I'd endeavour to make it a long twilight, and you know' – she bit on her lip now and shrugged her shoulders – 'I did, I did, because a lot of the lads shouted for encores; and you're not supposed to, you know, not in that type of concert, not until the very last; but I gave them three, and ones they could sing to. She was livid, and as I came off the stage' – she now giggled – 'I said, "The full moon's coming up". You see, two comedians were following me and they really do hog the stage, and I found myself saying to her – I couldn't help it: "It'll likely blot out the stars tonight." And you know, the place had to close by ten, and so she hardly got a look in at the end. Afterwards, I felt a bit of a cat, but she got up my nose, as Meg would say.'

His face was bright now as he said, 'Will she be there tonight?'

'Oh, yes, yes. She's a local lady, and one of some importance where war savings is concerned.'

'Aye, money talks. Anyway, there's one thing, you can hold your own . . . I think I knew that from the first. Remember the day I brought you home?'

'Yes, yes.' She nodded at him. 'Oh yes, I remember that day, and I've never really thanked you for it; but I do now. You gave me the chance of a new life that day, and a mam and dad. Did you think it strange to hear me call your mother and father "Mam" and "Dad"?'

'No, no; not at all, because Mother took to you straight away. You are her daughter; she looks on you as such.'

'And you're my *big brother*.'

He didn't answer for a moment; then he said quietly, 'Yes, looking at it that way, I suppose I am.' And he found himself unable to stop voicing his thoughts again, for now he said, 'You're beautiful, you know, Lizzie. You've grown into a beautiful woman. I wouldn't have believed it. I remember when I came into the house weeks back and saw you, I thought you were somebody else. I couldn't place you. It came as a kind of shock and a reminder that a number of years had passed over me, and . . . and that I'd missed out on so many things.'

Her face was flushed as she now said on a laugh, 'I don't know about beautiful. I think your eyes must have been affected, too.'

'Aw' – the word had a rough note in it now – 'don't be mock modest; you're not like that: you know what you look like; you know what you are. Go on, get yourself away, else I'll stop being civil to you.'

She was laughing as she said, 'Ta-ra, Geoff.'

'Ta-ra,' he answered her.

She had gone some steps when she looked back towards him, and she called, 'I'll say something to you when I get back if I've lost that bus.'

He made no further comment, but simply watched her hurrying away. Then he drew his lower lip tightly between his teeth, before turning about and making for the house.

The hall was full. Lizzie had opened the second half with some Chopin – an étude followed by a waltz – and

144

she was now standing to one side in the wings to allow a quartet to pass her when a voice in her ear said, 'There's your fellow along there. He's waiting for you. Here, give me your music, I'll see to it.'

Automatically she mumbled, 'What?' as she looked at the stage manager, but then turned quickly to see, there at the end of the passage, Andrew, his hand raised in greeting.

Her heart light, she pushed her way towards him, and, also in an undertone, greeted him, whispering, 'Why? When did you arrive? It would be next week, you said in your letter.'

'Come on. Come on.' He took her by the hand and pulled her through a back room and into another passage where she grabbed her hat and coat from a peg; then they were in the street, and there, in the soft twilight, they stood gazing at each other.

'Oh! Andrew, how long have you got?'

'Not long. Listen, I have to get the midnight train back. Come on, let's walk.' And almost roughly now he took her by the arm and led her along the street.

'Where to?' she said. 'Shall we go home?'

'No, no; there's no time for that. Just let's walk out in the country.'

'What . . . what is it, Andrew?'

She heard him sigh before muttering, 'There's something in the wind. I don't know exactly what. My leave was due in a fortnight's time and everything was arranged, the licence and everything. I'd had a letter back from Richard and he said he'd love to be best man. Anyway, the adjutant called me in this morning and said he doubted if I'd get a week, perhaps a couple of days, if that. There's been a lot

145

of transfers of late from the minesweepers to the big ones.'

'You . . . you mean . . . you might have to go over . . . overseas?'

'Could be; but I don't know. It's all hush-hush, and yet we hear of changing of plans and so on. Anyway, he gave me twenty-four hours. I got in just half an hour ago. I phoned the house and Meg answered. She told me where you were.'

'Oh! Andrew.' She clung tightly to his hand. 'Oh! Andrew, you seemed so safe on the shore job, well, I mean, not safe, but each rescue attempt did seem to me to be a quick dart out and back to base. Oh! Andrew.'

'Don't worry; it mightn't happen. Anyway, listen.' He laughed now. 'I'll likely be safer on the high seas than I would be ashore or in London these days. My goodness! London, Lizzie. You have no idea; everyone living there's a hero, or heroine. Oh yes, the women are heroines all right.'

'Oh, Andrew, don't make me feel so awful, stuck here in the food office. I wanted to join up, you know. I tried . . .'

'Don't be silly. That's the only thing that gives me peace of mind: to know that you're safe, at least comparatively so.'

They had walked by the river, then climbed up countless steps, only to find themselves in the town again and, laughing, had retraced their steps, then gone on walking until they reached the open country.

'What time is it?' she said.

'Ten to nine.'

'Must you take that train?'

'Yes, if I want to get back by tomorrow morning; at least, before twelve o'clock when I'm on duty again.'

She stopped suddenly and brought him round to face her, saying now in a whisper, 'You're . . . you're not just saying this about getting two days off to get married? It doesn't mean that you're going straightaway . . . I mean abroad?'

'No, no.' He held her hands tightly. 'I . . . I just wanted to see you, and . . . and tell you myself. I know you had made arrangements and booked the cottage in the Lake District. Well, we'll still go, but it might be for only a day, you see.'

When they came to a field with a broken gate they paused and looked across it to where a stretch of woodland appeared black against the deepening twilight, and, as of one accord, they crossed the field and entered the wood; and before they lay down in the shadow of some brushwood, he took off his cap and coat and laid them aside, and she did the same with her coat and hat; and then they were enfolded in each other's arms. In the shadow of the bushes their faces appeared dim to each other and his voice had a faraway sound as he said, 'You're . . . you're not sorry about the other time?'

'No, no, Andrew, never.'

'That's . . . that's been worrying me.'

'Oh, my dear, don't let it worry you.'

'I . . . I won't feel at peace until we're married . . . what if something happened? I mean . . .'

'I'd . . . I'd be glad.'

'Not unless we were married. I couldn't bear to think of anything like that happening to you.'

'It's happening to others, it's happening all the time, dear.'

'It might be, but not to you. Oh, not to you.'

She pressed herself gently from him and peered at him now and, her voice low and her words earnest, she said, 'It doesn't matter what happens to me, Andrew, so long as it happens to me through you.'

'Oh, Lizzie, Lizzie; I feel the luckiest man on earth. I know what I'm going to do after this is over; I've got it all planned out. I say I've got it all planned out. It was Richard who put it into my mind quite some time ago. I told you; remember? He suggested that I should go in for farming proper, and I jumped at the idea because I knew I could never stick Father's business, even if I were given the opportunity. Then, in the last letter I had from him he said, after the war I must definitely go in with him. He . . . he seems to be a lot steadier. He thinks the world of you, you know. I think he envies me a bit and I can understand that. And, oh yes, I'm glad he's getting rid of Janis. She's no good to him or anyone else, not even to herself . . . Would you like to be a farmer's wife?'

'I would like to be your wife, Andrew, whether you were a farmer or a dustman.'

'Oh, Lizzie. Lizzie.' Their lips met tight and hard, their bodies merged. The twilight became deeper and even when they could no longer see each other they still lay pressed close together.

Again she said, 'What time is it?'

He looked at his watch and the illuminated hands showed twenty minutes to eleven.

'We'd better be getting back,' he said.

'Oh, Andrew, Andrew.' Again they were clinging together.

When at last they dusted themselves down, put on their coats, and made their way across the field to the road, the distant clock had struck eleven. It wasn't until they were walking swiftly towards the town again that he said, 'How on earth are you going to get back? Look, you had better stay in an hotel.'

And she answered, 'I'll phone home. Dad'll bring the old bus. He always keeps a little petrol in reserve.'

It was almost half-past eleven when they reached the station and from where she rang the house. It was John who answered, and she said, 'Hello, Dad. Do . . . do you think you could come and fetch me? Andrew is getting the twelve o'clock train.'

His answer was sharp. 'You should have let me know before. Bertha's been worried to death.'

'I'm sorry, Dad, but there was so little time.'

His tone remained stiff as he said, 'Aye, all right, all right. I'll come straightaway.'

Coming out of the box, she said, 'It's all right. He's coming. You have time for a cup of tea?'

'Just about. The train isn't in yet.' He looked towards the platform.

They each drank two cups of tea but left the buns they had ordered untouched.

When the train puffed into the station, Lizzie, suddenly experiencing a dreadful feeling of panic, threw her arms about him and muttered, 'Oh, Andrew, Andrew. I . . . I wish you weren't going.'

'It's all right, my love, it's all right. I'll be back. Anyway, I'll phone you tomorrow.'

'What time?'

'Well, between half-past five and six, when you get in. Oh, wait a minute' – he paused – 'I don't know where I'll be at that time. Anyway, if I'm to go out, I'll phone the house first and leave a message. How about that?'

'Yes, yes, dear. Please. Please do. Oh! Andrew.'

There was bustle all about them but she could not release her hold on him, and he, too, held her tightly. Then, as if coming to herself, she said, 'Oh, you'll not get a seat.'

'Yes, yes, I will. There're not so many travelling at this time of night.' He opened the door to hand and stepped up into the carriage, pulled down the window and hung above her. In the green light hanging from the station roof, they could hardly make out each other's faces.

'Don't worry, darling. Everything will be all right. Next time it will be—' he pointed to the third finger of his left hand and, smiling now, he said, 'I've got it.'

'You have?'

'Yes. Woolworths.'

'Oh! Andrew, Andrew.' She forced herself to smile, then added, 'A tin one will do.'

A whistle blew. The train let off a great belch of steam; they couldn't hear themselves speaking. As the train began to move slowly, she did not walk along the platform but stood staring after it, a devastating feeling of loss consuming her.

When the train had disappeared into the blackness beyond the end of the platform she asked herself, 'What's the matter with me, anyway?' and turned slowly and went out of the station. There, standing on the kerb, was John, and beside him, Geoff. They both peered at her, and when she didn't speak, John flashed a shaded torch into her face, saying, 'You all right?'

'Yes.' Her voice was low, small.

John got behind the wheel and it was Geoff who helped her into the back of the car. He hadn't spoken, nor did he during the journey back home.

Indoors, Meg greeted her with: 'You all right, lass?' Then looking more closely at her face, she said, 'Whatever you say, you don't look it. Here! I've just made some cocoa. It's nice and hot; get it down you. Give me your things.' And she pulled off Lizzie's coat, then took her hat. John asked, 'Is she asleep?'

And Meg answered, 'No, I don't think so, although she's taken her pill.'

He walked quickly up the kitchen and out of the far door; while Meg, looking at Geoff, said, 'You want another cup?'

For answer he merely nodded at her; then sitting down on the settle by Lizzie, he asked her quietly, 'You all right?'

'Yes. Yes, I'm all right.'

'You don't look it. Is he for draft?'

'Draft?'

'Yes; posting?'

'Oh, well, he . . . he doesn't know; perhaps, nothing sure.'

'Well, then, you've got nothing to worry about.' And at this he rose, saying, 'Good-night then.'

'Good-night,' she said.

'Good-night, Meg.'

'Good-night. Good-night to you. Sleep well.'

151

When they had the room to themselves Meg went over to Lizzie and, peering into her face, she said, 'What's happened? Not had a row or anything?'

'No, no.' Lizzie shook her head widely.

'Then what's got you?'

'I . . . I don't know.'

'Wedding isn't off?'

'No; but he won't get a week; only two days at the most. But it's all fixed. He's got the licence, and' – she smiled now and pointed to her finger – 'the ring.'

'Aye well; that's a good sign. Both are necessary. It won't be long now, lass.' She patted her shoulder. 'So don't you worry: your waitin's over; it's been overlong, what with one thing and another.'

'Meg.'

'Aye, lass?'

'I got the most dreadful feeling on the station when he left me; dreadful. I've never felt like that before in my life. I can't explain it.'

'Oh, that's nothing, lass. I used to get it every time my lad joined his ship, and there was no war on then. If you care for somebody, it's natural-like. If you didn't feel like that you wouldn't care so much. That's natural-like an' all. Go on now, drink up your cocoa an' off you go to bed. As for me, I don't think I can make the stairs. It's been a long day.'

'I'm sorry. I'm sorry, Meg, to keep you up.'

'You don't keep me up, lass; it's meself that keeps me up. I keep goin' just to stop meself thinkin'. I can't get over that Shields do, I just can't. Aw well, there's one thing I suppose I should be thankful for; I've got neither kith nor kin to worry about. Yet I seem to worry about everybody else, and you in particular. Come on, get out of that seat and up those stairs.'

She tugged Lizzie to her feet; then after she'd seen her leave the kitchen and close the door behind her, she stood looking towards it, saying to herself, 'What made me say I felt like that every time my lad went to sea? I never did. I never did.'

2

The following morning John was unable to go to work. He was running a temperature. Bertha had got up, but she too wasn't feeling well, and so Geoff had phoned for the doctor.

At half-past eleven, Doctor McNeil came puffing down the stairs, to see Geoff waiting for him in the hall. 'Cold,' he said, 'a summer cold. A couple of days in bed and he'll be all right. 'Tisn't him I'm worried about; it's your mother.'

'What do you mean?'

'Just what I say; I'm worried about her. She's had three attacks in the past two years. Her heart's ticking like a time bomb . . . could go off at any minute.'

'You mean . . . ?'

'Aye, yes, I mean; that's what I mean, it could go off any minute. She doesn't make a fuss. She's not that kind. But she wants peace and quiet and no worries.'

'Well, she certainly gets that here. She . . . she may have worried when I was away but . . .'

'Yes, yes, she did. And now you're back, that's off her mind. Still, things crop up. Look after your father. See that he takes care of himself. That worries her. She's just been on about him tramping around in all weathers and coming home wet. Well, I must be off.'

As an afterthought he added, 'By the way, how are *you* feeling?'

'Oh . . . All right, pretty good.'

'Have to attend the hospital?'

'Yes, every now and again for a check-up.'

'Your arm? Is it moving any better?'

'No; not much.'

'No; and I don't suppose it will. You've just got to face up to that. Well, I must be off. Why people get colds in the summer, God only knows. Probably pollen.'

Meg was holding open the front door for him and he passed her as if she weren't there, and after she had closed the door on him she turned to Geoff and said, 'Queer customer, that. I wouldn't want him to see me out; he'd give me a sharp push into me box just to save time.'

Geoff smiled as he said, 'Very likely; and yet if he did, you'd likely push the lid up and say, "Not so quick, there; hold your hand a minute, will you?" '

She laughed aloud now, a belly-shaking laugh. It was the first time since he had come home that he had joked with her. She'd thought for a time that he objected to her presence in the house, until she realised he was the same with everybody. She watched him now going up the stairs one at a time as might a child who wasn't sure of his steps, and she thought, he's coming round. They said he had been a bit of a joker; always ready with an answer. He could be likeable if he kept it up.

She made her way to the kitchen thinking, what a nice house this is; a happy house. If she didn't think about Shields and the people who were gone, she could and would forget at times that there was a war on . . .

At twelve o'clock the phone rang. Meg answered it. It was Lizzie saying, 'Has there been a call for me?'

'No, lass.'

'Well, I didn't really expect one but, you see, Andrew said he might try to phone if he could, but he likely will have rung by the time I get home . . . How's Dad?'

'Doctor says he's got a summer cold.'

'And Mam?'

There was a pause before Meg said, 'Oh, all right, she's much the same: tellin' me I still don't know how to make a proper rice puddin'.'

Lizzie laughed, then said, 'Bye-bye,' and Meg answered, 'Bye-bye . . .'

Lizzie got in at about ten to six; Bertha was in the kitchen, and straightaway she asked her, 'Anyone ring?'

'Not for you, girl,' said Bertha. 'Anyway, he'll likely be out on patrol; they drop into the sea every day, they say, those young airmen. Mad-hats, some of them are. Go and tidy yourself; your tea's all ready. Guess what we're having?'

'I wouldn't know.'

'Kippers.'

'Kippers!' Lizzie's face stretched into a broad smile. 'Where did you get them?'

'You won't believe it. Ted Honeysett came to the door this afternoon. "Four pairs," he said, "would you like them? Straight from Craster." And he asked after John. He's not a bad old stick. I've always said that.'

'No; not if he brings kippers. What did he ask for in exchange, a couple of pheasants or a salmon?'

'Go on, and don't be cynical.'

'Don't be cynical, she says,' Lizzie said as she went up the room; 'I bet you a shilling there's a few birds missing in the next few days now he knows Dad's not around.'

'Well, here's one who doesn't blame him.' Meg came out of the pantry, her voice loud as she called up the room. And Lizzie answered on a laugh, 'Of course you wouldn't! Have you thought about exchanging duck eggs for any of his merchandise?'

'No; but that's an idea. An', for your information, I picked up four this afternoon, an' from Hobson's ducks this time. Ryebank has his hemmed in, the mean beggar.'

Lizzie went through into the hall laughing, and on to the cloakroom. After washing her face, she dabbed it with some pale pink powder and applied lipstick to her mouth. Then, leaning towards the mirror, she passed one lip over the other and stood gazing at herself. He said she was beautiful. Geoff had said she was beautiful. Andrew had said she was beautiful too, and many times. Was she really beautiful? She had considered she was pretty, but beautiful? Now Miss Thompson, in the upper office, she was beautiful, and smart. Where she got her clothes from on the clothing coupons she was allowed, everybody guessed at, but nobody knew for sure, because they were quality suits she wore. She looked like something out of *Vogue* magazine. Yes, she was beautiful. But then, she was so slim. She was the kind of woman who could wear a sack and appear attractive. There were people like that. She didn't consider herself one of them. Well, there were her hips, which were quite full, as was her bust. Her waist was only twenty-six but her bust was thirty-four. No, she couldn't see herself as really beautiful, not all-over beautiful. Anyway, as long as Andrew thought she was beautiful, that's all that mattered.

By ten o'clock she'd still had no word from him, and she sat in the sitting-room with a sick feeling in the pit of her stomach. She'd busied herself all evening, running up and downstairs and helping Meg prepare the meals for the following day, and a few minutes ago she had persuaded Meg to go to bed, telling her she was intending to wait up for another hour or so, because Andrew was bound to phone no matter how late it was.

Geoff was sitting opposite her, sunk in the easy chair, one leg thrust out stiffly, the other bent at the knee. He was reading. He did a lot of reading. She was surprised at that. She rarely saw him sitting down without a paper or magazine or book in his hand. Yet, he never conversed about anything he had been reading. He was now reading a book by George Orwell. She had remarked, 'Funny title, *The Road To Wigan Pier*,' but he hadn't taken the opportunity to expound on it. He had simply raised his eyebrows and shrugged his shoulders before saying, 'Look, why don't you go to bed? I'll stay up till twelve o'clock. I'll come and wake you if he calls. He could be anywhere.'

'He said he would . . .'

'Lizzie,' – his voice was strident now – 'you know what work he's doing; he could be called out at any time. They don't parachute from planes into the Channel at regulated times.'

'I know that. I know that.' Her voice was as sharp as his. And he came back at her, saying, 'Well, if you know that, why are you sitting there worrying?'

'Because he said that he would phone when he got in this morning, or, if not, at dinner time; he . . . he couldn't have been on duty all the time. And anyway, if he was in dock he would have phoned.'

'Well, that means he wasn't in dock; likely he was sent out as soon as he arrived. They don't just make short trips. They can be out for a day . . . two days, I should imagine, looking for fellows.' His voice dropped here, and he added, 'Look, I can guess how you're feeling, but it'll be all right; and you'll feel a great big silly-billy when that phone rings; it could be any time, perhaps first thing in the morning.'

He now pulled himself up from his chair, dropped his book on to a side table, then came over to her and, his voice quite gentle, he said, 'Go on upstairs; I'll take over phone-guard, ten till twelve. I promise you I won't fall asleep, and when he comes on that phone I'll greet him gently, I'll just bawl into it, "What the bloody hell do you mean, sir, keeping her waiting all this time? You stay there till I go and fetch her or you'll have my boot up your backside. D'you hear?"'

She hung her head now, laughing. She had never heard him swear before or use his sergeant-major's voice. His mother didn't like swearing. His father never swore except for an occasional 'damn'. As for crudeness like 'boots up backsides', well, she was sure he wouldn't have said that in front of his mother, because it had to be admitted the Bertha was a little pi about some things. And yet, because he had spoken in this way, he suddenly seemed to be more ordinary, more likeable. In a way, it brought back the shadow of the man she remembered.

She made to stand up, but he was so close she had to put her hand on his shoulder and, looking into his face, she said meekly, 'Yes, sir. I'll do what you say, sir. Thank you very much, sir.'

He went to swing round and almost overbalanced, so that automatically she thrust out her hand to steady him and they stood smiling at each other for a moment until she said, 'Drunk again. This'll be the last warning you'll receive, Lieutenant. You should know by now there's no drinking allowed when on phone duty. Any more of it and you'll not only lose your pips but your stripes too; you'll be stripped naked.' At this she burst out laughing and thrust her hand over her mouth and, her eyes shining, she said, 'I didn't mean that. I meant, stripped of your stripes.'

'I don't believe you. You meant it, all right. You've got a nasty mind; that's what comes of working in the food office.'

She moved from him, still laughing, and half-way up the room she turned, saying, 'You don't mind?'

'Go on, get yourself to bed and go to sleep. I'll wake you if need be.'

'Thanks, Geoff. Good-night.'

'Good-night, Lizzie.'

Stripped of his pips, his stripes . . . stripped naked. Funny that she should say that. Odd. That had been part of the nightmare. It had continued intermittently until a few months ago, but now it didn't matter any more. From the time of his promotion the fear must have been in him that he'd do something, lose his temper, hit out at one or other of those

160

he couldn't stand, and then he would be stripped: lose his pips and be stripped naked.

There was no call from Andrew that night nor yet the next morning, and Lizzie went to work feeling sick with apprehension. She had made Geoff promise that, should a call come through, he would get in touch with her at the food office. It didn't matter if private calls were forbidden, she'd risk being hauled over the coals.

She phoned home at dinner time. No, Meg said, there'd been no call; but not to worry, there would likely be one by the time she got back for her tea . . .

She ran all the way from the bus and came into the house panting.

Bertha, Meg, and Geoff were seated round the table. They all looked at her, and it was Meg who said, quickly, 'No luck yet, lass, but stop worryin', no news is good news.'

Bertha put out her hand and touched her arm, saying, 'There'll be a reason, dear.'

'He . . . he couldn't have been sent abroad, I mean, straightaway?' She was looking at Geoff, and he shook his head and said, 'No, not like that. Troopships have to be got ready and be seen to get ready. He would have known. Likely it's nothing to do with being sent overseas. When he told you there was something in the wind, it could mean anything, being sent to Land's End, or John o'Groats, you never know with Air Sea Rescue, or torpedo boats. Yes, he's likely been sent to pick up Germans in the North Sea; perhaps just off the coast here. He's maybe nearer home than you think. Come on, get your things off and have some tea.'

She looked at Bertha and asked, 'How's Dad?'

'His temperature's gone down a little, but the cold's settled on his chest. He'll be in bed for a few days, I think.'

'I'll slip up and see him.'

'No. Have your tea first; then you can go and sit with him for a while.'

'Until the phone rings,' Meg's voice followed her up the room.

And she repeated the words to herself, 'Until the phone rings . . .'

The phone rang twice during the evening. The first time was to see if Mr Fulton could stand in for Mr Carter's Home Guard duty, because he had gone down with a cold.

Geoff's reply to this had been, 'That makes two of them.'

The second call came from Mrs Hobson to ask if one of them would drop in at the farm; there was a bit of butter going. It was Geoff who again answered the phone, and he thanked the farmer's wife very much and told her he would call in the morning.

Each time the phone had rung Lizzie had appeared at the top of the stairs, and when she saw Geoff replace the receiver on its stand, she turned about and went into her bedroom again. There, throwing herself on the bed, she gathered up handfuls of the eiderdown and gripped it and buried her mouth in the pillow, muttering, 'Please, please, don't let anything happen to him! It's . . . it's important that nothing should happen to him. Please! Please!' And on the second occasion, she raised her head and looked up towards the ceiling: 'I should have told him, but . . . but I wasn't sure. I'm still not sure. Yet it could be. Oh, please, please! keep him safe . . .'

She did not drop off to sleep till two o'clock in the morning. And she was awake again when Meg brought her a cup of tea at half-past seven. 'Get any sleep, lass?' she asked.

'Not much, Meg.'

'Well, that's no way to go on. You'll make yourself ill. You goin' into work the day?'

'Yes, I'll . . . I'd be better there.'

'Aye, I think you will. But as I've said again and again, no news is good news. If anythin' had happened, you would know.'

'Would I?'

'Aye, of course.'

'I'm not Mrs Bradford-Brown, Meg; not yet.'

Meg seemed to think for a moment; then she nodded her head, saying, 'That's true, that's true. But somebody would have been informed and they would have let you know.'

When she was ready to leave the house Geoff said to her, 'Why don't you go in on your bike? You wouldn't have to wait for the bus, then.'

'It's a long haul back,' she said. 'It only saves ten minutes, and . . . and I often don't feel like it at the end of the day.'

He came to the door with her. 'I'll let you know as soon as I hear anything,' he said quietly.

'Thanks, Geoff.'

She walked away from him, thinking about how kind he had been to her these last few days. She didn't know what she would have done if he hadn't been at home. He no longer seemed the wounded soldier, more the sergeant, the lieutenant, the man-in-charge.

Geoff watched her through the gate, until she was hidden behind the hedge bordering the road.

For all his talk about Andrew being held up here or there, he felt there *was* something awry; and when Meg kept saying that no news was good news, that might be true if you were abroad, but not on this little island.

He turned to go indoors. Anyway, if anything had happened to him, she'd likely be the last to know. His address would still be shown as The Hall and it wouldn't be on his papers that the door was closed to him. Likely, the squadron leader, or whoever was in charge down there, even being aware of his forth-coming marriage, would imagine it was a family affair and that the girl was known to his parents. It wasn't likely that Andrew had told him what a pair of outcasts they both were.

Shortly after lunchtime there was a ring at the front-door bell. Bertha was upstairs sitting with John; Geoff was in the sitting room, and Meg was about to doze off in the rocking-chair in the kitchen. But she roused herself, reaching the hall as the sitting-room door opened and Geoff appeared. Nodding at him, she said, 'I'll see to it.'

When she opened the door her mouth fell into a slight gape. Standing on the step below her, but still seeming to look down on her, was that young woman Janis. She looked smart, even elegant, and Meg recognised her right away. This was the one who had come into the bedroom that day; Mr Boneford's wife that was, or perhaps wasn't now, she didn't know if the divorce had been finalised yet.

164

'May I see Mr Fulton, please?'

'He's in bed with a cold.'

'Then Mrs Fulton?'

'She's upstairs with him.'

Meg's voice was raw. She did not turn round but she knew that Geoff had moved from the doorway and was coming across towards her.

'What would you be wantin'?' she asked.

'I would like to speak to one of the family, please.'

'It's all right, Meg. I'll see to this.' Geoff was pressing her gently aside and was staring into the face that he hadn't seen for five years, and although the sight of it brought no quickening of his pulse, he found the muscles in his jaw tightening. It seemed a full minute before Janis said, 'I've . . . I've news of Andrew. I thought they . . . er . . . she should know.'

'Andrew?'

As he stepped back, he had to press Meg still further away. He took her hand from the door, then said, 'Come in.'

Janis passed him and he closed the door, then led the way into the sitting-room. Once inside, he turned and closed this door before walking up the room.

She followed slowly, her eyes flicking from side to side as if she were surprised at the brightness and comfort of the place.

He had turned to face her, and, pointing to a chair, he said, 'Won't you sit down?'

She sat down and stared at him for a moment. His voice sounded different, he looked altogether different. She had been told that he limped badly, but she had seen worse. He looked older. His uniform suited him too.

Geoff did not sit down but stood with his hand resting on the back of a chair, and he said, 'Andrew? What's happened to him?'

She lowered her head. 'He's . . . he's dead,' she said.

'What!'

'They . . . they heard last night. I didn't know until . . . well, about an hour ago. I'm not at home now, you know. I . . . I had called for some of my things. I' – she wetted her lips – 'I thought she should know. It . . . it was only fair. They didn't see it like that.'

'What do you mean, they didn't see it like that.'

'Well,' – she held out one hand, the palm upwards – 'you know what happened, don't you? They wouldn't recognise her. But . . . but I thought . . . well, as I said . . .'

The tone he had used so far had been a good imitation of Harry Cole's voice coming from the back of his throat, high up, slow, not drawled, but each word separate. Harry had been good at mimicking; he had made them all laugh at times. But now he forgot for a moment about Harry's voice, forgot that the first thought that came into his mind when he saw Janis a few moments before was the word 'uncouth'. Now, instinctively, he wanted to show her the cultured individual he had become. But instead his voice was almost a bark as he said, 'You mean they weren't going to let her know?'

She pulled herself up, shaking her head as she said, 'I'm sorry. I'm sorry.'

166

'Sorry! What kind of people are they, anyway? When . . . when did it happen?'

'Yesterday morning.'

'Yesterday morning?' His brows came together.

'He . . . he was passing through London. There had been an air-raid. Apparently he and other servicemen had been trying to get a woman and her children out of a bombed house and the place collapsed. Three of them were killed, and . . . and, I suppose, the woman and the children too, by what I can gather. His squadron-leader phoned last night.'

'Bombed house?' He moved his head in disbelief. 'It didn't happen at sea, then? A bombed house, you say. It's hardly believable.'

'Yes, yes, it's hardly believable.'

He saw her gulping in her throat, and he remembered that she was talking about her brother and he said, but for a different reason, 'I'm sorry, heart-sorry.'

She made no reply for a moment and then she said, 'We were never close, but nevertheless, he *was* my brother, and he was a good man.' She looked up at him now, saying, 'You'll tell her?'

He made no answer, so she went on, 'They were going to be married, I understand?'

'Next week.'

'Is your father very ill?'

'No, no.' He shook his head. 'It's just a heavy cold.' His eyes wandered from her before turning to her again and saying, 'If he had been on duty we would have known about this sooner, I suppose?'

'I doubt it.'

'What do you mean?'

167

'The servants don't even know yet. I wouldn't have known myself, but I happened to come in as they were getting ready to leave for Portsmouth. His body has been taken there.'

'You mean to say they didn't . . . they wouldn't . . . they would have gone and not let her know? By God!' He shook his head. 'You've got wonderful parents.'

He had expected her to come back at him with a defensive remark, but when she said quietly, 'I agree with you. They are unique, so understanding. I suppose you know I'm being divorced?'

'So I heard.'

'I, like Andrew, got shown the door because of it: I have ruined their standing in the county . . . Have you seen Richard since you came back?'

'No; there was no reason why I should see Mr Boneford, was there? We're of different worlds, aren't we?'

She had walked half-way down the room before she said, 'Companion-in-arms, one could say; and this war is acting as a great leveller, except some people won't recognise it.' She turned and looked at him: he was just a step behind her and there was a tremor in her voice as she said, 'If you had seen Richard, you would likely understand the situation better.'

He gave a slight shrug of his shoulders, and his tone was again that of Captain Cole: 'The situation has nothing to do with me.'

'No, no, of course not.' She made another movement with her hand as if flicking something away. It signified that she had made a mistake by suggesting that he would understand a situation that really had nothing to do with him.

168

As he passed her and reached out to open the door, she stopped and said, 'You'll be wondering, when I'm gone, why I should have bothered to come and tell the girl about Andrew. Well, it's this way. I feel I owe her a debt: I suppose you've heard she saved Richard from committing suicide, and in doing so put herself in quite a lot of danger. Well, if he had succeeded with his intention, I would have had it on my conscience for the rest of my life . . . Huh! It was in this very house he told me he was divorcing me; to be exact, in your bedroom. I noticed your school trophies were still on the wall. I thought it was ironic. I don't blame him for divorcing me; he did the right thing, and I'm glad to be free, or will be when it's all over. Anyway—' Her tone now lost its airy note and took on a tinge of sadness as she went through the doorway into the hall, saying, 'That's why I felt I owed it to her not to keep her in suspense, because if they'd had their way she wouldn't have known anything about it until it was all over and he was buried. Of course' – she nodded her head – 'she could've phoned the yard, but that would have been a bigger shock, I think.'

He opened the front door for her, and when she was on the step she turned to him and said, 'Goodbye, Geoff. I'm glad you've made it. You've been lucky.'

He did not say 'goodbye and thanks for coming', but watched her walk down to the gate, where her horse was tethered. He saw her mount with the agility of a boy, then cry, 'Get up there!' as she put the horse into a quick trot.

Wherever she was now living, or working, she was still able to keep a horse. She'd always need to have a horse. He closed the door; then stood still, staring down at the telephone to the side of him. My God! Andrew dead! And they've known since yesterday morning. Those swines, the pair of them! By God! he hoped they would run into a raid and be blown to smithereens, he did that . . . or no, just wounded, disfigured, like her husband had been, or made limbless. Aye, a quick death was too good for either of that pair. But how was he going to break the news to Lizzie?

As he continued to stare at the phone his thoughts jumped and told him, she's more beautiful than ever she was. Yet the sight of her hadn't touched him. Well, thank God for that. She had remained a torment in his mind and body for months after he had left. But, eventually, war and the blood of war had willed him clear of her. Yes, indeed, thank God for it. But Lizzie. Lizzie? Should he go in to Durham and see her? No; he couldn't tell her that in a public place; far better wait till she came in. Yes, far better.

He turned to go towards the kitchen and saw Meg was already standing at the hall door. 'Trouble?' she asked.

He nodded. 'Andrew. He's . . . he's dead.'

'Oh God Almighty! *Oh, no! No!*'

She turned and, putting a forearm against the stanchion of the door, she laid her head on it and began to cry. And going to her, he put his arm around her shoulders and led her into the kitchen, saying, 'There, there. Now look; you of all people have got to keep up. She'll need you.'

After a time she said to him, 'Who'll tell her?'

'I will,' he said. 'I will.'

*   *   *

He waited for the bus, and when it arrived he helped her down from the platform. The conductor said, 'Ta-ra! then,' and rang the bell. She did not reply but stood looking at Geoff, and he at her.

After a second or so she said, 'What is it, then?'

He swallowed deeply, 'We've . . . we've had news.'

She put her hand to her throat, then quickly undid the top button of her woollen coat and pulled the revers aside as if to give herself air. 'What is it?' she said again. 'Tell me.'

He put his hand out and caught her arm and, drawing her towards him, he looked down into her face. He had said that he would tell her; but this was as difficult as anything he had ever had to do. When men dropped dead around you, somebody else did the telling. He had never cottoned on very much to Andrew, mainly because he was a Bradford-Brown, but there had been something deep between Lizzie and Andrew, something that he envied. And now he had to tell her it was no more, finished, gone under a fall of bricks. No glorious end of dying in battle, just a pile of bricks and mortar tumbling on you.

He began, 'When he got to London, he went to help some fellows. They . . . they were trying to release a woman and—' His voice droned on, embroidering the tale, and she listened to him, her eyes stretched wide, her mouth agape. And when he saw her eyes close while her mouth was still wide and heard the agonised groan emerge, he said quickly, 'Oh, don't, Lizzie! Don't! Come on! Don't!' And he pulled her to him and gripped her tightly with his good arm, pressing her head into his neck in an effort to stifle the weird sound she was making.

'Come on home! Come on home!'

When he pushed her gently from him he was amazed to see that her face was dry; that she wasn't crying. Held tightly in the curve of his arm, they walked back to the house.

Bertha and Meg were in the kitchen and both went to her, although neither of them spoke, but simply led her to the settle and pressed her gently down, then sat on either side of her, each taking a hand while she stared straight ahead. They made murmuring sounds until she turned and looked from one to the other and then said pityingly, 'No! Oh, no! Not Andrew! Oh, no! Oh, Mam! Not Andrew!'

She now looked up at Geoff, who was standing in front of them and as if she were telling him something new, she said, 'We were going to be married soon; days, just days.'

At this, Meg rose from the settle, tears streaming down her face, and she muttered, 'I'll . . . I'll make a fresh pot of tea. That's what I'll do. This one must be clay cold, I'll make a fresh pot,' and she ground the kettle into the middle of the fire, took the teapot from the hob and poured the quite fresh tea down the sink, then almost dropped the teapot into the sink again as Lizzie said, 'And I think I'm going to have a baby.'

Meg did not turn around, but kept her plump body bent forward over the sink, and she heard Bertha gasp and say, 'Oh, no! girl. Not that! No! No!' Then Lizzie's voice, in a tone holding a faraway sound and like that of a child protesting, said, 'Why not? Why not? But he didn't know. I should have told him. I meant to, but I was keeping it as a wedding present.'

'Come and lie down in the sitting-room.' Geoff had his hand on her elbow to help her rise.

'No. No.' She shook off his hold; then got to her feet, saying, 'I'm all right. I'm all right. I'll go up to my room.' She paused and stared at the table, then turned to Bertha who had her head buried deep on her chest, and she said quietly, 'I won't want any tea.'

She had reached the far door when Geoff said hurriedly, 'Go with her, Meg. Get her into bed. She's in shock. I'd . . . I'd better give the doctor a ring.'

After Meg had left the kitchen he sat down beside his mother and, taking her hand, he said quietly, 'These things happen. They're happening all the time. Don't take on.'

She looked up at him. 'It shouldn't have happened to her,' she said; 'she's . . . she's never played around.'

'She wasn't playing around, Mam. She cared for him, a bit too much, perhaps; and what's done's done. You're not going to hold it against her, are you?'

'No. But what . . .' she bit on her lip, 'what'll she do? I'm so sad: she'll be on her own with a child to bring up.'

'She won't be on her own, will she, Mam? She'll still have us.'

'Yes, yes, of course. But . . . but it's different from having a husband.'

'She'll get a husband all right. There's plenty who'll come flying.'

'I don't know. I don't know. There's still a feeling about . . . well, children being born like this. I . . . I would have thought she could have waited. I've . . . I've been so careful in bringing her up, and I *have*

173

brought her up. She shouldn't have done it, not her, after all the care I've taken of her.'

'Look here, Mam. She's a young woman, and we're in the middle of a war. The old ideas have died and they haven't died hard either; they've been thrown over in the night, you could say. You've got to look at this differently.'

When she put her hand below her breast and pressed it, he said, 'There now, there now. Don't you get yourself agitated – you know what the doctor said – and just think she's going to need you.'

'Yes, yes, of course. It's only,' – she shook her head – 'you're right, you're right; but do as you say: I think you'd better get the doctor, because she was acting strange-like; she wasn't crying, and that was odd.'

As he went up the room and into the hall he thought: things don't die hard with people like his dear mother. She had lived in a cocoon all her life and, strangely, put respectability above caring. He shouldn't be surprised, yet he was.

And Lizzie hadn't cried. It was a bad sign, that. He picked up the phone.

3

The doctor had left some pills for Lizzie and she slept throughout most of the following day and night. On the second day she refused to take any more; and that morning at ten o'clock, she got up and dressed and went downstairs.

Bertha said, 'Oh, lass; you shouldn't.' And Meg said, 'Let her be, it's the best thing. Could you eat anything, Lizzie?' And Lizzie answered, politely, 'No; thanks, Meg; just a cup of tea.' She drank two cups of tea, then rose from the table and left the kitchen without a word.

She sat in the sitting-room staring out of the window, out on to the border where the daffodil leaves had been tied into neat knots, with behind them some large, orange-coloured poppies that were drooping their heads with the weight of their petals. The far border of the small plot was showing the dusty blue of the wild geraniums. It was the only part of the garden that remained for flowers, for the rest was under cultivation for vegetables. But she wasn't seeing any part of the garden. She was feeling strange: her mind was not in the present at all; it kept going back to when she first went to the typing school, and she used to cycle both ways. And she could see a young man on horseback. He would often stop and smile at her. And there was the time when she had climbed the stile and a nail had

175

caught her stocking and laddered it right up the back, and she was twisting round to look at the damage when the rider came over the hill. He had jumped down from his horse and said, 'Can I help you?' And she had pointed to the stile and said, 'That blooming nail!' whereupon he had laughed. And when she had said, 'I've spilled my blackberries through it,' he had said, 'I'll help you to pick some more.' And he had. It was from that day she had given him her heart, all of it. And now she hadn't any left. She could feel nothing, because he was gone. He was dead. And so was she and she'd never come alive again. Never! Never!

She heard voices outside the door: Meg was saying, 'Geoff's gone into Durham to get his dad's medicine. He won't be long. She's in here.'

When the door opened, she did not turn round, but glanced at Meg when she came to her side, and she, bending over her as one did over a sick person, said, 'You've got a visitor, dear.'

She didn't want visitors. She didn't want to see anybody, nobody. She wanted to be alone, left alone in this emptiness where there was only herself, not Andrew, nor anything inside her, nothing.

'Hello, Lizzie.' She looked up into the scarred face looking down at her, and she said softly, 'Oh, Richard.'

Meg now said to him, 'Would you like a cup of tea?' and he said, 'Yes; yes, I would, Meg, please.' And then he was sitting down by Lizzie's side and holding her hand, as he looked into her face, the lid of his good eye blinking rapidly over the deep sorrow that lay there.

'Oh, Lizzie. What can I say? I . . . I only heard last night.'

Some part of her mind moved as she thought, he must have come straightaway. It's a long journey. But she didn't say anything, just stared back at him.

'He was the nicest fellow I knew. We had plans. He may have told you: when it was all over we were going to work together. Oh! Lizzie. Lizzie.'

Something was happening deep down in her throat. She managed to press some words upwards: 'I'm going to have a baby, Richard,' she said.

His eyelids blinked rapidly, but not in unison; and then he said softly, 'I'm glad. I'm glad, Lizzie. He'll still be with you, then; you won't have lost Andrew when you have his child.'

'Oh, Richard.' Her voice was high and she repeated, 'Oh, Richard!' She was calling to him now over a long distance. 'What am I going to do, Richard? I . . . I can't live without Andrew. Oh, Richard.'

She was on her feet now, her mouth wide open, the lump in her throat threatening to choke her. She struggled for breath. When she felt his arms about her she clung to him. They were in the water again, going over and over. She was swallowing the water. It tasted dreadful. She was yelling something, but she couldn't hear what she said for the rush of the water.

He held her more tightly to him, crying, 'There, there. That's it, my dear, that's it. Let it come. You'll feel better now.'

'Oh! Richard. Richard.'

'I'm here, dear. I'm here. Come. Come.' He led her stumbling towards the couch, and when he went to ease her down on to it, she kept her hold on him, and he fell by her side and held her again like a child. But when her sobbing increased, he looked anxiously towards

177

the door; and when it opened he saw the tall soldier pause for a moment, then come hurrying forward.

The man did not speak to him but, putting his hand on Lizzie's shoulder, he shouted, 'Come on! Come on! Now stop that! You'll make yourself ill.' Then to Richard he said, 'Let me have her.'

But when Richard attempted to rise from the couch, she clung to him again, crying, 'No! No!'

Meg and Bertha now both appeared on the scene, and Bertha, putting her hands gently on Lizzie's shoulders, said, 'Come along now. Come along. That's enough. That's enough. It's all over. It's all over, dear. You'll only make yourself ill.'

Bertha's face was close to Richard's, but she kept her eyes averted from him until he said, 'You had better phone the doctor.' then turning his head, he looked up at the grim-faced Geoff and added, 'Put your arm round the back of her. We'll get her upstairs that way.'

Geoff hesitated for a moment before he obeyed what had sounded like an order; then, almost roughly, he bent and put his arm under her oxters and tugged her away from Richard's hold. But once on her feet, Lizzie pushed at Geoff with a force that almost made him lose his balance, and then gasping, stood looking from one to the other, and her words distinct and spaced, she said definitely, 'Leave . . . me . . . alone . . . I'm . . . all . . . right . . . so . . . please . . . leave . . . me . . . alone.'

They all stood staring at her as, pushing past Meg and Bertha she went to a straight-backed chair and sat down; and there, her head drooping, she gasped, 'I . . . don't . . . want . . . the . . . doctor . . . just . . . leave . . . me . . . be.'

'I'll get you a cup of tea, dear.' Meg was scurrying away down the room now. And Bertha, limping towards Lizzie, asked quietly, 'Wouldn't you like to lie down, dear?'

'No . . . No, Mam.' She shook her head. 'I'll . . . be all right now. I just want to be quiet.' She turned to Richard and said quietly, 'I'm sorry, Richard.'

'Oh, my dear.' He came towards her and took up one of her hands and held it between his, while Bertha, looking at her son who was staring at the visitor, said, 'Did you get Dad's medicine?'

Geoff blinked; then turned his attention to his mother, saying, 'Yes. Yes.'

'Well, come along and take him up a dose, please.' She now looked at Lizzie, saying, 'I'll be back in a minute, dear.'

It was some seconds before Geoff followed her, and there was one thought in his mind as he crossed the hall and that was, My God! I'm lucky.

Back in the room Lizzie said again, 'I'm sorry, Richard. I suppose it had to happen, but no . . .'

'Oh, my dear Lizzie, please. I take it as a great compliment . . . no, something more, that you could turn to me, me of all people.'

She looked up into his face: perhaps it was because her eyes were still flooded with tears, but the pink, stretched skin seemed more prominent, more puckered, seeming to have eclipsed the good patch that was left. She put her hands out to him and he held them as she said, 'I remember telling you I'm going to have a baby.'

'Yes. I'm so glad for you.'

'You really are?'

179

'Oh, yes, truly, and—' the skin of his face moved up, his thin lips spread showing a surprisingly good set of teeth as he said, 'I'm putting my claim in now, to be the godfather, boy or girl.'

She brought his hands together within hers as she said brokenly, 'You're such a good man, Richard; Andrew said that. Andrew liked you very much.'

He made no reply and she looked away from him. It was odd that she should speak of Andrew. She had been feeling she would only be able to voice his name again to herself. Over the past two days her mind had been elsewhere; somewhere, but not here. It must be like this, she supposed, if you were going mad, your mind going somewhere else. But she was back into reality, and reality was pain. Now she wanted to cry out against the loss of her love. She wanted to wail again, Oh, Andrew, Andrew, but she mustn't, she mustn't ever cry again like that; it had been terrifying. For a time she had thought she was drowning, as when she and Richard had been in the river. She looked up at him, asking quietly, 'How are you?'

And quietly, he answered, 'Niggling. I can say that to you. Strange, isn't it? That I haven't got to say to you, Oh, I'm feeling fine. Oh, I'm facing up to it. Such ludicrous statements. In fact, someone did say to me, "You must face up to it"; and you know, I have to, for my parents' sake. Said another way, I put on a show, because they're so troubled, they're so concerned for me. You see,' he took his hands away from hers and pulled a chair closer to her, then sat, his elbows on his knees, staring down at his joined hands as he said, 'They are not young as you would expect the parents of someone of my age to be. My mother was forty-two when I was born, and my father was forty-five. It was his third marriage. His two previous wives had died and left no issue, as they say, and he didn't expect any when he married a woman of forty-two; but there, dear Mama, she gave him me, and I altered their lives. They brought me up in love, and now they are so unhappy for me. Would you . . . would you come and visit sometime . . . soon? I . . . well, I told them you would. You know, I've asked you before. It's like this—' He now drooped his head still lower over his hands, until all she could see was the crown of his head. His hair was thick here and had a wave in it. It was a deep brown colour. She thought he must have been a good-looking man . . . She brought her attention back to what he was saying: 'They can understand me making a man friend here and there, but not a woman. So, Lizzie, if one day you would come and visit us, you would be doing me not only a great favour but offering me something far deeper than that, something that as yet I cannot find words to express.'

For a moment she forgot the pain that was like an abscess beneath her ribs, and she said, 'Oh, Richard. Yes, of course, I would be only too pleased, and . . . and I must tell you, that at the moment I feel closer to you than anyone' – she spread her hand wide – 'here; I suppose because you . . . you knew Andrew, and as I said, he liked you. You see, although Geoff was quite civil to him, he couldn't forget he was Mr Bradford-Brown's son; nor could Mam or Dad come to terms with the difference in our positions. Meg seemed to be the only one who took us both for what we were; two people in love who wanted to get married.' She bowed her head now and muttered, 'A week, ten days, and it would have been done; but . . . but somehow that's of no consequence now. We couldn't have been closer. You know something, Richard' – she looked up at him again – 'I would have been full of regret at this moment if . . . well, if we hadn't come together. We were married. In both our eyes we were married.'

'Yes, yes of course you were, my dear; and . . . and you'll be all right. Don't worry. You'll be supported by your family too. He . . . Geoff, seems a very capable fellow.'

'Yes. Yes he is.' Her mind springing away from the pain and going off at a tangent again, she thought, I wonder if he's thinking that's the man, or one of them, who was with my wife. She had heard Bertha telling the doctor that it was Richard's wife who had brought the news. Why her? she wondered. It was a question she would have to ask later.

The door opened and Geoff entered. He came straight to her and placed a hand on her shoulder. It was firm and protective. 'How are you feeling?' he asked her.

'Better.' She nodded at him. 'Much better.'

'Good.'

He looked across at Richard, staring him fully in the face for a moment, before saying, 'I'm sorry you had to run into this.'

Richard made no reply whatever, but going to Lizzie, he leaned towards her, saying, 'I'll write and make arrangements. Perhaps you could come for a few days. It would make a change for you. It's rather lovely up there, you know, at this time of the year.'

'Thank you, Richard. Yes; yes, I will.'

'Soon?'

'Yes, soon.'

'I'll leave our telephone number with your mother.'

'Do. Do. Goodbye, Richard. And thank you.'

'Goodbye, my dear.'

Her mind registered the fact that he had called her 'my dear' a number of times during the last hour or so. He was such a nice man, and it was such a great pity he was so scarred. Fancy his parents being old, and them worrying because he had no woman friend, no-one who would look at him.

When the door had closed on him, Geoff said, 'What was all that about? You going to stay there?'

'He's invited me. He . . . he was a friend of Andrew's, you know. They were to go into partnership after the war.'

'Oh yes?'

'Yes.'

'What kind of partnership?'

'Farming. He has an estate in Scotland.'

'Nice for him. Anyway, it's a good job he's got something to keep him busy.'

She recalled that Richard had hardly spoken to Geoff, seeming to ignore him. They clearly hadn't liked each other. Well, they wouldn't, would they? Richard's wife had been a great disturber of the peace. He had lost his other friend through her. Why was it that it was she who had to bring the news about Andrew? But what did it matter? Why was she troubling herself about anything? The pain was filling her chest again; how long would it last? For ever, and ever, she thought. They said time healed. Such sayings were . . . stupid, spoken by people who had never known loss.

4

To Lizzie, the months that followed were strange. Every member of the household seemed bent on doing his or her bit to take Lizzie's mind off her loss when she was in the house. Meg chattered constantly and told funny tales about the happenings along the Tyne: 'Did you ever hear of Jessie Bugs and Wiggie? Oh, they were famous in Gateshead,' she said. 'Then there was the blind bellman in Felling. He was like a town crier. And oh, you must have heard of Tommy on the bridge. He was barmy. It was a wonder they didn't lock him up, because there he was on the bridge, every day for fifty years. Her mother said she used to stand and watch him waving his arms about. Then did she ever tell them about the time when the Raffertys' house caught fire? She had? Oh well, she still laughed about it herself. She could see Peggy Rafferty hauling the bairns out of the house – nine of them she had – and when one of them said, "Where's me da?" "Up in bed," she had said; "and I hope he fries; an' he will with all the whisky he's got in him." And she would double up with laughter before ending, "You see, I didn't really know that Pat was up there. But the men made a dive, just in case, and got him down. The bed was alight and he was still asleep."'

On and on her tales would go and sometimes the tears ran down her face, so heartily did she laugh.

Bertha had taken to relating the happenings of her own childhood, when the place had been a busy little farm. But strangely, it was John who seemed to monopolise the conversation. Talking pointedly to Geoff, who hardly opened his mouth, he would recall various events from earlier in the war. And this would catch Lizzie's attention, for he had never previously given them any inkling of having a detailed interest in the war.

He would nearly always start with, 'You should have been here, lad. July 1940, it was, about the middle of the month when it started. The bombers would come over, often the fighters with them – and it developed into the Battle of Britain. Dowding was a marvel. He had to fight not only the German Air Force but the bloomin' government. "Protect the convoys," they would say; "look at all the ships they're sinking." But no, he kept our boys going and they brought down three hundred of their planes. Then what d'you think they did, the Germans? They set out to destroy the bases in Kent, where the fighters were stationed, and they bloomin' well nearly succeeded an' all. We lost over one hundred and eighty planes there. Then where did they turn to next? London, of course. But lad, you could understand that, 'cos we went over there and bombed Berlin and some of their other towns as well. It was a kind of retaliation, but by God! what a retaliation! And we all thought we were for it; that they would land at any time.'

On and on he would go while Geoff sat across the table staring at him, trying to still the whirling in his own mind that his father's talking always engendered, the whirling that was full of sand that parched his throat, making him unable to swallow. He would feel his legs and feet leaden, when he would hardly be able to lift one foot in front of the other. Then, miraculously, they would come alive and he would run, before throwing himself flat on his face, barking to the others, every other word a curse, his mind always yelling at him; if only he could see the bloody enemy! Then he did. Quite unexpectedly he did. He saw the fellow about to stick a bayonet into young Fairbanks and he fired and he fired and he fired. He had to lift the corporal to his feet because, for a moment he was stiff as if he, too, were dead. Then he jabbered, 'Thanks, Sarge. Thanks, Sarge. Thanks, Sarge.' He had looked around for other Germans, but there were none. Where the hell had the fellow come from . . . ? And his father was going on and on again.

'What did you say, lad?'

He looked at his father. 'Nothing. Nothing, except Lizzie looks tired. She should go to bed.'

Lizzie was indeed feeling tired; she felt tired all the time these days. Especially she was tired of listening to war talk. She thought that John had become very insensitive. Why did he keep on about the war? And Geoff was kind. She didn't know how she would have got through these past weeks without him. He would see her to the bus in the mornings and he would wait for her coming back at night.

And as her body became heavier she became, in a way, tired of that too. The first awareness that she was carrying a baby had filled her with joy. But now all she was filled with was a dull ache.

She was about to start her holidays and she had decided to accept Richard's offer and stay at his place for a few days. Twice recently he had called to see how she was and they had talked about Andrew. He was the only one she could talk to about Andrew; nobody else mentioned his name.

Last night, she had suddenly made up her mind to go to Scotland: she felt she must get away from the claustrophobic atmosphere in the house; they were all so concerned for her; nobody acted naturally.

When she told Geoff what she was planning to do, she saw immediately that he wasn't pleased. 'Why do you want to go there?' was his reaction.

'It'll be a change,' she had answered, 'and he's invited me several times.'

At this, he had muttered, 'You . . . you don't mind being with him, looking as he does?'

She had shown her indignation in her answer and by the tone of her voice. 'No, I do not mind being with him. He can't help looking as he does. I would have thought you'd have understood that. Anyway, he's the same person underneath, and I find I can talk to him.'

'And you can't talk to me, is that what you mean?'

'No, no, of course not,' she had rapped back. 'But you are different.'

'Yes, by God! I am.'

She was amazed and confused when he turned from her and hurried away, his limp very much in evidence. And with a touch of defiance she went to the phone and got through to Richard, hearing the pleasure in his voice when she asked if it would be convenient for her to come on Monday. 'Yes, yes,' he said, and eagerly gave her directions. He would meet her at Edinburgh station. If she caught the connections her train would get in about 6 p.m.

187

Bertha, too, was surprised at her proposed visit. And for the first time she mentioned Andrew, saying, 'You haven't forgotten Mr Boneford was married to Andrew's sister, have you? and . . . and we don't know if the divorce has been granted yet.'

Bertha's tone had surprised and apparently hurt Lizzie, for she had cried, 'What difference does that make? I'm not proposing to marry him, am I? I'm merely going to stay with his parents.'

'Now! now!' John had come to his wife's aid. 'There's no need for you to take on like that, Lizzie. Bertha was merely saying . . .'

'I know what she was saying' – Lizzie's voice was quiet now – 'and I'm sorry. But I want to get away. And, let's face it, it's the only place I've been invited to. You wouldn't want me to visit my stepmother in Gateshead, would you?'

They were shocked – this wasn't the Lizzie they knew – but they made allowances. She had been bereaved, not of course of a husband, but of a lover, and she was carrying his child. Yes, they must make allowances.

Meg was the only one who seemed to think that the forthcoming trip would be good for Lizzie, and when they were alone, she said so: 'That's right, lass. Get yourself away. You need a change. And there's another thing; you'll be killin' two birds with the one stone by givin' that poor fellow a bit of female company.'

So Monday came and Geoff not only saw her to the bus, but went with her to the station, and got her ticket for her and saw her into the compartment. Just before the train left he said, 'Don't forget about us, will you?'

'Oh, Geoff.' She shook her head. 'Try to understand, will you?' At this he nodded at her and smiled, saying, 'Aye, yes, I'll try to understand, but I'll be looking forward to your coming back. Phone us the night, will you? Let us know you've arrived all right.'

'I'll do that. And tell Mam I'm sorry if I upset her. I didn't mean to.'

As she sat back in the corner of the compartment and the train moved out of the station, she saw him walk towards the exit, then turn about and stand looking back. And when she could no longer see him, she let out a long heavy sigh . . .

The journey seemed endless. She did not gaze out of the window at the passing countryside because her thoughts were turned inwards.

It was now early September and she was almost five months pregnant: the bulge was in evidence, and her mind seemed to have affected her body, because she never felt well. Mrs Logan, who worked in the lower office, had said that she always felt happy and healthy when carrying, and she'd had four children. You must cheer up, she had told her; it isn't good for the baby to worry.

It was strange, but the general consensus seemed to be that you could sorrow and show it if you had lost a husband, but if it was someone who had not put a ring on your finger, and had left you with a child, well then, that was different. You shouldn't somehow feel the same, nor expect the same kind of sympathy or consideration, a view expressed by one of the girls when she imagined Lizzie to be out of earshot: 'You can't expect to have your fun and not pay for it, can you? It isn't that people don't know what's what these days.'

People could be cruel. People *were* cruel. The world was mad. She wished she could escape from it. At times she felt desperate, so lonely, more so when she was in the house and they were making a fuss of her. She could understand now how Richard had felt when he had tried to end it all . . .

He was waiting on the platform. He ran along by the side of the train when he saw her standing at the window, and the train had hardly stopped before he had opened the door, holding out his hand for her case, then helping her down on to the platform.

'Oh, I'm glad to see you, Lizzie,' was his greeting.

'And I, you, Richard. I . . . I hope I haven't put you out by coming.' It was inane, but she'd had to say something, and he countered it with, 'Don't be silly, put me out? I've been counting the hours all day,' then he added quickly, 'and so have my mother and father. They are so anxious to see you. We'll have to take a bus first, but Matty will be waiting on the outskirts.' He turned his head towards her. 'Matty is . . . Well,' he laughed, 'I sometimes have to wonder just what Matty is. He's . . . he's like one of the family. He seemed to be an old man when I was born, but he came to the house when he was ten. His father was the stockman. But he himself is a Jack-of-all-trades and master of quite a few. You'll like Matty.'

She looked at Richard. He was dressed in breeches with leather leggings, a green tweed jacket, and a tweed hat with a soft brim. This was pulled well down on one side, so acting as a shield. He looked smart; at least, his body did. And he seemed entirely different from when she had last seen him. There was more life in him; in fact, you could say he was lively; and he talked easily. Well no, she wasn't right there: he was running on from one thing to another as if he were excited or embarrassed.

On the bus, he continued to talk. Then after what seemed a long ride he said, 'This is it. And there's Matty.' He helped her off. 'He doesn't bring the trap into town,' he explained, 'because Pedro doesn't like cars, and he's the only one that suits the trap . . . the horse.' He laughed and she laughed with him, saying, 'Yes, the horse.'

The man standing by the horse's head smiled at her. It was a tight smile, accompanied by a narrowed glance, and when Richard introduced Lizzie to him, he inclined his head and said one word, 'Ma'am.' And Lizzie said, 'How d'you do?'

A minute or so later they were all seated in the trap and bowling along a narrow road; and she looked about her, saying, 'This is nice . . . nice country. It reminds me of some parts of Durham.'

'Oh—' Richard turned his head to the side, his good eye seeming to twinkle at her as he said, 'With all due respect, ma'am, you won't find any scenery like this in Durham, an' you ain't seen nothin' yet.' My! My! This was a different Richard. She smiled widely at him. Of course he was on his own ground, his home ground. When he leant towards Matty and said, 'I'm right, aren't I, Matty?' the older man nodded without turning his head and in a voice holding a deep burr, he answered, 'You are that, Mr Richard. You are that.'

She looked at the lean profile of the driver. He was what could be called a dour Scot, this one.

'How long will it take us to reach . . . your home?'

'Oh; little over half an hour. That's if Pedro keeps up his spring.'

By the time the half-hour had passed, she had to admit that the scenery was very different from that she was used to in Durham. She had always imagined Scotland to consist mainly of rugged mountains, gorges, and miles of barren screeland, although on her two visits to Edinburgh, each had been by way of the Cheviots. This, however, was like another land, soft and mellow. They passed through villages with glowing gardens, through woodlands with soft tinkling streams. But then, of a sudden, the scene changed: they were entering wilder country, with the hills in the distance seeming to touch the sky.

'We'll soon be there,' Richard said. 'You're not tired?'

'No; not at all.'

'It's been a long journey.' He paused, then said, 'Am I going to apologise that we are off the beaten track? No, for that would be a lie. And anyway I daren't, not in Matty's hearing.' He put his hand out and punched the older man between the shoulders and was answered with a grunt.

When they entered a wooded lane the horse's trot turned to a walk, and Richard said, 'If I was blind drunk I would know I was reaching home. He's a character, is Pedro.' He stabbed his finger towards the horse's swaying rump. 'Strange, but right from the very beginning when he was put into the trap, he refused to run once he had reached our land.

This' – he waved his hand from side to side – 'is the beginning of the estate. It's odd, isn't it, that a horse should behave like that?'

'Yes, it is indeed. I wonder why?'

'I don't know. None of us do. It's as if he knew he was on his home ground and so that was that; from here on he could take it easy.'

After the horse had walked about a mile, she looked at Richard in surprise, saying, 'This . . . all this is the estate?'

'Yes; but it's mostly rough grassland. We've got bits under cultivation here and there where possible. It's the labour, you see; you can't get it today. There's three land-girls come twice a week and help out, but we have only Jock, he's the stockman, and a young boy left to see to the outside of the farm. Anyway, you'll do the rounds tomorrow.'

The horse now turned and, walking between two iron gates, entered a drive and continued past a stone lodge set back to the right.

The drive was mostly overgrown with grass through the shingle, except where two ruts showed the passage of a heavy vehicle and between which the horse now walked sedately.

The drive seemed never-ending until, nearing the end of a dark tunnel of overhanging trees, Lizzie was able to see the long, low, ivy-covered house, fronted by a low terrace, with the early evening sun glinting in its windows set deep in cream-coloured stone.

When the trap stopped opposite the front door two figures appeared on the terrace and looked towards them. He had said his parents were old, and

for a moment she couldn't imagine that these figures were they, that is until they came towards her.
The man, although seemingly straight, was indeed, as
Richard had said, an old man. His hair was white
but still thick, and below it his whole face sagged
into jowls that went to form his neck, but his eyes
were bright and clear and blue, and his handshake
was firm when he greeted her, saying, 'Glad you've
got here at last. Had a good journey?'

'Yes. Yes, thank you.'

'This is my mother,' said Richard. 'Mother, this is
Lizzie,' and he turned to Lizzie, saying, 'She knows
all about you.'

Lizzie and the woman looked at each other as
their hands met, and for a moment Lizzie thought
that she must be years younger than her husband;
but then she noticed the metallic glint of the brown
hair, the white streaks near the ears, and then the
folds of flesh beneath the eyes; yet while the mouth
was young and the cheeks were young, it was the
neck that could not deny age. But overall, the face
was kind, and warm, and welcoming.

'Hello, Lizzie.'

'Hello, Mrs Boneford.'

'Oh, not Mrs Boneford!' The tall man was already
walking back into the house, saying, 'She's Edith
and I'm James. Let's settle for that, eh, Lizzie?' He
turned and grinned at her over his shoulder, and
she laughed, saying, 'Right, James!' and it was amid
laughter that they entered the hall.

Lizzie stopped and gazed about her in wonderment.
She had read about such halls and seen them in
pictures of noble houses. But this wasn't a noble house.

194

From the outside it looked a homely house, on the large side, perhaps, but homely. But here was a long room made austere by its stone walls, the same colour as those outside. At one end was a deep-set fireplace holding an iron standing grate flanked by two huge fire-dogs. There was no fire burning but the grate was piled high with half-burned logs and there was a pile of ash underneath it. The floor was made up of square stone slabs partly covered by two carpets, one red and one blue, both fading into a neutral harmony.

At the opposite end of the hall from the fireplace, a shallow black-oak stairway rose to a half-landing before turning again and at the head of the further flight she glimpsed part of a gallery.

A number of doors went off the hall, and to the side of the fireplace a deep stone archway led somewhere. The ceiling was beamed with the same type of wood that went to make the staircase, and round it was a wooden cornice from which oil paintings hung here and there by means of chains.

'Would you like a cup of tea first, or would you rather go to your room and get settled in?'

Lizzie put her head slightly to the side and gave a small smile as she said, 'I'd love a cup of tea.'

'Good; so would I.' Edith now turned to her husband, saying, 'Tell Phyllis we're ready, will you, James?'

And Lizzie watched this elderly gentleman turn smartly about and answer like a young fellow might, saying, 'Will do,' only to stop abruptly when a voice came from the far end of the hall, saying, 'I'm here, ma'am.' And to this, the master of the house retorted, 'Yes, of course you would be, being nosey again. Can't get you to come at a run first thing in the morning, though, can I?'

Her mouth slightly open, Lizzie looked from Richard's father to what was evidently a middle-aged maid. She was wearing a blue print dress with a white collar, and a small matinée apron hung from her ample waist.

Lizzie's mouth opened still further when this person answered in a broad Scottish accent, 'If I got to me bed at a decent hour, I'd rise from it in time to see to your wants . . . you'll be wantin' your tea now, ma'am?' She turned to her mistress, and Edith Boneford smiled and said, 'Yes, please, Phyllis.'

Richard, who had taken Lizzie's coat and hat, was now guiding her through the arch and, bending his head towards her, he said on a chuckle, 'You'll hear a lot of that kind of exchange. They've been going at it for years.'

'Really?' It was a small whisper.

'Oh, that's nothing; wait until they get really started.' As he opened a door for her, he said, 'You'll likely find us a very strange household.'

She made no answer. It might be strange in one sense, but already it was warm, so warm. Even the house seemed to embrace her. And now she almost gasped as she entered the drawing-room, which was, in every way, in contrast to the hall. At first she could take in only that the walls were a pinkish grey and the carpet was blue, and the upholstery was rose-coloured. There was a large chintz-covered couch and two velvet-covered ones. There were numerous tables and china cabinets. She had never in her life seen any place so beautiful; in fact, she had never imagined *any* place could be so beautiful, yet showing such use, for when she sat down on the couch she saw the velvet on the arms was worn to its base.

From where she sat she was looking at another open fireplace; but here the fire was burning in the low hearth.

When Richard and his mother were seated, and his father took up a position with his back to the fire, Lizzie was again slightly surprised when his wife said to him, 'For goodness' sake! James, sit down. You're taking all the heat. I'm frozen.' She turned now to Lizzie adding, 'I'm always cold; and, you know, he always does that.'

What could she say? She looked from one to the other; then towards Richard, and he was smiling widely at her. His scarred mouth looked relaxed, his one brown eye wide, he looked . . . happy? She questioned the word . . . well, certainly different.

'What's she up to? It would be all ready. Mary would have everything ready. I'll go and see.'

'Leave it, Father. I'll go.'

With Richard's leaving the room, a silence fell until Edith Boneford said quietly, 'How are you feeling, my dear?' And before Lizzie could answer, James leant forward from the end of the other couch and softly he, too, enquired, 'Yes; how are you feeling?'

She looked from one to the other and answered quietly, 'Very well. Yes, very well.'

'When is it expected?'

She was slightly surprised to get this question from Richard's father and she thought it might have brought a reprimand from his wife; but no, Edith was looking at her, waiting for her answer, and she said, 'About the middle of January.'

197

'Oh, that's a cold month.' Edith made a little motion with her head. 'Have you anyone at home to look after you?'

'Oh, yes, my mother, and Meg, a friend who is staying with us.'

'I thought your mother was an invalid.'

'Well, not that kind of an invalid. She has a bad leg, but . . . but she gets about. I'll . . . I'll be all right . . . well looked after. And Geoff is at home. He is well . . . well' – she put out her hands in a helpless motion – 'I don't know whether Richard has told you, but Mr and Mrs Fulton are not my parents. I went to work for them when I was fourteen. Then they sort of adopted me. Their son, Geoff, was in the army, and he's only recently returned. He was wounded, but now he's at home all the time and is a very practical fellow.'

'Oh, yes, yes, I've heard about him.'

The strained note she detected in Mrs Boneford's voice embarrassed Lizzie for a moment; but then she was surprised at Mr Boneford's next words. 'We're . . . we just wanted to say that if you should need a maternity home, you'd be very welcome here. You see, we were very fond of Andrew. He was a different kettle of fish from his father. Couldn't stand that man.' He now rose to his feet and went to the fire and once again took up his position with his back to it. But this time his wife didn't chastise him, she simply continued where he had left off, saying, 'Yes, we were very fond of Andrew. As James says, he didn't take after his father, nor after Alicia. I was amazed at Alicia closing the door on her own son. She should have stood up to that bully of a man. But then, Alicia could never bear a scandal of any kind. Of course, did she but know it, she must have already lost some face when she married Bradford-Brown.'

Lizzie was certainly embarrassed now. Judging by their conversation, it was as if they didn't know that she, Lizzie, was the reason for Andrew's family forbidding him the house. On the other hand, if they did know, and of course they must do, they were being tactless, to say the least. And yet, there might be some other reason. She couldn't fathom it.

When the door opened and Richard entered pushing a tea trolley and Phyllis the maid followed carrying a large two-handled silver tray that seemed as much as she could manage, Mr and Mrs Boneford's conversation turned a somersault.

'Have you any wellington boots?' This was from Mrs Boneford. 'Well, of course, you wouldn't have thought about bringing them, but it's been raining rather heavily lately and there's boggy parts.' Whereupon her husband took up the thread, saying while pointing to her open-toed sandals: 'Go round in them,' he cried 'and we'll have to stick you in the brook up to your knees to get the mud off,' only for his voice to change when he asked quietly, 'Do you think you'll be up to tramping the hills?'

'No; she won't, Father,' and Richard, pushing the trolley over to his mother's side, added, 'If she does the farm and round about, that'll be enough. You're not taking her on one of your so-called short treks.'

'I wasn't thinking about taking her on one of my . . . short treks. Anyway, I'm sure she'd come if I asked her, and she'd be up to it, wouldn't you?' and without waiting for an answer he left his position by the fire to sit down in a high-backed, deep-winged chair.

In the meantime Phyllis had placed the heavily laden tray on a sofa table at the head of a couch, and was about to offer a plate of scones to her master, only to be greeted with, 'We have a guest. Haven't you got eyes?'

When the whispered yet quite audible answer came back, 'Yes, I've got eyes, but you always demand to stuff your kite first,' Lizzie was forced to droop her head and bite on her lip. Then Phyllis was standing in front of her offering her the plate of hot, buttered scones. There was a quirk to her lips and a twinkle in her eye, and when she said, 'He's showing off,' and this was greeted with laughter both from Mrs Boneford and Richard, she thought, It's like a comedy. Yet, a comedy would have never got away with a maid cheeking her master like this, and in front of the mistress and the son of the house. It was indeed an odd situation.

A few minutes later, as Phyllis went to make her departure, her master shouted after her, 'Don't forget I'm taking you in first thing in the morning.'

'You're not!' came the laconic reply.

'We'll see. I'm not having you squawking your eyes out and not being able to do your work,' a statement, which caused the maid, if she were a maid, thought Lizzie, to turn quickly about and throw at her master: 'Aw, you! Fiddle-faddle!' before going out and closing the door softly after her.

'I'm sure you must think you've landed in a madhouse,' Richard was saying, 'Those two are no respectors of persons. You wouldn't think they were in love with each other, now would you? And if one's little finger aches, the other nearly goes up the lum.'

'It's true. It's true.' Mrs Boneford was handing her a cup of tea. And when Lizzie took it from her, her hand was shaking, for she found that she wanted to laugh, not just in an ordinary way, but almost hysterically. She had a strange feeling on her; it was as if, like Alice, she had entered another world and had discovered what she hadn't recognised before: that she had been tensed up for weeks, but that since entering this house that tenseness had disappeared, leaving her feeling very much at ease with these people, strange as they might appear to be in their nonconformity to what she imagined were the rules that governed such an establishment . . .

The conversation at dinner was such that at times she almost spluttered over her food, as Edith Boneford related some incidents of the early days in this house, where she had apparently come as a bride nearly thirty years ago.

And when Mary Catton, the cook, who was older still than Phyllis, came in to help serve the meal, the banter included her too.

It was three hours later when the reason for all this was made clear to Lizzie. She was in her dressing-gown sitting by the side of a single four-poster bed in a comfortable but definitely old-fashioned bedroom. The carpet, particularly by the side of the bed, was threadbare; the furniture was heavy solid mahogany. There were no modern conveniences; the ewer and basin stood on the marble-topped wash-hand stand, the bathroom, she had found out, being at the end of the corridor. Mrs Boneford had told her she was putting her in what was called the dressing-room, as it was next to theirs, and opposite Richard's, so

201

should she need anything or anyone in the night, they would be at hand. She was made to think they considered the birth to be imminent.

Then came a tap on her door. When she called, 'Come in,' Edith Boneford entered.

She was dressed in a long velvet dressing-gown with a deep collar. Her appearance was completely changed. She looked old now, fragile.

When Lizzie got to her feet, Mrs Boneford said, 'Sit down, child.' It was nice to be called child. Then, indicating the side of the bed, she added, 'May I sit down?' leaving Lizzie to ponder further on the strangeness of this woman in asking if she might sit on one of her own beds. This was courtesy at its finest.

Once seated, she did not begin to talk, but stared at Lizzie for some seconds, and then she said, 'You will have been puzzled at the charade you've witnessed since your arrival . . . well, my dear, I feel I must explain. You see, it's a kind of play we indulge in. We're all in it. We all have our parts, particularly James and Phyllis, as you have no doubt noticed. It's for Richard. We pretend everything is as normal as it was before the war.' She gave a small smile as she added, 'Even then, James and Phyllis would indulge in their little repartee. You see, they've all been with us so long, Mary, Phyllis, and Matty. There were others, but they have died; and the younger ones . . . well, they're in the services; Matty's two sons are at sea, and Mary's only boy was killed in the first months of the war.'

She now bent over and unbuttoned the bottom button of the dressing-gown, smoothed the button-hole round with her fingers, then slipped it back over the button, before she went on, 'You have no idea what it was like when he first came home. He hid himself away like some wounded animal. Yet, his face has much improved from when we first saw it in hospital. And what I've told myself time and again, and even said to him: there are so many men worse off than himself, and at least he has part of his face as it was. What broke him up finally was when Janis couldn't bear to look at him, couldn't bear even to be near him. He was absolutely torn apart at that time. It was about that time too, that I first heard of you. We were sitting having tea in the drawing-room, just as we were today, and he looked at me and said, "I came across a young girl last week who looked me straight in the face, Mother; not a nurse, not one of the hospital crowd, but an ordinary girl from outside." Then he added – she now bent forward and touched Lizzie's hand – "But she wasn't an ordinary girl, she was beautiful, and she looked me straight in the face; and I could tell by her eyes she wasn't forcing herself; nor did she turn her head away; and we talked." That . . . that was the first time he met you. And later he told me that you and Andrew were in love and of the reaction of his parents. Then' – she swallowed deeply now, and her lips trembled as she went on to say – 'about the time when he found out about Janis and his so-called friend – it wasn't Janis's first escapade by any means, but it seemed to be the last straw – that's when you stepped in, literally, my dear, and saved his life. Oh, yes, yes, he told us' – she nodded – 'he had been quite prepared to finish it. And as he said later, his act could have finished both of you.'

She now straightened up and with her hands, one cupped inside the other on her lap, she made a small clapping noise and her expression lightened as she said, 'That . . . that incident has been the turning point in his life. He . . . he now has the will to live. I'm sure you gave it to him.'

At this Lizzie shook her head. 'Oh no. Oh no. He's . . . he's a brave man. He would have faced up to things on his own.'

'I doubt it, my dear. I doubt it. This thing called pride, it's different in a man from that in a woman. No matter how plain a man looks there's a vanity in him. A woman admits it and despairs over it at times, but not so a man; even ugly men are attractive, but there's a difference between ugliness and a face becoming a grotesque mask. No, my dear, your friendship has given him the courage that he lacked before. You see he was a very handsome fellow, not that he was ever openly vain about it, but nevertheless he was aware of the figure he cut. When he was in his full regalia and his kilt swinging, oh' – she shook her head slowly – 'there wasn't, to me, a more beautiful sight. And so, I hope you see, my dear, why we act as we do, talk as we do. He's aware of the play, and he joins in so that we won't worry about him. But we do all worry about him, of course. Anyway' – she rose from the bed – 'he goes back in a fortnight's time, and they are going to do something with the eyelid. If they manage to lift it up it'll make all the difference. I think it is that part of his face which is the worst.' She now flapped her hand at herself, saying, 'I've talked too much and you're tired.' Then her voice again changing, she said, 'I . . . I felt I had to tell you so that you wouldn't think we were all idiots.'

Lizzie too had risen to her feet and now she held out both her hands to the older woman, saying, 'I . . . I think you're all marvellous. I think he is too.'

'You do?'

'Oh, yes. I admire him. He must have gone through hell a number of times.'

'You're very understanding, dear. I can see why Andrew was willing to give up everything for you, materially that is. Good-night, my dear.' She leaned forward and kissed Lizzie on the cheek, then went quickly from the room.

Slowly Lizzie got into bed, although not to sleep. She switched out the bedside light, and as she lay staring into the darkness, strangely she wasn't thinking of Richard alone, and what her friendship had done for him, but of Geoff. She found herself wishing that Geoff liked Richard. Then she asked herself why. But she avoided a straight answer, telling herself it would be better all round if the three of them could be friends, because she would like to come again to this house, for she liked everyone in it. But she knew her visits would annoy Geoff, and she didn't want to annoy Geoff, for he had been so kind to her during these past months, almost like a . . . a brother . . . a close brother.

Never in her life had she known such contentment. She could not say happiness, because she associated that with Andrew, and the feeling for Andrew had brought excitement, followed by pain. The pain was still there, but dulled somewhat and more so since she had come into this house. They were all so caring towards her. But she still had to prove to them that she was capable of tramping, not only around the farm, but through the whole estate.

She had met the land-girls and was introduced to them as Mrs Brown. That had been thoughtful of Richard; but it had an odd sound; Mrs Brown. Yet, that's what she should have been at this time, a missis. But did it matter? No, she wouldn't have minded still being Lizzie Gillespie so long as Andrew had been alive. And inside her he *was* still alive. Every kick the baby gave informed her of that.

They were walking back from the farm. The night was closing in and she was feeling pleasantly tired. An hour ago she had gone to meet Richard, who had been doing his daily stint with the cattle. He was now carrying a large can of milk and she herself a basket lined with straw on which lay three rows of eggs. They had walked in silence for some way; then he said, 'Are you feeling tired?'

'No,' she lied brightly; 'I never felt better, I mean, less tired. Not that I'd be able to do the rounds with your father again.'

'He's thoughtless. He should never have taken you out yesterday.'

'He didn't take me any distance, really, but he strides and I think it irked him a bit when he had to trot by my side instead of gallop.'

He laughed. 'Mother refuses to go walking with him now. Odd' – he shook his head – 'he won't admit to age. You can't imagine he'll be eighty next birthday, can you? At times I fear for him in case his defiance brings him to a dead stop. And yet, he says that's what he wants; and I suppose it is the right way to go, to be brought to a full stop in the middle of whatever you've loved doing all your life; and his has been walking or marching at the head of his men. Huh!' he laughed gently. 'It used to be funny when Mother was drawn into his little walks. She would stop and plump herself down on the hillside and call to him, "General! Your battalion's fallen out."'

Their laughter joined; and they walked in silence again for some way, and it was she who spoke next, saying, 'You know, Richard, I can't tell you when I've enjoyed myself so much as these past few days. I feel I'd like them to go on for ever . . .'

When he paused in his step, she turned to him blinking rapidly and saying hastily, 'Well, what I mean is, to feel so contented in my mind, because since Andrew went I've been . . . well, I've been full of turmoil. You understand?'

'Yes, yes, I understand; and I'm so glad to hear you say you've found contentment here. I wish . . .' He paused for a long moment and looked down, then repeated, 'Yes, yes, I understand. There comes a time when pain has to cease or ease. If it didn't, you'd go out of your mind or try to finish it.' He turned his face towards her again. It was his good side, his brow and the left-hand side of his face was shaded by the soft tweed hat, and in the twilight she saw once more the man whose portrait in oils hung on the gallery wall. He was in full regimental uniform and, as his mother had said, he had been a handsome man. 'Oh, Richard.' She put out her hand to him and he gripped it and held tightly on to it as they walked along the hill path down towards the house.

She had not meant her impulsive action to be taken so far, and after a time she withdrew her hand as gently as she could. 'If I don't look out, we'll have scrambled eggs.'

He said, 'You know I'm going back into hospital shortly?'

'Yes; your mother told me.'

'They are going to have another go on me; not that I can see they can make much improvement.'

'Nonsense!' Her voice was sharp. 'After each visit it's been better.'

'You think so?'

She detected a slightly excited note in his voice, and she nodded firmly, saying, 'Yes, yes, I do.'

'They . . . they are going to try something further on my eye. It's a delicate business.' He paused; then sighed gently as he said, 'You know, it's wonderful that I can talk to you like this, Lizzie. I can't to Mother or Father, or anyone else, and I'm always amazed at the way you take me as a whole man.'

'You *are* a whole man. Don't talk so silly. You're . . . you're the nicest whole man I know.' And she smiled.

'Oh, Lizzie.' He did not look at her, but continued to walk on, his eyes now cast downwards, and quietly he said, 'You don't know what that means to me, that . . . that someone like you can see me as a person, not turn from me, not feel forced to make polite conversation about the weather, the war, ration books, or in some cases, the niceties they're being deprived of.' He glanced towards her. 'This really is what happens when my mother brings together a few friends, for my own good, mind, she says. God! It's always another kind of torment. Anyway,' – his voice changed again – 'I'm going to take you to see Paddy tomorrow. He's in charge of an out-station up in the hills. He's an RAF radio wallah, a grand fellow. You'll like him.'

They were approaching a gate leading to the yard when he said, 'We'll go through the kitchen because Mary always likes a bit of a crack.'

Before they could even place the eggs and milk on the kitchen table Phyllis greeted them with, 'There you are then! I thought you'd never get back. The phone's rung twice for you, Mrs Brown. It's from your home. They want you to get in touch right away.'

Lizzie cast a quick look in Richard's direction, and he said, 'I hope nothing's wrong,' and she answered, 'I . . . I don't know what it can be.' Then turning to Phyllis she said, 'Thanks, Phyllis,' before hurrying out and into the hall in order to phone home.

There was little delay before a voice said, 'That you, Lizzie?'

'Yes. Yes, it's me. What's the matter? What's the matter, Geoff?'

'It's Mother. She's very ill. She had a heart attack this morning. She . . . she wants to see you.'

'Oh. Oh, I'll come right away, but,' – she looked to the side where Richard was standing, then she said, 'Well, I . . . I can't get away tonight, but . . . but first thing in the morning.'

The voice came at her now, harshly, 'Why can't you leave tonight?'

'Well,' her own voice rose, 'it's after seven o'clock, and . . . and we're miles from the station, and . . . and I don't know about trains. I'll get the first one tomorrow morning.'

'You might be too late. She mightn't be here to-morrow morning.'

She gritted her teeth, then said, 'Wait a moment,' and putting her hand over the mouthpiece, she turned to Richard, saying, 'If I left now, would I be able to get a train back to Durham tonight?'

He thought for a moment, then shook his head, saying, 'I doubt it.' He now turned and looked at the grandfather clock, saying, 'It's twenty-five past seven. You wouldn't be able to get to the station before half-past eight; the timetables are so erratic now. I know there's one leaves around seven in the morning; you could get that.'

She thought a moment, then spoke into the phone again, saying, 'The earliest train, Geoff, is seven in the morning, and if I get the right connections I could be in Durham at around eleven. I . . . I could phone you from the station to let you know what time to meet me.'

There was a pause on the phone before the voice came back, saying, 'Well, if that's all you can do, that's all you can do. I phoned you over an hour ago.'

'Yes, you might have done' – her voice was as sharp as his now – 'but I happened to be out at that time.'

'Yes, you happened to be out at that time. Well, all I can say is I hope you're in time to see my mother.'

She heard the phone click down, then turned and looked helplessly at Richard and to where his mother and father were now standing in the archway, and very much like a child, she said, 'I've got to go home. Mam is very ill.'

'Oh, my dear.' Edith Boneford walked towards her. 'I'm so sorry. But what a pity. Oh dear me! dear me! About trains?' Mrs Boneford looked at Richard, and he said, 'I think the best bet is to wait for the seven o'clock in the morning train.'

Lizzie now asked Richard quietly, 'Could I risk going in and trying to get a connection?'

He looked first towards his mother, then to his father, and it was he who said, 'There was one used to leave around ten. It would likely land you there in the middle of the night.'

'I think I'd better try for it.'

'Well, if you aim to catch that one,' – Edith Boneford's tone was practical – 'it's now just on half-past seven, so you have time for a bite to eat. And, Richard, what about getting the truck from the farm? It may not be so comfortable but you'll get there in half the time.'

'Yes, yes,' he nodded, 'that's a good idea. Yes.'

Lizzie did not hurry up the stairs, and when she reached her room she sat on the side of the bed and, bending forward, she placed her tightly gripped hands between her knees, and while she prayed that nothing would happen to Bertha, she also thought, Geoff shouldn't have spoken to me like that. He's taking too much on himself. Then saying aloud, 'I'll have to phone him again,' she rose to pack her case.

She had just placed it on the floor by the side of the bed when there came a tap on the door, and after calling, 'Come in,' she was surprised to see James Boneford walking slowly towards her.

He stood there, his white hair hanging over his forehead in an untidy mass, unusual because he always wore his hair sleeked back. Her thought was that he must have been running his fingers through it. She watched him wet his lips, then run his fingers round the inside of his collar before he said, 'There'll be no time for a private word downstairs, but . . . but, Lizzie,

211

'I . . . I just wanted to say . . . well, I wanted to thank you for what you have done for my son . . . thank you in a personal way. He has been sort of . . . well, a new man since he made your acquaintance. You saved his life, and for that I also want to thank you.'

'Oh. Oh, Mr Boneford . . . James, please, please, don't. I've done nothing except talk to him; and I like talking to him. It's been my pleasure.'

'Talk to him, huh! Poor chap. He couldn't get people to look at him for two minutes, never mind talk to him. He has gone through hell. It's been hell for all of us because . . . because we care so much. But for him, a special kind, yes, a special kind.' His upper lip moved, seeming to push his neat moustache into his thin nostrils; then he said, 'If only that other one, the one that was his wife, had had one spark of your compassion, how different things would have been; but then . . . then' – he gave a twisted smile – 'had she been different we wouldn't have met you, and we've all been very pleased to meet you, Lizzie.'

She almost said, 'Thank you, sir,' for his manner and tone were reminiscent of the regiment, stiff, polite, but very meaningful, so different from when he was sparring with Phyllis. Impulsively she leant forward and kissed him on the side of his stubbly moustache, and, his arms reaching out quickly, he held her by the shoulders and kissed her back, a hard dry kiss to the side of her nose. Then he turned and almost marched from the room, leaving her standing with the tears rolling down her cheeks. And she was made to think, Oh, if only I could stay here.

They were, as usual, to eat in the small dining-room, where the table held eight, ten at a pinch. The table in the main dining-room, when fully extended, she understood, could seat eighteen. The chairs there were upholstered in hide; but in the smaller dining-room they were Hepplewhite and the padded seats showed much use. It had once been the serving-room to the dining-room proper, she had been told, and off this was a butler's pantry and other sundry small workrooms. The pantry had two doors, one leading into a corridor from which was the entrance into the one-time servants' hall, which itself had access to the kitchen. Excluding the attics and the servants' quarters there were twenty-six rooms in the house and seemingly countless passages, in which Lizzie had become lost more than once during the past three days.

When she came downstairs she found there was no-one in the drawing-room and she imagined they were not down yet and that she was a little early for the meal which, at this time of the evening, took the form of a supper. Or perhaps, she thought, they were already in the dining-room.

Intending to make her way there, she walked through the archway, turned to her left and went down one of the two passages. But it wasn't until she came to the end of the passage that she realised she had taken the wrong one, for this one led to the kitchen quarters, which she recognised by its worn green-baize door leading to what Mrs Boneford had called the hatch room, which in turn had an entrance to the small dining-room.

As she opened the door she was immediately brought to a halt by Mrs Boneford's voice saying, 'Richard! Richard! Listen to me.'

Then Richard's voice, harsh-sounding, replying, 'No, Mother, no, I can't do it. I won't do it. I won't spoil what there is between us.'

'Don't be silly, Richard. Don't be silly. I'm telling you to ask her. Tell her you'll wait; that it doesn't matter how long. If you don't, you'll be sorry, because someone will snap her up. A girl like that won't be left alone long at any time, and certainly not now, not now.'

'Mother! Mother! Listen to me. She likes me; she looks upon me as a friend; what's more, she can look at me. I want her to go on looking at me, but if I do as you ask, she will leave me and I shall never see her again. What is more, Andrew is still fresh in her mind. It's no time since he went. So, in ordinary circumstances, it would be indecent.'

'Oh, Richard, my dear, you . . . you don't know women. You picked wrong in the first place. I hinted as much but you wouldn't listen. So please listen to me now. That girl needs someone to love her and the child that is coming. She likes us all here, I know she does. Your father thinks she's a wonderful person, and . . . and don't forget Mary has taken to her; and, as you know, Mary is a barometer. She did not like Janis from the first time she saw her. But with Lizzie . . . well, you know what she said to me yesterday? "Missis," she said, "that should have been the one."'

'Mother, for God's sake! be quiet, please, and listen to me. Once and for all, I'm not in a position to ask her to marry me now, and when I become so, I wouldn't. I couldn't. Even if they patch me up so that I won't scare the children, in my own mind I shall always be a monster. I'm thankful for what I've got: we are friends, we can talk. When I don't see her I know she's there and I can call and have a word with her. She would even come here, as now, and I would have her company for a while; but more than that, Mother, oh no! You don't know what you're asking. To think that at some time I might propose to any girl! No! And to someone like Lizzie? Good lord, never!'

In the silence that followed, Lizzie, her hand over her mouth, now lifted one foot carefully after the other, hoping not to cause the boards to creak, and returned the way she had come.

In the hall she met Mrs Boneford coming from the other passageway and, she, seeing Lizzie, straightaway hurried to her, saying, 'What is it, dear? Are you feeling ill? You . . . you look so white.'

'I . . . I . . .' Lizzie could find nothing to say.

'Look, I don't think you should go tonight.'

Now she could just find words to say, 'Oh, yes, I must. Yes, I must.'

'Well, come along, dear, and have something to eat. It's going to be a long journey . . .'

The fact that she could hardly eat anything and that she had little to say except 'Please' and 'Thank you' was put down to the fact that she was worried about her mother. And when, some time later, she bade goodbye to Mary and Phyllis, and was embraced by both James and Edith, she still could find little to say except to thank them, which she managed to do warmly, while they in turn told her how much they had enjoyed having her and that she must come and stay for a longer period . . . and before the baby was born, because very often, in the winter, they were snowed in up here. The last words Edith said to her were, 'That would be wonderful, if we were snowed in and you had the baby here, now wouldn't it?' and she had managed to smile as she replied as lightly as she could, 'I cannot stand the cold.' And to this James had cried, 'I'll have a fire roaring in every room for you, my dear . . .'

She and Richard had little to say to each other as they drove through the night. Twice he ran the vehicle off the road, on each occasion fortunately, on to a grass verge and not into a ditch. When he apologised profusely, he said that he was more used to driving the horse and trap.

Altogether, it was a rough ride, and she was thankful when they reached the outskirts of the town and left the rutted country roads behind.

In the station she phoned home and it was Meg who answered. 'Oh, is that you, lass? Oh, I'm glad to hear your voice. Oh, I am. And you're on your way. Oh, that's good news; she'll be happy. Here's Geoff.'

'You're getting the train then?' he said.

'Yes,' she answered briefly, 'but it's a slow one. I don't know when I'll arrive; probably sometime in the middle of the night. I'll . . . I'll phone you from the station.'

'I'll make enquiries about connections and I'll meet you there.'

'Very well. How is she?'

'Not good. Not good at all.'

'I'll . . . I'll be there shortly.'

'Right, Lizzie. Right.' His voice was softer now.

She put the phone down and looked along the platform to where Richard was coming towards her.

'There's one goes at half-past nine; you're lucky. Come on,' – he picked up her bag – 'it's in already.'

Each dim-lit carriage showed that the train was already full, and so, at the end carriage, he said, 'You'd better get in; but don't stand, sit on your case in the corridor. If there are any decent ones among them, somebody will soon give you a seat.' He opened the end door of the carriage and pushed her case in; then they stood staring at each other in the dim green light cast from the lamp above their heads.

'I'm . . . I'm sorry you've got to go like this, Lizzie, but phone me and tell me how she is, will you?'

'Yes; yes, I will, Richard.'

She watched the skin of his face move like stiff parchment before he said, 'It's been a wonderful three days for me.'

'And . . . and for me too, Richard.'

'You'll come again?'

'Oh, yes, yes. Yes, I'll come again. I'd like to very much.' She could say this because she could hear his words: 'I'll never ask her to marry me.' So that was that, and it was just as well.

Marry Richard? She had never even given it a thought; and yet hadn't she been aware that he more than liked her? Yes, but as he said, he would never expect her to marry him.

She held out her hand. 'I . . . I'd better get in. Goodbye, Richard, and . . . and thank you.' She could lean forward now and put her lips to his. It wasn't cruel. It was a kind of payment for his kindness, and a liberty she could take because she knew, in a way, that he would expect nothing more from her.

He did not respond to the kiss but stood perfectly still, until, after mounting the steps into the train, she

217

put out her hand to pull the door closed when, swiftly, he pushed it closed.

A whistle blew.

'Goodbye, Richard. I'll phone you.'

'Goodbye, Lizzie.' That's all he said. He didn't make any move towards the window and the last she saw of him was the outline of a tall man standing under a dim green light.

The journey was a nightmare. No-one offered her a seat. Other people were standing in the corridor. Sitting on her case she looked an ordinary young woman, just as able to put up with the discomfort of the journey as the rest of them.

Things lightened a little from Newcastle to Durham. She did finally manage to get a seat, flanked by snoring soldiers and breathing in the stale smell of beer and spirits.

When at last she arrived in Durham, the dawn was about to break, and as she stumbled from the compartment it was almost into the arms of Geoff. The first words she said were, 'What a journey! What a nightmare!'

He took her case from her and walked by her side, and as they passed through the barrier, she gave up her ticket to a bleary-eyed porter. Then they were on the pavement and she stopped and drew in a long breath of air before she said, 'How is she?' And he, looking down at her, said, 'She died at half-past one this morning.'

PART FOUR

What Price Marriage?

1

It was two months since they had buried Bertha, and it seemed that her dying had changed every personality in the house. The most noticeable was that of John: the words 'lost soul' could have fitted him, for he went out to work in the morning, returned for his midday meal, went out again in the afternoon, came in at half-past five, and sat in the sitting-room, and from whichever chair he chose to sit in, he directed his gaze towards the piano, as if he were seeing Bertha sitting there.

At times he would talk, mostly to Geoff, and about the war. Things were turning. The Americans were making a difference. It was all those destroyers they were sending. Look how they were sinking the U-boats. This year alone, they said, fifty had already gone to the bottom.

When he talked of the war it was as if he was concerned for what was going on, but they all knew he was only repeating the headlines that he glanced over each morning. He was a lost man. Bertha had been his stay. In a way he had gone back to his young days, when he had relied on his brother. The only definite stand he had made on his own in his life had been to marry Bertha. And now she was no more; except what he conjured up of her when he gazed at the piano.

Geoff too had changed, but in an opposite way from his father, for he had taken over control of the house. It was as though he had appointed himself head of it. The only time he seemed to leave was when he went to the military hospital for a check-up. On one occasion he had been kept in for two nights, and when he returned his anxiety was evident. He seemed to be concerned not so much about his father's welfare as about Lizzie's.

Lizzie had been working up till a week ago, when she had caught a cold. The weather was bitter: already there were sleet showers, and hoar-frost covered the windows in the mornings. Although she insisted it was only a cold, Geoff also insisted that she should have the doctor, and after an examination the doctor advised that she should give up her work at once and rest: her legs were swollen, and she admitted to having felt unwell for some time now.

As the doctor was leaving on this particular morning, he addressed Geoff as if he were the husband, saying, 'Take care of her. She'll go her time if she rests.' And Geoff had answered as a husband might, 'Yes; yes, I'll see to that. I'll insist on it.' And that's what he had said to her when he returned to the bedroom.

'You know what the doctor's just said?'

'No. What has he just said?'

'You've got to go careful; if you want to run your time, you've got to rest; so you do what you're told.'

'Look,' she said; 'stop making a fuss. I've only got a bit of a cold; I know how I feel . . . inside,' she added.

'You might think you do, but I should imagine the doctor knows better. So I'll write a note to your office tomorrow morning.'

'You'll do no such thing. I'm still able to walk; I'll

222

go in and tell them myself. Now, Geoff, please' – she held up her hand – 'leave this to me.'

He came to the bed and looked down at her, and after a moment, he said softly, 'I worry about you.'

She blinked and turned away from him as she said, 'I'm . . . I'm grateful, Geoff, I am, I am really; but there's no need. Babies are born every day and there's Meg to help me.'

'She's old.'

'Old!' She rounded on him now. 'She might be old in years, but she's still spritely and has got a head on her shoulders, more than most.'

'You mean she could handle things better than me?'

'Yes; yes, perhaps I do in this case, she being a woman.' She now smiled at him, and after a moment he smiled back, saying, 'There are male nurses. I've had experience of them; one in particular. He had a voice like a nancy boy, but a pair of hands on him like a navvy. You know, I once said to him, "It's a pity your hands can't change places with your voice," and he said, "What! What!"' He had now taken on an effeminate tone. '"You are a funny fellow," he said. "Not half as funny as you, chum," I answered. And, you know, he flounced away like a saucy girl. He caused more fun in that ward than a whole concert party of comedians could have done.'

'Poor soul!'

'Yes, you would say that,' he nodded at her.

Talking of hospitals reminded her that she hadn't asked him about his leg for the past two or three days, and so she said, 'How's your leg?'

'Fine.' He slapped his thigh. 'But look, this arm is

223

better.' He raised his left forearm breast high. 'I've never been able to do that before, so the muscles must be getting to work again. I never thought it would happen.'

'Well,' she smiled, 'that's what comes of being domesticated. There's nothing like a bit of housework to firm up your muscles.'

'By! you're right there. I just thought this afternoon, if the lads could see me now.' The smile left his face; and she asked quietly, 'Do you miss the army?'

He paused, as though thinking, before answering her, then said, 'Yes and no. At times I miss the companionship, the bustle, the excitement . . .' – he looked over her head to the head of the bed – 'egging them on, yelling one minute; then another time scarcely breathing, signalling to each other like the deaf and dumb. Those were the worst times, quiet times, easing forward on your belly, part of you sick with fear, the other half clean mad to get up and rush forward-and-shoot-and-stab-and-maim-and-kill.'

'Geoff! Geoff!' She had pulled herself up, her voice sharp now, and he blinked his eyes and brought his attention to her again, saying, 'There I go. There I go.' And, his mouth wide now, he laughed: 'That was a prelude to the big picture.'

She looked at him and said quietly, 'Men *are* frightened then; I mean, of going into battle?'

He turned abruptly from her, his voice harsh now as he made towards the door, saying, 'Any who say they aren't are bloody liars, or are already mad, and should never have been let out of the loony bin.'

She lay back looking towards the closed door. In a way, she thought, he's as maimed as Richard, only his

224

scars aren't visible. And yet, once or twice at night, she had heard the pain of them. On one occasion he had yelled and she had hurried out on to the landing, there to see Meg already standing outside his door. This had happened recently; since his mother had died.

As she lay there she heard the faint tinkle of the phone ringing downstairs, and a short while later, when Meg brought her up a cup of tea, she asked casually, 'Who was on the phone?' And Meg, dropping herself down on to the side of the bed, said, 'Mr Richard.'

'Oh, why didn't you tell me?'

'Geoff answered. He told him you were bad.'

'Oh, nonsense! Good gracious, you'll have him on the train, coming to see what's the matter with me. Geoff did that on purpose.'

'Why would he do that, lass?' Meg's gaze was penetrating.

'Because . . . because he doesn't like Richard, that's why.'

'Well, perhaps he has his reasons.'

'What d'you mean by that?'

'Just what I say, lass. You've shown a great deal of interest in that fellow, you know, when you're supposed to be just friends.'

'Well, Meg,' – she leaned towards her – 'let me make this clear to you; that's what we are: friends, and that's what we are likely to remain. I'm sorry for him. I always have been, and, with those in his condition, a little kindness can only help.'

'Aye, well,' Meg slid from the bed, 'you know what they say, lass, pity is akin to love.'

'Oh, don't be silly, Meg.'

Meg now turned sharply and, leaning her hands on

225

the bed, she brought her face close to Lizzie's, saying, quietly but firmly now, 'You're no fool, lass, but . . . but I'm goin' to say this: I think you're closing your eyes to somethin'. Him down there' – she thumbed towards the floor – 'is no relation to.you, not even a second, or third, or fourth cousin, and it's evident to anybody with eyes, how the wind's blowing from his direction.'

'Meg, please!'

'All right,' Meg straightened up; 'you can say "Meg, please!" in that tone of voice, but just let me point out one obvious thing, lass; he's not runnin' round you like a broody hen just to keep himself warm. Even before he lost his mother, I could see the way his mind was workin', especially, I can tell you, when you went away for those few days to Scotland. My! My! he was like a bear with a sore skull. And you know one of the last things Bertha said to me, do you, before she went? She said, "Lizzie will always have a home here as long as Geoff remains." That's what she said. Now, lass' – she wagged her finger at her – 'don't look at me like that. I'm a slight bit older than you and I've seen life, and I've known sorrow, and you can't live on sorrow. There comes a time when you say to yourself, I've got to go on. What am I goin' to do with me life? You've got a bairn comin'. It needs to be brought up in a good home, and you won't find a better one than this, nor anyone much better than Geoff. Oh, he's got his faults, who hasn't? and at times he talks as if he's God Almighty. But he's got this house, 'cos his dad won't marry again, ever, I know that, and he'll have a decent pension, and he's goin' after a light job. You could be settled well and comfortably for life, lass. Think about it and ask yourself, what's the alternative?' She

226

grinned now, her eyes lost in the wrinkles, 'That's a big word for me, isn't it, "alternative"?' And as she finished, 'And you do like him, don't you?' Lizzie turned her head away and looked to the side of the room. And when Meg repeated, 'Well, you do, don't you?' she said quietly, 'Yes, I suppose I do. But liking and loving aren't the same thing.'

'D'you know somethin'? I'm goin' to tell you: me mother had a hell of a life with me da. He could drink like a stranded whale. I said to her once, "Why do you stick it? Why don't you walk out on him? You don't love him. You can't," and she said, "No, I suppose not; but I like him, and I've found that that's much more lastin' than love." I was young at the time when she said that to me. I didn't believe it, but I proved it to meself years later. If you start with lovin' somebody and yet know they're not companion-like, it's rarely, rarely that you grow to like them. But if you start liking them, nine times out of ten you end up by lovin' them. But then again, there's all stages of love. Eeh! here I go on. Anyway, lass, would you like me to phone Richard and tell him that you're not dying, because, as you say, if he thinks you're real bad, he'll land on the doorstep, as like as not.'

Lizzie thought for a moment, then said, 'Yes; yes, please. And tell him I'll phone him tomorrow.'

'I'll do that, lass. Now settle down and enjoy your sniffles . . .'

When Meg left the room she left behind a big question mark in Lizzie's mind. It came at the end of 'Could I marry Geoff?' There was a long pause before she could give herself the answer, 'Yes, perhaps,

227

but . . . but not yet awhile; not until the pain of Andrew eases off.'

It was the day before Christmas Eve when, descending the stairs and poised on the second step from the bottom, the bulge of her stomach seemed to pull her forward, and she would have toppled and fallen had Geoff, who happened to be crossing the hall, not hopped quickly towards her and caught her; and she lay against him for a moment, his arms about her, but the mound, although pressed tight to him, kept their faces at a distance, and they remained still and looked at each other. When he said quietly, 'Third time's catchy time,' she said, 'What!'

'Third time's catchy time. Surely you remember?'

Slowly she disengaged herself from him and said, 'What should I remember?'

'Well' – he turned and pointed towards the kitchen door – 'it should happen one time, many years ago, that I almost knocked a young lass on to her back when I pushed open that door, and I caught her and she said to me, "Third time's catchy time."'

She laughed now, saying, 'Good gracious! I don't recall that, but fancy you' – she paused – 'remembering it!'

He walked beside her towards the sitting-room, saying, 'There's lots of things I remember about you in those few days I knew you before I went abroad. And it is odd, but I always thought of you as the little girl until I came back and saw the young woman. You were a shock, you know. And—' he leaned forward to push open the door for her while saying, 'don't forget I saved you from the factory.'

228

'No; I've never forgotten that, Geoff.' She had half-turned to him as she passed into the room.

'Oh' – his face was serious now – 'I meant that to be funny: I wouldn't want to claim a medal for it. Who knows, if you had gone there you would likely have finished up marrying the owner.'

'Yes, you're quite right,' she laughed; 'stranger things have happened; he might have wanted a nurse in his old age.'

He chuckled as he said, 'That's right; but I cannot see you pushing a wheelchair.'

His manner now becoming serious and with a deep sadness in his voice, he said, 'It's going to be an odd Christmas without Mam, don't you think? And I'm worried about Dad. He doesn't seem to care any more what happens in or outside the house. Funny,' she had slowly let herself down on to the couch and he now dropped into a chair opposite her. 'Some men can only love once. They don't seem to have it in them to change. Whether that's a good or a bad thing, I wouldn't know.'

It was on the point of her tongue to say, 'Wouldn't you?' because having dwelt on a future that appeared might be linked with his, she had, naturally, thought about his early association with Richard's wife.

There were times when she had a longing to see Richard, a feeling she couldn't really understand, except that maybe she found it easy to talk to him, and yes, laugh with him. It would seem that they shared the same sense of humour.

Bertha used to talk about Geoff and of the great sense of humour he had. She, herself, agreed that he was a great joker, but thought his joking was one-sided. It

229

was always he who seemed to enjoy the joke most, with the victims of his practical jokes rarely enjoying the fun.

She looked at him now and wondered why she was dissecting him. It was silly and unkind, because they now got on so well. He was so thoughtful, and she should be grateful that she had him. And she was. Oh yes, she was.

The telephone rang, and as Geoff made towards the door, it opened and Meg called, 'It's Mr Richard.'

'I'll take it,' said Geoff.

'No, no, please, Geoff, I'll see to it.' Lizzie pulled herself up from the couch, and she didn't look at him as she passed him, although she was aware that his eyes were hard on her.

Taking up the phone, she said, 'Hello, Richard.'

'Hello, Lizzie. How are you?'

'Oh, I'm all right, fine. And you?'

'Fine. I'm . . . I'm in Newcastle. Do you think I might call on you?'

'Oh, yes. Yes, please do. Where have you come from? The hospital?'

'No. No; home. But I had business at this end, and I thought I'd like to drop in on you.'

'I'll be delighted to see you.'

'Any snow there?'

'No; none at all. The roads are clear.'

'Then I guess I should be with you in just over an hour.'

'That'll be lovely, Richard. Bye-bye.'

When she turned from the phone, Geoff was waiting by the sitting-room door, and he didn't move as she passed him again to enter the room, although he mimicked her, 'Delighted to see you. That'll be lovely;' yet after she had again lowered herself on to the couch, he stood over her, saying more seriously, 'I hope you realise you could be giving him ideas.'

She looked at him. 'Yes; yes, Geoff, I do realise that I could give him ideas, one of them being that he has a friend; and no matter what you think or what you say, that's how it's going to be: he's going to remain my friend.'

'Oh. Well, if that's how you see it . . .'

'I do.'

'Well, we'll need to have a straight talk about it, won't we?'

She stared up at him. 'I don't get your meaning.'

'Oh, Lizzie, you get my meaning all right. I'll . . . I'll wait until the child's born, and then we'll have things straight, eh?'

He waited for an answer, but she gave him none; then he turned abruptly from her to march from the room.

She had sounded very determined when she said she would keep up her friendship with Richard. But she couldn't have it all ways, could she? Geoff was the kind of man who would not share with anyone. Odd that she was being made to choose; but then she had her future to think about, and that of the child: this was her home, and she had been happy here and, with time, could be again, perhaps. Anyway, she had to stop thinking of herself, for now she was all John or Geoff had: once the war was over, Meg would go back to Shields, for that's where her heart lay, as was proved by her constant trips to see how the town was faring.

Well, it was settled then. What she'd have to do now

was break it gently to Richard where her intentions lay, and he, being the fellow he was, would understand any cooling off on her part. But, knowing how he felt about her, would he? Poor Richard. Why was it she was already feeling his loss . . . ?

It was not the one hour but almost two when she opened the door to him, and on greeting him she was immediately aware of an improvement in his face. But she made no remark on it.

In the kitchen he shook Meg warmly by the hand. He had been carrying two flat parcels which he placed on the table and now, pushing one in Meg's direction, he said, 'A Happy Christmas, Meg. That's from my mother.'

'For me? A present from your mother? Now isn't that nice!' She looked towards Lizzie, and added, '*Isn't* that kind of her, and us not havin' met up?'

Turning now to Lizzie, Richard said, 'That too is from my mother, and don't ask where she got the wool from, because I would only have to say she has friends at court . . . and on the islands.'

Lizzie and Meg each now opened her parcel; and Meg was the first to hold up a Fair Isle jumper and her exclamations of delight filled the kitchen: 'Eeh! I've always wanted one of them. I have . . . I have really, Mr Richard. I really have. And to think your mother knitted this for me.'

'Well, no; she didn't knit that one; she had someone knit it for you; and I had to make a guess at your . . . bust line.'

Putting her hands under her ample breasts and pushing them upwards, Meg said, 'You're a clever lad to do that. And you'd have to guess both ways, 'cos when I have them in me camisole they go up by three inches.'

They were all laughing at this when Lizzie held up a soft angora cardigan, exclaiming, 'Oh! Richard, this is beautiful. It's so soft. Oh, what can I say? I must phone her later. Did . . . did she knit this? I do know she knits.'

'Yes, she knitted that and took pleasure in doing it. Anyway, how are things with you?'

As she laid the cardigan gently back on to the tissue paper, Meg answered for her, 'She'll tell you how they are in the sitting-room; the tea's been here waiting a half-hour or more. What held you up?'

And he turned to her, saying, 'Your bus didn't know I was coming and went off without me. I had to walk from Fuller's crossroads.'

'Oh, well, you'll be ready for a cup of tea, then. Go on and I'll fetch it in.'

As they left the kitchen Richard asked, 'Is Geoff in?'

She paused for a moment before saying, 'No; he . . . he went into Durham to do some shopping. He should be back at any time.'

In the sitting-room they sat looking at each other; then they both spoke together and laughed, and he said gently, 'You first.'

And she, looking at him tenderly, said, 'Your eye, they've done a marvellous job on it; and your lip too.'

With a slight shake of his head he said. 'I don't know about marvellous, but it is a small improvement.'

'Small! Wonderful job. Was it very painful?'

'No, not really; not this time, anyway. It's when

they graft that it stings a little. It's funny, you know, but it isn't the places they put it on, it's the places from where they take it off that hurt the most.'

She looked down now as she said, 'I've never asked you, Richard, but were you injured other than on the face?'

He paused before he said, 'Yes. Down to my waist on this side.' He pointed. 'Odd that it missed my neck.'

'Your mother's bound to be pleased.' She smiled widely at him and he nodded at her, saying, 'They're both over the moon. However,' and the pleasure sank out of his voice as he ended, 'they . . . they can't do much more, except build up the lower lip. The skin will always remain very much the same, I think; perhaps weather a bit.'

'Oh, it isn't all that noticeable.' They again looked at each other in silence for a moment, and then he said, 'You lie beautifully, Lizzie.'

'I'm not lying.' Her voice was high now.

'All right, you're not lying, you're just being kind, as always. Anyway, to get off me, how are you?'

'Fine. Fine, except' – she made a face at him – 'I get a little weary now and then. Anyway, the time's galloping on.'

He now said, 'I've got to ask you this, because Mother insisted, although I said it was a stupid question: wouldn't you like, she said, to come and have the baby at our place? And I said to her, "It isn't what Lizzie would like, it's what you would like, isn't it? It's a stupid question." '

'But a very nice one. Thank her so much. Under other circumstances it might have been a good idea,

234

but . . . well, Geoff seems to have got everything arranged. He's . . . he's worse than Meg.' Yes, this was the way to put it. It was a good opportunity, so she went on, 'He's got it all planned out. He's made the small bedroom into a nursery and brought his own cot down from the attic, where his mother had stored it all those years ago, and he's painted and papered. Papered, I say, with the help of Meg.'

'Is his arm still bad?'

'No, it's improved amazingly, although I doubt if it will ever be completely right.'

With his next words, he took away the need for her to do any more gentle breaking of the news, by bringing it directly into the open.

'Are you going to marry Geoff, Lizzie?'

The straightforwardness of the question left her blinking and her lips moving one over the other as if searching for moisture; but then, for a moment, she was saved from answering by Meg's forcing the door open with a jerk of her buttocks and her entering the room carrying a tea-tray, saying, 'Shall I cut into the Christmas cake, Lizzie?' and being answered by Richard, putting in quickly, 'Not for me, Meg. I . . . I haven't a sweet tooth. I see you have my favourite scones there, so those will do fine.'

As Meg placed the tray on the table she said, 'John's just come in. He's having a cup and a bite in the kitchen. He's half-frozen, but he's going out again. He's frightened them beggars will get the grouse. I say, let them have them. I said to him, "Didn't you say it was the open season right up to the first of December? Well, can't anyone take what they want up till then?" And he smiled, he actually did. That

235

was something. But they're wily beggars, those grouse-grabbers. Probably some of the lads from the camp' – she nodded towards Richard, saying, 'and who's to blame them, eh? And they won't stop then, that's certain, 'cos like me, half of them wouldn't know when one of them birds say, "Cinch! it's the second of December; you can't touch me."'

'Oh, Meg.' He flapped his hand towards her, then asked, 'How are the ducks going?'

'Oh, they've gone on strike, Mr Richard. It's them bloomin' farmers; they've got them penned in now, but they get out now and again and I often come across a stray egg.' She leaned towards him saying, 'Some night I'm going out on the rampage and pull up all the wire.'

'Do that, Meg. And look' – his voice sank to a whisper – 'give me a ring when you intend to go into action and I'll come and give you a hand.'

'I'll do that,' she whispered back to him. 'That's a promise. I'll do that.' Then she went out laughing.

Lizzie poured out the tea; then she offered him the plate of scones, and he had bitten into one and drunk from his cup before he said, 'You didn't get a chance to answer my question, Lizzie.'

She found herself thinking, oh, dear. Oh, dear, when it should have been quite simple to say, Yes, but her hesitation brought from him the reminder, 'The question was, are you going to marry Geoff?'

Now she answered, 'I . . . I don't know. I suppose so.'

He took another bite of the scone and after he had swallowed it he remarked, 'It would be sensible, I suppose.'

236

'Yes, yes,' she agreed, straightaway adding. 'And there's a child to think about; it . . . it would give it a name.'

'Oh, Lizzie. Lizzie.' He had been about to drink from his cup, but he put it down into the saucer with a clatter, saying, 'Don't marry just for that. It . . . it doesn't matter any more about . . . I mean about names. Please don't let that be the reason. If . . . if you like him, then yes. I know that Andrew must still be in your mind and there's plenty of time ahead, but Lizzie, please, I say this to you as a friend who . . . who holds you most dear, don't marry just to give the child a name. Look at me.'

She looked at him and he said, 'Promise me that?'

After a moment she muttered, 'Yes. Yes, all right, Richard, I promise you that.'

She was surprised at his next words because they were almost the same as Geoff's had been. 'We'll both have to understand, Lizzie, that if you marry, things will be different. Most men, especially those of Geoff's character, wouldn't approve of a friendship like ours. You understand that, don't you? Perhaps you've thought about it already. I'm . . . I'm sure he has.'

'Oh, Richard.' She looked away.

'Please, please don't be upset; I'm just talking common sense, for once in my life. We can have dreams and fantasies but when it comes to living, they have to be pushed into the background and cold facts have to be looked at straight in the face. Oh, Lizzie, Lizzie, you're not crying?' He leaned towards her. 'Oh, my goodness.' He left his seat to sit on the couch beside her and, taking her hand, he said, 'I . . . I wouldn't for the world upset you, you know that, but . . . but

I thought I'd better . . . well, I'd better bring things into the open. Please don't cry.'

What she did then was spontaneous: she leaned her head against him and when his arms went about her, she muttered, 'Oh, Richard, I'm sorry. I'm sorry.'

He put up his hand and gently stroked her hair, saying, 'Now what have you to be sorry about?'

It should happen that at that precise moment the door opened again and Geoff marched into the room. Lizzie lifted her head quickly from Richard's shoulder and now they both looked towards him, and as she went to withdraw from Richard's arms, he held her steadily for a moment; then slowly he relinquished his hold on her and, rising to his feet, he looked into the scowling face of the man standing in front of him and he said calmly, 'She was upset. She had been talking about Andrew. Naturally she . . . she cried.'

Her head down, Lizzie too rose from the couch, muttering, 'Ex . . . excuse me,' and went hastily from the room. And there the two men were left standing, staring at each other.

Geoff had to make an effort to speak, and when he did his voice was little above a growl as he said, 'I'm going to marry her.'

'Oh, yes, yes, so I understand.'

'You what?'

'Just that, just as you said, you're going to marry her.'

'How d'you come by that?'

'Just . . . just observation.'

The tone of this fellow annoyed Geoff. He felt like the corporal or the sergeant again, appearing before his superior officer; and they were always supposed to know better than anyone else. Always in the know. He watched him now put out his hand and lift up the cup and saucer and finish his tea, then calmly replace the cup on the table before saying, 'Well, I'd better be off. Your buses are very erratic, you know. Goodbye.' And with this he walked from the room, his back straight, his step firm, definitely still the soldier.

Geoff ground his teeth. He had never liked the fellow. Even before he had met him, he had never liked him. The sound of his name put his teeth on edge: Captain Richard Boneford. He had the idea that if it wasn't that the fella looked like a bloody gargoyle, Lizzie might have had ideas in that direction herself. Anyway, he'd get this thing settled. Let them get Christmas over and then he'd put it to her. As soon as the bairn was born or perhaps before the bairn was born, they'd get married, so it would be in his name. But why wait till after Christmas? Well, if he put the question now there'd likely be an up-and-downer, because he could see she was upset. No; he'd ask her on New Year's Eve. Yes; then they could start a new life the following day.

He was to wonder later about this business of a life being planned from the beginning, or why did he leave the asking until New Year's Day?

2

On the afternoon of Christmas Eve Geoff went into Durham. Even the jeweller's shop was crowded. There seemed to be plenty of money about, and people were spending it on things they would have thought twice about, more than twice about, a few years ago. But there wasn't much choice in the way of presents.

When the assistant said, 'But what size ring, sir?' He stuck out his little finger, saying, 'Her third one looks as big as that.'

'Fingers are deceptive, sir; but anyway, the lady can change it or have it altered to fit.'

So he came out of the jeweller's with a ring which cost him twenty-five pounds, and as there would not be a bus for another hour and a half, he decided to have a drink.

He did not often frequent the bars or canteens in the city, so he had no favourite place and went into the first bar he came to. It was just on six o'clock and, who knew, there might be some whisky on tap. He felt the need for something to warm him up.

After the dim grey streets the place seemed brilliantly lit, and he stood for a moment against the blacked-out door and gazed about him, his eyes blinking in the strong light. The far end of the long room was crowded with people standing near a counter, with others sitting at bench tables. In front of him was another counter. It too was thick with people; but going off to the side was a short corridor which, he could see, led to a bar, and he was about to step towards it when a woman emerged, accompanied by two soldiers, both corporals. And it was evident that she was remonstrating with them, for when one, laughing, caught hold of her arm, she wrenched it away. And as her voice came to him, saying, 'I meant no such thing. You've got the wrong idea,' it caused something inside him to give a slight start. And then she was staring straight at him; but not until she was within six feet or so of him did she recognise him, which caused her to pause in her steps before hurrying forward and exclaiming loudly, 'There you are! You're late.'

The two soldiers then stopped and were staring at the officer. One grinned as he stepped to the side, saying, 'Our mistake, miss. Our mistake;' but the second one, seeming to stand his ground, remained still until Geoff said, 'You need a further explanation, Corporal?'

The tone of the voice and the manner of the officer had an effect on the corporal and he muttered something, gave a desultory salute, then turned about and joined his companion at the counter.

Looking into her face Geoff asked quietly, but sarcastically, 'What is your intention now, Mrs Boneford?'

Her head was down as she muttered, 'I . . . I want to get out of here.' At this he opened the door and let her pass out into the darkness, and after a moment's hesitation he followed her.

When they stood side by side in the darkness, he

said, 'They appeared to think, at least one of them did, that he had been led up the garden.'

'He hadn't been led up the garden.' Her voice was stiff, her words seeming to come through her teeth. She had now turned and was walking up the street, he by her side, and she went on, 'They're a nuisance. Have been for some time.'

He asked now, 'You work there?' and there was a note of surprise in his voice.

'What's strange about that?'

'Huh! Only that I couldn't imagine you serving in a bar.'

'I'm not in the bar. Beyond it is another part of the canteen.'

They walked on in silence for some seconds until he said on a laugh, 'Anyway, hello. Apart from once, long time no see.'

She did not answer him immediately, and when she did her voice was flat: 'I've seen you a number of times in the town,' she said.

Another silence ensued before he asked, 'You going for the bus or have you a car or perhaps a horse waiting for you?'

'Neither the one nor the other; I now live in town.'

The stretching of his face indicated his surprise, and he said, 'Oh! Have you far to go?'

'No; I'm practically there.' Her dim torch, which she had been playing on the pavement ahead of them, was now lifted and he could see that they were passing a number of doors set in twos and divided by a few feet of wall and window from the next two.

She couldn't be meaning that she lives here, surely,

242

he thought, because these are little more than two-up, two-down houses.

When she stopped abruptly he had to retrace one step, and he switched on his torch and directed it towards her face as he said, 'You live here?'

'Yes, I live here,' and her tone implied, 'Now come back with something funny about that.'

He did not, but just stopped himself from saying, 'Alone?' and instead, gave her the usual seasonal greeting, 'A Merry Christmas, then.'

'And to you,' she answered. Then, opening her handbag, she fumbled in it for a moment before taking out a key, and as she inserted it in the lock, he directed his torch-light towards it, and she cast a glance at him over her shoulder, saying, 'Would . . . would you care to come in?'

Her voice sounded practical; there was no subtle invitation in it, but there was a long pause before he replied, 'Well, yes, thanks. I have more than an hour before the bus goes. Yes; thank you.'

It was all very polite.

Once inside the door he was conscious of standing close to her in the blackness, and she said to him, 'Don't move until I switch on, or you'll fall over the bike.'

The shaded electric light showed up a narrow passageway almost blocked by a bicycle leaning against the wall, and as he followed her, pushing past it, she switched on another light and said, 'Come in.' And he went into what was evidently the sitting-room-cum-kitchen, and stood for a moment dumbfounded as he looked about him, while she said, 'Sit down. I'll put a match to the fire.'

He walked past a round table off which, it was evident, she ate her meals, for a white lace cloth lay on it, together with a small cruet set.

As the gas fire plopped into flame, she straightened up, pulled off her hat and coat and threw them on to a chair; then looking at him, she said, 'Take your coat off for a minute. You'll feel the benefit when you go outside.'

Slowly and slightly awkwardly because of his left arm, he shrugged off his greatcoat, then handed it to her, together with his hat.

They were standing now looking at each other, each aware of the awkwardness of the situation, and when she said, 'Would you like a drink?' her voice sounded high, as it was wont to do when she was about to laugh; but at the moment it seemed the only recognisable thing about her, for now in the light of the room, divested of her brimmed hat and turned-up collar, he saw a much older version of the girl he had remembered for so long after he had left the country, even a different version of the woman who had called to tell them about her brother. She was so much thinner. It prompted him to ponder how old she would be now, and he decided she must be around twenty-six. And he told himself that he had seen women of thirty-six who looked younger.

'Would you like a drink?' she asked him again.

'It all depends on what you have to offer,' he said.

She walked towards a wooden cupboard at the side of the fireplace. And when she opened it, he saw there were three bottles on the top shelf, two of beer and one of wine.

Her head turned towards him, she said, 'I can offer

you beer or sherry—' she made a motion with her head to the far end of the room where there was another door, 'or tea.'

He knew how difficult it was to get bottled beer unless you stood in line for it; as for sherry, it had never been his drink; and so he said, with a touch of his old self, 'Since I joined the Salvation Army I've drunk nothing but tea.'

She did not smile, only slanted a quick glance at him, then went down the room and into the kitchen.

He stood looking about him. There was a chintz-covered couch with the springs at one end evidently the worse for wear; and the two armchairs were odd. There were three single chairs and a china cabinet, which he noticed was supported by a block of wood where apparently the bottom of one leg had been snapped off. He couldn't believe that this was where she lived. The place, he had to grant, was clean and tidy, but he imagined that even the servants up at the house would, at one time, have turned up their noses at the furniture. And then there was the house itself, or flat, as such was called nowadays. The working man's home. What must she feel like living here, after having been brought up with two silver spoons in her mouth?

She called from the kitchen, 'Do you take sugar?' and he replied, 'No; thank you.' And when, a few minutes later, she entered the room carrying a small tray on which were two cups and saucers, she said, 'You're still standing? There's no extra charge for sitting.'

He waited until she had placed the tray on the table and seated herself on one of the single chairs; then having followed suit, he took the cup and saucer that she was handing to him and said quietly, 'Thanks.'

When silence again fell on them and they both sipped at the tea, he shook his head, nipped at his lower lip; then with a wry smile he looked across at her, saying, 'The things that happen. It's strange, isn't it?' He stared at her. And she answered his look for a moment before, taking up a spoon from the saucer, she began stirring her tea slowly as she said, 'I find nothing strange any more. I don't think anyone does really, not in this war. Who, for instance, would have imagined that Janis Bradford-Brown or Mrs Boneford couldn't handle two thick-headed corporals. But' – and she smiled now – 'I've got to admit that I was beginning to lose my nerve. Well, you see, it was the third time this week. I think I could have managed one but not two together.' The smile suddenly slid from her face as if it had never been there, and he saw the muscles tighten as she went on, 'Everybody's so broad-minded now, except seemingly when one has been divorced. Oh,' – she flapped her hand in the air – 'I'm not squealing; at least, not against Richard; I mean, him not playing the gentleman and taking the blame; but it's just annoying the ideas some fellows get into their heads about a divorced woman. You can remain married and have two or three strings to your bow, and if you're diplomatic, doors will still swing open for you, but if you should be careless and be found out, then God help you.'

He said nothing, just continued to stare at her, as he thought, that's what has aged her, the bitterness in her; it's buried deep.

'Anyway, that's enough of me, what about you? How are you? You got it in the leg and arm, didn't you?'

'Oh, as you see, I'm fine, both extremities doing very well, thank you very much. I was always lucky.'

'Yes, yes.' Her voice was quiet now. 'I think you were. You . . . you were determined to rise, weren't you? My goodness, I was mistaken, you know, all that time ago. I could never see you as an officer.'

There was a little grimness in his own tone now as he answered, 'That was your lack of perception.' As he used the word another came into his mind: 'uncultured'.

'I hear . . . you're going to be married.'

'What!' His eyes narrowed; his jaw was thrust out. 'Where did you hear that?'

'Oh, it's got around; perhaps from your evacuee. I . . . I don't know. I just sort of heard it. I think it was from Florrie Rice, who is still in the kitchen up at the house.'

'Well, I'm afraid you heard wrong; what I mean is—' He stopped.

'What do you mean? You're either going to be married or you're not. You should know.'

'I've never said any such thing, nor has Lizzie.'

'But . . . but you *are* going to marry her?' The words were slow and he didn't answer for a full minute when he said, 'That was the idea. She's got a child coming, you know.'

'Oh, yes, I know.'

'And, you know, you'll be its aunt and your parents its grandparents. What do they think about that?'

'Well,' she nodded slowly, then again stirred the remaining tea in her cup before she went on, 'I wouldn't like to tell you.'

'Well, I can't say that it would have mattered very

247

much to them what Andrew did; after all, they threw him out, didn't they?'

'Yes, in a way; but only in a way. They thought it would bring him to his senses, but when he was killed it . . . well, it broke them up. There was me before that, but Andrew's death put the finishing touch to them. It was the only thing really that got me to go back at weekends.'

'You had cut adrift too?'

'Oh, yes. Andrew's death brought sympathy for them from people even knowing about the breach: but my doings . . . oh dear me!' She smiled and her face took on a sadness now as she said, 'I've no need to tell you, Geoff, that I'm not made to be a martyr; had anything else happened to Richard, I . . . I could have stood it. If he had lost both legs or both arms, or been flat on his back for life, I . . . I could have stood it, yes.' She moved her head in small nods now. 'But as it turned out, his face' – she drew in a long breath – 'I tried, I honestly tried, but I couldn't bring myself even to look at him. It was dreadful for him, for I realised he was the same under the skin, but . . . well, I suppose I'm not the probing type, either. Anyway, I was given my marching orders; but seemingly now they are glad to have me back in the fold; in fact, they wanted me to return home for good. But no, oh no! once you've been out of the corral, so to speak, the sight of the railings is enough for you. Still, I visit at weekends.'

She now glanced at her wrist-watch, saying, 'Which reminds me, Father's picking me up at eight o'clock. I'm spending the holiday there, but it certainly won't be a merry Christmas, I know that. I'd rather be in the canteen, although at times I can't stand it there, either.'

'I thought you would have been in the Forces?'

'I did too. But apparently there is something wrong with my eyes.' She put her hand up and pressed her fingers against her temples. 'I should be wearing glasses all the time, but I hate them, except for reading . . . Would you like another cup of tea?'

'Yes; yes, I would.' He was about to hand his cup to her when the doorbell ringing brought them both to a stillness, and again glancing at her watch, she muttered apprehensively, 'That . . . that could be Father.'

He rose to his feet, saying, 'But it's not half-past seven yet. Couldn't it be a friend?'

'No. I . . . I have few friends, and those I have I wouldn't entertain here.'

'Oh.' And he raised his eyebrows, which brought from her the muttered gabble: 'You . . . you know what I mean;' then, 'Look, Geoff,' and it was the first time she had used his name, 'would you mind going out the back way?'

'Why?'

'Oh!' She made an impatient movement; 'you shouldn't need to ask, but if you want an explanation, there would be hell to pay if he found you here: your name . . . well, that of . . . your house, everything infuriates him. He would have had your father out long ago if it wasn't that he needs him so much. There's hardly anyone left. Please! Please!'

The bell continued to ring persistently now and she held out her hand to him and drew him into the kitchen, saying, 'The yard door leads into the lane.'

'Well, presumably you'll let me get my things on.'

She flew from him and picked up his coat and hat and pushed them at him, the while pressing him towards the back door, saying, 'Another time, Geoff. Another time. Please.'

He was standing out in the dark pulling on his coat when the voices came to him, hers high saying, 'I was in the lavatory; I couldn't get here any quicker.'

He directed his torch towards his feet and found his way down the backyard to the door. It was bolted and, as if he were on an exercise, he withdrew it quietly back, before passing through into the lane.

It wasn't until he was on the front street and walking towards the centre of the town that he found the chuckling sound he was making was turning into hysterical laughter. There had been fellows in hospital who had begun like that in the middle of the night: just quietly chuckling; then it had risen into a yell. Mostly those without legs; they always yelled they were going to walk out.

Well, he'd better stop now that he really was out and away, for there had been that pull on him that could easily have about-turned him and taken him back inside. No! he *wasn't* going to return to the time when every minute of his life had been filled with her. Oh no! that wouldn't happen again, not to him. Anyway, she was far removed from that girl; she was now a woman; and she certainly hadn't improved in looks; and what was more, she had been around. The girl he remembered had been his and his alone. She was a virgin when he had first taken her; as he was too. They had both been young and gropingly innocent.

On the bridge he stopped and looked down to the steely water that was reflecting a star here and there, and he asked himself why had nothing come of it, for they hadn't been wise. Wise? Good lord, no! They had known nothing about preventatives; and so did it mean that neither of them was capable of producing a child?

The thought brought him to Lizzie, and his hand went to his pocket and to the slight bulge of the jeweller's box. What was he going to do about that now, eh? What? The question rang loudly in his head. Well, nothing had altered, had it?

That was a damn silly thing to say . . . nothing had altered, had it? There she was looking years older; and as if she'd been around. He'd say . . . and some. Yet, she still gave off that same body magnetism, as she had done as a girl and a young woman.

He walked on, pushing his way through the throng of people and the zig-zagging of flashing torches on the pavements. It wasn't until some time later when he was on the bus that he asked himself again what he was going to do about it. And the answer he gave himself was that he'd wait and see. Anyway, he hadn't committed himself in any way to Lizzie, had he?

Hadn't he? If he hadn't said it in words he'd said it in actions. Well, not really: he'd acted as a brother might, and in her extremity she needed someone to be kind to her, just like a brother. He wasn't committed. Anyway, everything lay in the future. He'd mark time and see which way the wind blew. Yes, that's what he would do, mark time. Because you couldn't trust your feelings at a time like this, not really.

. . . In the name of God! what had come over him? Was he mad even to think that he could wipe

out the last six years and pick up where they had
left off? And no matter what he told himself, there
was still Lizzie; and he liked her, he more than liked
her. And except for her one lapse, she was clean.
Yes, she was clean, whereas . . .

3

It was the beginning of January. Christmas and New Year had been quiet times, and only Meg seemed to notice any particular change in Geoff. She remarked on it to Lizzie, saying, 'You two had a tiff or something?'

'Tiff? Geoff and I? No. No. What makes you think that?'

'Just that he's quiet like, all of a sudden. Well, not quiet, but not so ready with his quips; no life-and-soul of the party, so to speak; stopped jokin'.'

'Now, Meg, would you expect him to be joking? Look how Dad has been over the holidays.'

'Well, just because John's been down, I thought Geoff would have made an effort, like he's always done up till now. Anyway, lass, how's it goin'?'

'Well, the way I'm feeling now, it could be any minute. No, no,' – she smiled and patted Meg's arm – 'it's just that I'm so heavy I feel ready to explode.'

'How many pills have you got left?' Meg went to the side table and opened a small box. 'Down to four,' she said. 'Oh, well, Geoff will call in at the chemist with the prescription this afternoon. It's made out for four lots and this is only the third.'

'I hope I don't need the four.'

'So do I.'

'Anyway, whenever you decide to let him out, or her, pick a nice day, will you? 'cos what with the

253

wind and these sleet squalls, things are gettin' me down. Eeh! I was drenched in a second afore I got back this mornin'.'

'Serve you right for going out when the weather's only fit for ducks,' Lizzie said, laughing.

'Well, that sayin' must be true, nice weather for ducks, 'cos there they were, nine of them, splashing about as if they'd never seen water afore. And I told you I picked up six eggs.'

'By! If Mrs Hobson only knew.'

'If those lips could only speak, and those eyes could only see,' – Meg went out laughing as she sang the old ballad – 'hoppin' mad she'd be.'

Lizzie settled back in the big chair at the side of the fireplace and began to think over what Meg had said about the change in Geoff. She herself hadn't been truthful in her answer: there *was* a change in him, but she couldn't lay her finger exactly on the difference, except that he was a little quieter, not so merry and bright, but he *was* still kind and concerned . . . or, was he still as kind and concerned?

Until now, his usual greeting in the morning had generally been jocular, along the lines of: 'Well, how goes the partnership?' or 'What has your lodger got to say?' But these last few mornings, in fact, for this past week, his enquiries had been somewhat subdued: 'How are you feeling, Lizzie? Did you sleep last night?' the usual questions that a kindly brother might ask a sister in the circumstances, but they lacked the warmth and concern of a . . . This line of thinking gave her the reason: Richard. Richard had phoned twice last week. That was it. Yes, perhaps, because after she had taken the calls, Geoff had made no remark about them, even though he had been passing through the hall on both occasions she had been on the phone.

Richard's reason for phoning, he said, had been because his mother was anxious to know how things were faring with her. She always felt warm, knowing the concern that he and his family felt for her. There *were* good people in the world. She had been so fortunate, in a way. First, there had been Geoff bringing her to his people, then Bertha and John had been so kind to her over the years. But since Bertha's going, John's attitude towards herself had definitely changed, and this saddened her. Then there had been Meg. Oh, Meg was like a star in a dull sky. She could say she was surrounded by kindness, so why didn't she feel at peace and joyful at the coming event? But need she ask that question? There was no Andrew to share the joy with her, and her child would never see its father.

Geoff came into the room, to stop some distance away from her and while buttoning up his coat he said, 'Is there anything more you want besides the pills?'

'Oh yes, a couple of pounds of bacon, fat; you know I like fat.'

He smiled. 'I'll tell them,' he said, then added, 'I've got your sweet coupons. What d'you fancy with those?'

'I don't suppose there's any chocolate. I would love a bit of chocolate.'

'I'll hunt around.'

'You're going to get wet.' She looked towards the window.

'Oh, it's just squalls; but I've missed the bus, so I'll have to walk to the corner. Anyway, I want a breath of fresh air, wet or snow-filled. You all right?'

255

'Yes; yes, I'm fine.'

'Good. Be seeing you then.'

'Be seeing you.'

There *was* something different. She looked towards the closed door. Could it be his father objecting to their association? Could be. But whatever it was it seemed to be worrying him. If he kept up this attitude, she would just have to put it to him; she believed in bringing things into the open.

As Geoff walked up the hill he was finding it hard going, as the wind was full against him and his hip was paining him a little. At the top, he leaned against the low parapet of the bridge and took a breather, telling himself if the bus got there on time he'd likely be able to see her coming off the afternoon turn.

Since the night he had scurried out of her back door they had met four times, but always it had been across the counter, and so over numerous cups of tea they had talked, ordinary talk, everyday talk. They even discussed the course of the war: things were looking up; there was this second front looming ahead. Then there was this division between the US High Command and Bomber Harris over the part to be played by RAF bombers. The RAF were still bombing Berlin and had been from November last year but, as some said, to little effect other than to the morale of the civilian population, for the Germans seemed to have an amazing amount of ammunition with which to hit back.

Sometimes other men and women at the counter would join in the conversation, each expressing his own armchair idea of the strategy of the war, even if it was expressed only as: who do the Americans think they are anyway? Bet when this is all over they'll spill it around that they did it alone. Big boys. Big heads.

'Well, we would have come badly off without the big boys, big heads,' would say another faction.

And so it had proceeded on each of the four occasions he had gone casually into the canteen for a cup of tea. But he knew and she knew; oh yes, she knew, it couldn't go on like this much longer. His aim in seeing her today was to accompany her to her house and have a talk.

And what then? . . . What about Lizzie? Oh God! Lizzie. Why had he been pushing so hard in that direction? He had never really cared for Lizzie; well, not in that way. There had been a need in him and she had been there to fill it, and he had played the daddy, and now there would be some explaining to do. But first he must talk with Janis. Strange, but even saying the name in his mind sent a quiver through him.

He was descending the hill when he was hit by a sudden squall of rain. One minute there was nothing, then it was as if his face was being bombarded with ice particles. He turned his head to the side and limped on; and it was then that he saw a woman pushing a bicycle along the river bank towards the shelter of the wood where it covered the steep bank and formed an archway that led to the barn . . .

He had put his good leg over the hedge and, with the weak grip of his left hand was holding on to the branches, while with his right hand he pulled his left leg upwards and over. And all the time he was calling, 'Wait a minute! Wait a minute!' But the figure below, head down, went on unheeding towards the shelter of the wood.

He slithered sideways down the bank, calling her name now, and he was still calling it as he, too, entered the shelter of the wood. Here he stopped in the comparative quietness, for as yet the rain was only seeping through the entwined branches in moderate force.

'Janis! Janis!' He could see through the dimness the blur of the figure standing waiting and he hurried towards it, and when he came up to her, he was gasping as he said, 'What on earth are you doing out here on a bike?'

She put up her hand and wiped the rain from her face before she answered, 'I'm on a bike because I don't happen to own a horse any more.'

'But why? I mean at this time . . . ?'

'When I tell you I'm looking for your father, it's likely that you won't believe me.'

'My father? Isn't he in the yard?'

'No; else I wouldn't be here. Brewster caught his fetlock on some barbed wire and Father's gone berserk. I phoned the vet but he was away on a job, and it's Rice's half day, and your father wasn't to be found.'

'He left the house over an hour ago, so likely he's at yon end of the estate. There's been some birds missing, hasn't there?'

'Oh' – she jerked her head upwards – 'don't talk about missing birds. Father's got that man Honeysett on the brain.'

'From what my dad says, I wouldn't think it was old Ted. This is a professional job. Ted spreads his over; he's not too greedy, like. But they must have had a big bag yesterday, because they dropped two dead ones near the west gate.'

They were walking on, now, close together one minute, separated by tree roots crossing the path the next. And then they were out in the open again; and there before them stood the run-down barn that had been their rendezvous for so many years.

He turned and looked at her and in a low voice he said, 'You're very wet. Why . . . why didn't you wear a mac?'

Her voice too was low as she answered, 'There wasn't time.'

It was he who said, 'Well, we might as well take shelter out of this until it eases.'

Slowly now they walked towards the building. The door was half open and was hanging on one hinge, and the grass and weeds from outside had encroached around the bottom of it. Putting his right shoulder to it he thrust it wide, allowing her to pass him while pushing the bike.

The atmosphere inside seemed to be colder than that without, and there was a dank smell of rotten vegetation. At one end the roof had fallen in and ivy was growing around the relics of the traps still hanging on the stone wall.

When she shivered he peered at her through the dimness, then asked, 'You cold?'

'No, no. It's . . . it's just that—' She looked around her. 'It hasn't stood the weathering very well, has it?'

'No; no, it hasn't.'

'It's like me.' She was staring at him now, and he at her and he asked, 'What do you mean by that?'

'Just what I say. It . . . it must only be a few years, six to be exact, since I felt young, with my body full of something that spelled excitement and adventure. I'd . . . I'd tasted the latter with you. Then came Richard, and then came war, and there followed—' She opened her mouth wide now as if taking in a great draught of air, and he watched as she put her arms around herself as a child might to hug itself with glee; however, her action was more like one of despair.

He fought back the desire to put his arms out towards her and he said, 'Well, you had everything going for you. What went wrong, besides your husband's . . . misfortune?'

She turned to him and there was a cynical smile on her face now as she said, 'Knowing me as you once did, don't you think that's a silly question to ask? You guessed from the beginning that I was the kind who not only baked her cake, then ate it, but wanted to have it whole and untouched besides. In short, I wanted it all ways. Being my mother's daughter, I didn't want the stigma that went with divorce: I still wanted to hide under the respectable cover of Mrs Richard Boneford and daughter, not so much of Ernest Bradford-Brown, but of Mrs Alicia Silton-Weir-Conway, whose uncle is an admiral and who has a bishop and several generals she can call upon, in fact, whom she did call upon, to attend my wedding to Richard. And of course I had to go and make matters worse in picking for a partner in crime or, in this case, sin, Richard's best friend. In fact, he had been his best man. It wasn't taken into account that he and his own wife hadn't lived together for the previous four years, except publicly at the hunt, and the ball, and the weddings. As it was, if I'd needed any lessons in whoring, she would have been the one to . . .'

'Shut up!' He brought out the words through his teeth. 'What are you trying to do? Appeal to my pity and understanding? What are you taking me for? If you want to empty yourself, there's a Roman Catholic church in the town; they hear confessions there.'

He watched her face, the eyes blinking, the lips quivering, the thin body seeming to swell underneath her coat. Then, flinging around from him, she went to grab the handlebars of her bicycle, but before she reached them, his arms went about her, the left one only able to rest on her waist, but the right one holding her in a vice-like grip tight against him. When his mouth fell on hers it was with a savagery that almost overbalanced her. For a brief moment she responded to him; then, her body slumping, she pulled her mouth from his and dropped her head on to his shoulder.

A broad black post attached to the wall supported the remaining roof beams, and as if he needed support himself, he pulled her the couple of steps towards it, and then they were both leaning against it. To the side of them, the rain dropped through a gap in the roof. Outside, the wind swished the trees and the tall grass into a background murmur.

'It had to come, hadn't it?' His voice was thick.

'You . . . You can't still think . . . think the same?'

'No, no, I don't. I think differently, but . . . but along the same lines.'

'Oh, Geoff, Geoff. You're . . . you're a fool, you know; I . . . I can't really change.'

'What d'you mean by that? Do you still want to play around?'

She went to pull herself from his hold, but he held her; and now there was an indignant note in her voice as she said, 'I'm . . . I'm not playing around. I mean . . .'

'You mean there's nobody on your horizon at the moment, but there could be in the future. Is that what you're trying to say?'

'No, no. But there's one thing I do know: *you* haven't changed; you're still—' she again made a movement to release herself, then said, 'aggravating.'

'Give it the right term; speak the truth.'

'Look, Geoff. I could have as many men as days in the year, and as many in one night as the days in the week, taking in the corporals. But there's been no-one. No-one since the . . . well, the divorce.' Her voice changed, taking on the old haughty note as she added, 'Perhaps it's because I'm particular: if I can't pick from my class I won't go beneath it.'

His thrusting her from him almost made her fall on to her back; then his voice now loud, he said, 'This could be exactly where we left off all those years ago. Do you remember? In this very place you said I was uncouth, and now you're telling me that you could have it off with people you consider worthy of your favours; but that, of course, they've got to be the officer type, the real type, not someone like me, dragged up from the ranks. By God! . . .'

'*Now you stop it!* It is my turn to say stop it, because you're as big a snob in your way as I've been in mine. Think of the other night with those two corporals, insistent, and persistent. All right, in the ordinary way they might have been quite decent fellows, but it seems they believe that war gives them a licence, especially if it's put around that you are a divorcée and that you've walked out on a poor fellow who's disfigured. Even the scum of the town consider you're fair game. As for the women, or at least some of them, they put you through it as much as the men, but in a different way. So yes, I meant what I said. I'm not going to take it back. I'm not anybody's piece for the night, yours or anybody else's.'

Again she made to move towards the bike and once more he held her, and now he was smiling as he said, 'We're a pair, aren't we? We always were, right from the very beginning, going at each other's throats one minute and being swallowed alive by each other the next.' As he felt her again shivering in his hands he said, 'That's true, isn't it? Listen, I want to tell you something. It's funny that we should be here now in this place, because I was on my way to meet you and walk home with you, and tell you what was in my mind. It was going to be, oh so different from this; polite, quiet. I meant to explain to you, that yes, I had been thinking about marrying Lizzie, but that now I know I couldn't. I knew it from the minute I met you on Christmas Eve. We . . . we could make a go of it, you and I. We're alike, you see, under the skin.'

'Oh, Geoff. No, no; don't take it that far, please. But as we're speaking the truth, I'll tell you that I too jumped back seven years . . . no, eight years. I felt the draw of you too, but . . . but when that's said, nothing . . . nothing has really changed. Let's be practical. You have no job, and you're living on your pension. Yes, yes, you have a home, but it's

263

also your father's home, and . . . and the girl's.' It was as if she couldn't bring herself to speak Lizzie's name, but she went on, 'And then there is a child coming. You have responsibilities. For my part, well, I'm depending mostly still on Father's gratuity, which allows me to rent that mansion that I live in, and to exist. Added to that, I have the little I earn. So there we are. And, Geoff, let's leave it at that for the time being; only know this, I'm . . . I'm glad you've come back into my life . . .'

He was about to put his lips to hers again when she stiffened as the sound of a motor-horn came to them. The road was only about thirty feet away, but from it the barn was well concealed by scrub.

She stood, her head back as she listened, and when there were four long blasts on the horn, she pulled herself from his arms, saying, 'That's Father. It's a signal he uses if I'm out in the grounds and he wants me . . . at least it used to be. But that's him all right; he must be on his way into town. I'll have to go.' As she grabbed the handlebars of the bike, he caught her arm and said, 'Are you as afraid of him as all that?'

She turned her face which was close to his and said softly, 'No; in fact, I'm not really afraid of him in the ordinary way, but I'd be afraid of him finding me here with you. Apart from the feeling that . . . that he would want to pay somebody out for the loss of Andrew, you'd be the next best thing. I'll get in touch.'

As she made for the opening, he pulled at her arm, saying, 'When?'

'I'm on duty tomorrow until two o'clock.' She now put her hand towards him in appeal as she said, 'Don't come out in case he should look over the top, please!'

'God!'

'Please, Geoff.'

'All right, go on.'

He watched her push the bike along to the left towards the open road that he himself would have taken if he had been returning home.

The rain was still falling steadily, and as he watched her disappear into the curtain of it, he heard a voice calling, 'I've got him. What's taken you so long?'

Her voice came as from the end of a tunnel, calling back, 'I've been right round. How's Brewster?'

'How do you think he is? I've got to get into Newcastle, then get back and give Fulton a hand until the vet comes. You stay with your mother until I get back tonight.'

Her voice came now as a faint echo, saying, 'I've got to go and . . .'

He heard the end of her father's words calling, 'You stay!' Then there came the sound of the car starting up.

Except for the splattering of the rain there was silence, and after stepping back into the barn, he lay against the beam and closed his eyes tightly, while his teeth clamped down on his lip. Why the hell had he taken any notice of her? Why hadn't he walked out and confronted that stinking, big-headed nowt, and asked him who the hell he thought he was?

Was this a new beginning? Was this how it was going to be? seeing her on the side? Scared stiff her old man would catch a glimpse of them? He didn't think he could stand that. But what if it were that or not seeing her at all? Because, no matter what she said, it was very obvious she was afraid of her father in all ways.

He pulled himself upright; then seeing there was some moss on his hand where it had touched the stanchion, he quickly took off his coat and grimaced in annoyance as he saw the green stain had also smeared his right sleeve and part of the back. Going outside now, he held the coat slantwise to let the rain soak into it. Then, taking his handkerchief, he rubbed at the smear; but it had little effect, for the mark seemed to show up even clearer on the fawn trench coat. Dragging it on now, he turned about and walked along the path Janis had taken a few minutes earlier, telling himself that he would have to go back home and change into his greatcoat, for it went against the grain of the spit-and-polish soldier in him to appear other than smartly turned out in public. He would tell them back home that he had slipped, which could easily have happened on a day like this.

4

Lizzie's child was born, during a snowstorm, at half-past two in the afternoon and after forty-eight hours of labour. Her tired body released a baby girl with a crumpled face and a comb of black hair, and weighing seven and a half pounds. The doctor handed the child to the midwife and the midwife handed it to Meg. And Meg, her face and body running with sweat, as if she herself had given birth to the child, cleaned it, wrapped it in a soft white blanket and took it to the bed for Lizzie to see, saying, 'There you are, lass. Look at her. You'll never see anything more lovely than that.'

Lizzie looked at her daughter. She wanted to put out her arms to hold her; she wanted to smile; she wanted to speak; but she was too tired.

The doctor said, 'There, there. Let her be.' Then bending over her, he pushed her wet hair aside from her brow, saying, 'That was a tough ride. You were determined to hang on to her, weren't you? Now you'll soon be all cleaned up; then you can just sleep and sleep.'

His voice was soothing. Her body was at rest, but her mind was still working. As though from a distant chamber a voice was calling, 'You have a daughter, Andrew. Andrew, you have a daughter.'

When the doctor moved from the bed, Meg said, 'What about its feed?' and he replied, 'She won't be able to feed it. You've got a bottle ready, I suppose? Nurse will tell you how to go on.'

'I don't need any instructions with regard to bottles or bairns.'

At this, the doctor and the midwife exchanged a small knowing smile; then he went out of the room and down the stairs, where he was met by Geoff, and without preamble he said, 'It's a girl.'

'A girl?'

'Yes, that's what I said, a girl. She's a fine girl; it's a pity there's no father to welcome it. Still, she's in good hands here. Your poor mother would have been such a support for her; but as long as that old dear up there is about, she'll act as a good substitute . . . And how are you these days?' The doctor was putting on his coat, and Geoff replied, 'Oh, pretty well.'

'Your leg seems to be more mobile than your arm.'

'Yes; yes, that's so.'

'I suppose you are more fortunate than some others; and now you've got an interest, a family to see to, even if it's second-hand. Well, I must be off; I hope I make it. The road's clear up to Fuller's crossroads corner, but after that, it's hard going.'

On his way towards the door he paused and said, 'By the way, I'm a bit worried about your father: he wants pulling out of himself. Time is not doing its job in that quarter. Perhaps the child will have some influence; a new life often has. Well, if possible I'll be in tomorrow . . .'

A few minutes later Geoff tapped on the bedroom door and he was greeted by a smiling Meg, saying, 'Come away in.'

He walked up to the side of the bed. The nurse was straightening the sheets over Lizzie's shoulders, and she explained, 'She's very tired.'

At this Lizzie slowly opened her eyes, gave a weak smile, then closed them again, and without saying a word he turned from the bed and to Meg who was holding the child out to him, saying, 'Look at that. Isn't she a bonny bundle? Go on, take her.'

He took the child from her and gazed down at it. Its eyes were half open, its lips were puckered, but the sight and feel of it brought to him no emotion whatsoever, other than to add to the worry already in his mind. And as he handed the child back to Meg she demanded, 'Well?'

'She's bonny.'

She narrowed her eyes at him as she hugged the bundle to her and repeated, 'She's bonny? Aye; I should say she is,' and she turned from him and laid the baby in the cot to the side of the fireplace. Then saying, 'I'll have to get that bottle,' she made to go from the room, and he followed her. But on the landing she stopped and confronted him: 'What's wrong with you these days? Sickening for something?' she said.

'What d'you mean?'

'Just what I say. Something on your mind?' It was a question.

'What should be on me mind?'

'You tell me; I'm askin'.' And with this she marched from him, leaving him to stare after her for a moment before making for his own room, muttering, 'Inquisitive old biddy!' He had once liked Meg . . . he had once liked many people; at least he had put up with them. Now, there was only one person on his horizon and she was obliterating the rest. What he was going to do about the whole situation he didn't know . . .

It was the following morning before he went into Lizzie's bedroom again. She was wide awake and the child was lying by her side. She smiled at him, but it was still a weary smile, and he asked, 'How are you feeling?'

Her smile widened as she said, 'Just as though I'd fought one of the big battles all by myself.'

'Well, I suppose it is a sort of battle.'

'You're telling me.' She turned and pulled the shawl away from the child's head, saying, 'Isn't she bonny?'

'Yes, yes,' – he nodded – 'she's bonny all right.'

She looked up at him now, her face unsmiling, and her eyes narrow. 'What's wrong, Geoff?' she said.

'Wrong?' His voice was high in his head. 'What makes you think there's anything wrong?'

She turned and looked at the child again before she muttered, 'Things are not the same. It's . . . it's as if you had something on your mind.'

He turned from the bed now, saying, 'Well, perhaps I have one or two things. We'll talk about them later on.'

'There really is something, then?' She was staring at his averted face, and he said, 'As I said, there's one or two things I want to talk about. Just wait till you get stronger and on your feet.'

As he spoke, the door opened and his father came into the room; but he paused before approaching the bed, and when she said softly, 'Hello, Dad,' he answered briefly, 'Hello.' Then he was standing looking down at the child.

When he made no comment, she looked up at him and said, 'I've . . . I've been thinking of Mam all morning and . . . and missing her. She would have loved her, wouldn't she?'

'No, she would not.'

The tone of his voice startled even Geoff, and he touched his father's arm, remonstrating, 'Dad! Dad!'

'I'm speaking me mind, lad, I'm speaking me mind. Your mother was upset about the whole business.' He now looked down on to Lizzie's startled face as he went on, 'She never got over it, you doing what you did. You were a great disappointment to her, lass. And to me an' all. It didn't help any, the state she was in; no, it did not. After all she had done for you; brought you up as if you were her own. She educated you, you know she did, you know she did.'

'Dad! Dad! That's enough! Come on. Come on.' Geoff got hold of his father's arm, and John, looking at him again said, 'Well, it had to be said. It's been on my mind for a long time, and it had to be said, because she thought the world of her.' He turned his glance down now on Lizzie's crumpled face, saying, 'It's no use cryin'; tears come too late. You weren't a babe in arms; you knew what you were doing. You could have waited. You could have waited. But there, what's bred in the bone comes out in the flesh.'

'Now, Dad!' Geoff was pulling him from the room, remonstrating all the while, 'That's enough! You're going too far.'

The door was still open when Meg came in and, going to the bed, she said, 'Now lass, lass, don't upset yourself like that. What's all this about? Has he been at you, the old 'un? If you ask me, he's goin' round

271

the bend, and has been since Bertha went. Blamed you, has he, for the bairn? My God!' And as she sat down on the edge of the bed she said, 'Now, now! Stop it,' and put her arms around Lizzie and held her tightly.

'Contrary old swine,' Meg went on, 'He may not go to any church, but he's a holy Joe under the skin. There now. There now. Give over. You've got the child to think about. Come on; dry your eyes.' She lifted up the end of her apron and rubbed it round Lizzie's face, saying, 'This house is not the same as it used to be, and it isn't only because of Bertha's goin'. There's something in the wind and I can't put me finger on it. Anyway, I don't suppose I'll be here much longer to . . .'

'What?' – Lizzie's voice had a break in it – 'What do you mean, not much longer?'

'Now, now; don't agitate yourself any further. Well, you know, lass, I'm a refugee . . . all right, an evacuee, but I've got a home back there to go to. I didn't tell you last week because you were just on your time; but you know when I went in, I went to see her at the office, the one who allocates houses; she's a very nice lass, not like most of them. Anyway, as she said, there's a choice now, but if you wait till this business is over, you won't be able to get a place for love nor money. She gave me the pick of two, and I decided on the one near the Dean's Hospital. It's a downstairs flat, and it's big an' all, with three rooms and a scullery. Of course, the water and the lav's outside.' She laughed now. 'That'll be the day when they're inside. That's what's been so good here, the indoor lav. Now I'll get me backside frozen again. Eeh! how common can she be, that woman.' She laughed; then

272

went on, 'And the lass said she would help me fix up with furniture and things . . . Don't look like that, Lizzie, lass. Look,' – she punched her gently in the shoulder – 'you could come and stay with me. Have a holiday. I'd take you down to the sands. When they get it all cleared again, that is. And you'd find the folks canny. That's on the whole, of course. There's the odds and sods, like there are in every place; but wherever you go you're sure to get one or two good neighbours. Now look; don't start cryin' again. I haven't gone yet, and anyway, as an old fellow said on the bus comin' back, we're all in God's hands. But—' her face became serious now and she nodded at Lizzie, 'a lot of people say that, don't they: we're all in God's hands. Well, the bus conductor came back to this old fellow with something that was very true. You know what he said? He said, "Well, if we are, He's got us into a pretty bloody mess." And, you know, that stopped people laughing for a time, 'cos it's right, when you come to look into it, deep like; 'cos what is He doin' lettin' all this slaughter go on? You know, that's one thing I could never understand when I was in the thick of it at the beginning of the war, them goin' into church and chapel prayin' after there was an air raid. What were they doin' that for? Thankin' Him for the dead and the dyin'? And them blinded and limbless? I was in a state once, you know, Lizzie, and I yelled that out in the street. 'Twas after I came up out of the shelter and some daft old bitch said to me, "You've got to have faith." Faith in what? . . . Eeh! there I go jabberin' on. Anyway the snow's stopped.' She ran a gentle finger along Lizzie's cheekbones, saying softly, 'Keep calm, lass, and get

273

your strength back.' She paused, and Lizzie asked flatly, 'Why? Because I'm going to need it?'

'Aye; aye, you could say you are.'

'What's in the wind, Meg?'

'I'm not sure, lass. I'm not sure. If I opened me mouth now I might be doing somebody a great disservice. But as you've said afore, things are not right in this house, and there's a reason for it; there's bound to be. Anyway, I'm goin' to phone your friends now and tell Mr Richard that you've got a daughter and you're puttin' her name down for one of those fancy schools; or is it just the lads they do that with?'

'Oh, Meg!'

'Now, now, stop it!'

Meg got off the side of the bed and slapped Lizzie's hand none too gently, saying, 'Don't let your energy drain away in tears. Just remember, you've got a lovely daughter; you've got good friends in Mr Richard and his family, and you've got me. Not that that is anything to brag about, lass, but you know what they say: any port in a storm.'

As Meg, standing in the doorway, wagged her finger towards the bed, Lizzie thought to herself that, in the mentioning of her friends, Meg had omitted both Geoff and his father. Yes, his father perhaps, but why Geoff?

5

Ted Honeysett glanced first to the left and then to the right along the main road before he slipped over the bank and into the brushwood; and a rabbit would have made no more sound than his feet on the undergrowth.

It was towards the end of March and the days were lengthening; although the day had been dull, with high winds and showers foretelling the approach of April. The pheasant season had finished on the first of February, but salmon fishing had started then, and the trout a few days ago. He was well acquainted with the dates, although they meant nothing to him. Yet, he had become wary of late, because he did not want to get involved with the big boys scooping both fish and fowl indiscriminately, and causing the landowners up the river to tear their hair.

Anyway, his purpose in entering the wood this night was not to do even a small amount of poaching, but some spying. Five minutes earlier, he had seen Mrs Boneford that was, or Miss Bradford-Brown that used to be, making her way along by the river bank, not on a bike this time, but on foot. And he smiled to himself as he thought he could tell her that she was taking a walk for nothing, because the signpost was lying on the grass again.

By! that signpost had been in some positions during the past weeks. By! it had. And then there were the notes stuck in the old elm. Well, the signpost was in the grass and the note was in the old elm, and she would have her journey for nowt the night. And it was just as well, if she did but know, because if he knew anything, sooner or later there would be a bang like a time bomb going off. What that pair didn't know was that the old man was on their track.

One night, he himself had been surprised by the unmistakable sound of someone moving carefully through the wood beyond the scrub bank: it had brought him into his natural stiff stillness. He hadn't known of anyone being in the wood; and yet, at the same time as that hussy and Geoff emerged into the open, he saw below him the figure of her father standing behind a beech tree. He had waited, holding his breath, fully expecting the old fellow to stride forward and knock hell out of young Geoff, at least with his tongue, for he'd be no match with his fists; even if Geoff Fulton had only one good arm, being in the army, he would have known how to use it.

Well, he smiled to himself as, bent double, he cautiously picked his way along the bank to where he had a view of the barn and also the end of the wood.

Pulling his old mac around his knees, he crouched on the ground to await events after the old fellow, hoping to confront them both in the barn, would find only his daughter there.

After raising his head slightly, his whole body stiffened and he could scarcely contain an audible sound of surprise as there, across the way on the mound at the end of the wood, hidden only by some low scrub, he saw a crouching figure; and what had brought the sound from him was the fact that he could also make out the butt end of a rifle resting across a low branch.

He straightened up from the knees, exclaiming to himself, 'Good God; he means to pot them.'

What action he would have taken next, he never knew, for suddenly there she was, the girl, or the woman as she was now, emerging from the wood: and she had seen what he had seen, for she was running hard at the figure and yelling, 'Stay where you are, Geoff!' And at this, the figure behind the mound stood up, and to his utter amazement, Ted saw they had clashed and were struggling.

He himself was standing upright now. When he heard the crack of the gun, he thrust his forearm across his eyes for a moment and screwed up his face. But the next instant he was bounding down the bank; and there she was, standing with her hands cupping her face, her mouth wide open, staring down at the sprawled figure with the blood pouring from his neck.

'My God! miss. What . . . what have you done?'

He was standing close beside her, and she showed no surprise at seeing him but said, 'It . . . it went off. It . . . it went off. I was trying to get it away from him. It . . . it went off. He . . . he was going to shoot Geoff.' And she looked towards the barn, seeming surprised now that Geoff wasn't visible; and he said, 'He's not there. He left a message.'

'What?'

'Well, you know . . . in the tree and . . . and,' – he pointed his finger, wagging it towards where the signpost lay.

'Oh! Oh!' She put up her hand and started to scratch the rim of her hair, then she looked at him as if seeing him for the first time and said, 'It . . . it went off, Mr Honeysett. It went off.'

He looked about him now, bewildered. The twilight was closing in. He brought his gaze back on her; then looked towards her father again, and now she muttered, 'What will I do? Get Mother?'

'No! No! Look, I'll go and get Geoff. He . . . he should be back now; it's . . . it's time for the bus. Look; come along, miss . . . missis.' He took her arm and led her towards the barn, and there, pressing her inside, he lifted his finger to her as if he were admonishing a child, saying, 'Now stay there. Don't move; just stay there. I'll bring Geoff. He'll know what to do. D'you hear?'

'Yes. Yes, Mr Honeysett, I hear.' She closed her eyes and nodded to him, then lay back against the wall of the barn. And now leaving her, he took to his heels and ran some way along by the river bank, then up on to the main road. And he continued to run until he had to stop to get his breath, and as he did so the bus came around the corner and stopped a few yards from him. But to his dismay the only passengers to alight were Mrs Ryebank and her daughter, which meant they had missed the other bus that stopped at Fuller's Crossroads and so would now have a good mile and a half to walk home. They would be going by the Fultons' place, and that meant he couldn't run any more without causing comment.

When he eventually reached the house, instead of going in by the front gate he went round the back, through the gate from the field and into the yard.

It was almost dark now and he looked about him, hoping for a sign of Geoff before knocking at the kitchen door where, he felt, his appearance alone would

278

ause comment. It was opened by the old woman, the
evacuee one, and he said to her, 'Is Geoff in?' And
he peered into the darkness, saying, 'Who is it?'

'I'm Ted Honeysett. Is he in?'

At that moment he saw the figure of Geoff. He was
pressing the old woman aside, and he came and stood
on the step and said, 'You want me, Ted?'

'Aye, Geoff. Have you . . . have you got a minute?'
He tried to make his voice sound ordinary.

'Yes, I suppose so.' He stepped out into the yard,
pulling the door behind him. And now, his voice
changing, Ted muttered, 'Come away over here for
a minute.'

'What's up? What's up with you?'

'Something's happened. Bad. She's . . . she's shot
her dad.'

There was a silence between them for a moment,
and Geoff didn't break it by saying, 'What d'you say?
What d'you mean?' and Ted growled at him, 'Did
y'hear what I said? I haven't gone off me head. I said,
something's happened. She's shot her dad.'

'My God! D'you mean that?'

'Aye, I mean that. Why d'you think I'm here? I've
run me bloody self out of wind. Got the shock of me
life. She . . . she came across him, her dad, the rifle
cocked for you.'

'*For me?*'

'Aye, for you. Who else? He thought you were
meetin' her. And she thought so an' all; she thought
you were in the barn; she hadn't got the note. Well,
I'll explain about that on the way. Get your coat, will
you, an' come? Bring a flashlight, and put a move
on, 'cos I've left her in the barn.'

'*You've left . . . ? You mean?*'

'Aye! Aye! I mean her, the one you've been meetin'. Look, I know what I know. Just get your coat, man, 'cos we might be in for a long session.'

A minute later when Geoff appeared at the kitchen door pulling on his coat, Meg said, 'Aren't you goin' to finish your supper?'

'I . . . I won't be long. Put it in the oven; I'll get it when I come back.'

He was out of the gate now hurrying along the road, Ted having almost to trot to keep up with him and between gasps trying to explain what he had seen: 'As I said, I could have told her you weren't there. She hadn't seen the note in the tree. Aw, man, it's no good makin' growling sounds; I get about, and you should bloody well thank your lucky stars that I do the night. But something's got to be done with him. I mean it's got to look like an accident, and . . . and it doesn't, as far as I can see. You . . . you know all about firearms; they aren't in my line; they never have been. You'll likely have to arrange that gun as if it had gone off on its own, or as if he tripped or something.'

They had almost reached the top of the bank when Geoff said under his breath, 'Why are you doing this, Ted? Why are you so concerned? You've never liked him, or her, or any of them, if I know you.'

'No; that's right. And likely that's why I'm doin' it.' They were down the slope now and on the river bank and walking carefully, and Ted went on, 'Me mind works as quick as me hands and . . . and I saw that she could skip off, aye, she could and leave him there, 'cos she was in a kind of panic, so nobody would know or think of accusing her.

280

But who's old Bradford-Brown been after for years?
Me. And only last week I had an up-and-downer
with him on the road, and that stuck in me mind.
I was comin' back from Hobson's, me flat cart full
of wood, branches an' that, and there he was in that
truck of his. And your dad was with him, and Peter
Rice an' all. And he makes your dad pull up and
demands where I got the wood from. When I said
I had bought and paid for it, he said it would be
the first time I'd ever paid for anything in me life.
And to that I said I wasn't the only one, but my
deals were small. And I thought he was goin' to
have a fit. He yelled at me, "I'll get you one of
these days. You see if I don't." And like a bloody
fool, I said, "If I don't get you first." So you see
what I mean about when they find him. Who will
they go lookin' for first? That's what flashed into
me mind. They'll have the polis on me afore I can
say Jack Robinson. And I'm not daft. I know Sergeant Winters and Constable McCabe have turned
blind eyes to me as long as I can remember, and
they haven't lost by it. But in the case of a kill-
ing, by! they would forget all about that. By! aye,
lad, they would. Then there was Rice and your dad
to bear witness to what I'd said; so I suppose it
was self-preservation, as they say, me jumpin' down
that bank and makin' meself known to her, else she
would have been off like a linty.'

They had reached the outside of the barn now
and Ted, his voice a whisper, muttered, '"Twas over
there.' He turned the dim light of his torch towards
the ground, picking out the outline of a body; and
then he said, 'I'll wait here a minute.'

When Geoff entered the barn he swung his torchlight towards the broad beam, and there she was, standing as if nailed to it, with her hands pressed tightly against it at each side of her. Not until he came close to her did she move or speak, and then she just muttered his name, saying, 'Geoff?'

'It's all right. It's all right. Don't worry. Everything will be all right.'

'I . . . I shot him. I mean . . . I didn't, I just struggled with him. He was going to shoot you. I thought you were in . . . in here.' She was gabbling now and he pulled her to him, saying, 'There, there now. Look, take hold of yourself.' He gripped her hands. 'You're as cold as ice,' he said. 'Here, take my coat and put it round you.'

'No, no. What . . . what am I going to do?'

Nevertheless, he pulled off his coat and put it around her, then said, 'Just stay there. Just stay there now; I'll be back in a minute.' He went outside again, and going to Ted, he said softly, 'Show me again where it is?'

Ted showed him, although he himself stood well away from the twisted body.

In the light of the torch, Geoff looked down on the heavily bloodied chin and neck. For a moment, he wondered if he might still be alive; but no, he had seen too many dead men not to recognise another. He swung the torch about and it showed up the gun lying some six feet away. For the moment he was back in the field: if a man tripped and his gun went off it wouldn't be six feet away. The picture in his mind showed him the position in which the gun and the man would be lying. He turned to Ted now, asking, 'You haven't touched the gun?'

282

'Me? No. By God! no. But she did. Her prints will be all over it.'

Yes, he had already thought of that. 'Stay there,' he said.

'What?'

'Just stay there a minute. I'll be back.' And at this he hurried further down the slope and into the barn again, saying softly now, 'There are some gloves in my pocket. I want them.' He not only pulled the gloves from his coat that she was hugging to her, but a large handkerchief from an inner pocket. Quickly he left her again. And now standing near Ted, he said, 'I'll want your help in a minute.' Then, putting on the gloves, he went and picked up the rifle and with the handkerchief, rubbed it clean. Up and down, up and down the barrel he went as if determined to give it a polish. Presently he returned to the dead man; and after turning him gently on his back and crossing the man's hands over his chest, he placed the rifle between them and pressed the fingers here and there on to the barrel. This done, he laid the rifle aside and taking his torch, played it on the ground over the mound before again addressing Ted, saying, 'You'll have to help me in this; I've . . . I've no strength in my left arm. Now I want him lifted up the bank to where the roots are. If he tripped it would be from there. Now clench your fists and pull them up under your coat sleeves.'

'What?'

'Do as I say. Clench your fists and . . .'

'Oh, aye, aye, I see.'

'Wait a minute.' Geoff swept the light of the torch around the ground, and at one point he went down on his hunkers and peered at the thin grass sprouting from the shale bank, then muttered, 'Most of it must have soaked into his collar and clothes. But let's get him up. I'll take the legs. It's only a yard or so.'

As soon as Ted touched the body he exclaimed, 'Oh, my God! My God!' And at this Geoff said, 'Shut up! Lift.'

Two or three minutes later, Geoff laid the legs down, then gently turned the body partly onto its side. After this, he picked up the gun and, flashing the torch towards the dead man's head, he took stock of where the gun would have fallen after firing. As near as possible to his guess, he laid it on the ground; then assiduously, he played his torch around the spot from where they had moved the body, and wherever he thought he detected a stain he pulled up the clump of grass, broke it into small pieces, then flung it, scattering it around.

'You've done this afore then?' Ted commented.

'No; not quite like this. Anyway, it isn't finished yet. If he's found by daylight, from the state of the ground it might be assumed there'd been quite a bit of a tussle. So I think I and my dad should be the ones to find him, then I can do a bit of ploughing around.'

'Eeh! My God! I never thought to witness anything like this.'

They were standing on the path outside the barn now, and Geoff said quietly, 'If I were you I'd go along to The Hare and have a drink, if they've got any in. I'll pop in there meself later. And . . . and, Ted, no matter what you've been doing to save your own skin, I want to thank you very much for what you're doing to save hers . . . and mine, because you seem to know as much about us as we know ourselves: you know how things are between us, and that whatever touches her affects me. So, I thank you for us both.'

'Oh, that's all right, that's all right. You're your father's son, and I suppose, in a way, I'm doin' it for him, 'cos he's been decent to me all these years, especially when I had the youngsters runnin' about. I always like to pay me debts in whatever way I can, even if it is with somebody else's property.' He stayed himself from laughing and said, '"Tis no jokin' matter the night though. 'Tis no jokin' matter the night. God, I'll not sleep until they find him an' hear what they say, 'cos bet your life, if they think it isn't an accident they'll be on to me. I know they will. I know they will.'

'No, they won't: it'll be an accident all right. Anyway, you stay as long as you can at The Hare, then walk home with somebody. By that time they should be wondering why he hasn't turned up. The main thing is, act ordinary. Go on with you now.'

'Aye. Aye, as you say, act ordinary; but it'll take some doing. Be seeing you. Be seeing you.'

Geoff now went into the barn, and saw that she was still standing with her back tight against the beam.

Putting his arms about her, he shook her slightly, saying, 'Now listen. Listen carefully. Everything's all right. It just looks as if he's had an accident. His foot's in a tree root, and when we find him that's what it'll be, the result of an accident. Now come on, you're going home. You're going in and you've got to try, whether you like it or not, you've got to try to act as if nothing has happened. You can do it.'

'I . . . I can't, Geoff.'

'Well, what is the alternative?' His voice was cold. 'Go back and tell your mother that you've shot your

285

father, because he was aiming to shoot me? And why was he aiming to shoot me? Because he's always hated my guts, and the very thought of his daughter lowering herself . . . once again, was just too much for him. So, no matter how you pleaded that you were trying to save me, you wouldn't have the shred of a name left. You think you haven't got much of a one now, but believe me, dear, they'd hound you, and you'd be unable to stand it. You'd have to clear out, and . . . and without me. Yes, without me, for, face up to it or not, as I don't like to, I'm handicapped, I can only really use one arm, and I'm lame. But on the plus side, I've a small pension and a ready-made home, and the responsibility of a father whose mind, at the moment, is not very stable, I'm afraid, not forgetting my adoptive sister and her child. So here I'm stuck, Janis; and you can be stuck with me, and in a way, happily, if you so wish, that is if you can defy your remaining parent. So what is the alternative for you? It's just as I said, you'd be out on your own, a real working girl for the first time in your life, and you wouldn't like it. Oh, no, Janis, you wouldn't like it. So, my dear, I'm going to take you as far as the gates and from there for the next few hours you are on your own. It's up to you. Go in and talk to Florrie Rice, speak to your mother, then go up to bed. Come on, there's no time to lose.'

Docilely she went with him, and she never spoke until they came up out of the woods and to the side gate that led to the stables, and there she clung to him for a moment, saying, 'I've . . . I've made a mess of everything. All my life I've made a mess of everything.'

'Yes, you have, haven't you?' His voice was harsh, but breezy. 'Well, now, this is a test. Don't make a mess of it, because remember: if you do, it's the finish of everything for both of us; and it will hit you more than it will me. Go on, now.' He was about to press her away when he pulled her to him and kissed her hard on the lips. Then he, too, was walking away along the main road towards home, thinking, why does this kind of thing always happen to me? First, the army, where he could have risen still further, and had meant to. Then to be left with a body that was handicapped. Next, to become entangled with Lizzie, only for that to be swamped with the revival of emotions that had never really died, and all to lead to this.

He had not mentioned how the loss of his mother had affected him, because Lizzie had been there to take her place; at least, in a way. It was quite true what old Meg had said in one of her bits of raw philosophy; a man didn't only want a wife; she had to be a mother, housekeeper, and loose woman all in one.

And it was Meg who greeted him when he entered the house, asking, 'Where've you been? It's kizzened up to cork, and it was a lovely bit of fish. Did that Ted bring you a salmon?'

'Salmon? no; but he wanted me to pick up a few bottles of whisky on the side.'

'Oh, good. You can get a couple for me when you're on.'

'I'm . . . I'm sorry.' He walked into the scullery now, saying, 'I didn't like the set-up, and the stuff wasn't sealed. I think somebody's got a still somewhere, so I let it go. Where's Lizzie?'

'Where would she be, but upstairs with the child? She's got nothing else these days to keep her occupied.' Her last words were merely a mutter, and he came back at her as if he hadn't heard, saying, 'What's that?'

'Nothing, nothing. Anyway, I've put your supper on the table. It's there for you, such as it is.' And with that she went out of the kitchen. And he came out of the scullery and looked at the plate of dried-up fish, which he pushed aside, then walked towards the fireplace and, resting his hand on the mantelshelf, he gazed down on to the brightly black-leaded hob. His mind was in a turmoil, yet, in it he was planning out the action he must take later on that night, because as indifferent as Mrs Bradford-Brown was to her husband, she would surely begin to wonder when he didn't turn up later on.

He had already decided to stay downstairs in the sitting-room until twelve, supposedly reading. If he had heard nothing by then, well, he would have to take it from there, wouldn't he? But about this other business at which that wily old woman would keep nudging; he would have to have it out with Lizzie, come into the open. But one thing at a time; let him get tonight over first.

It was twenty past eleven when the phone rang. He almost sprang across the room to the hall, and when he picked it up he immediately recognised the refined tones of Mrs Bradford-Brown. 'Is that John?'

'No, no; it's Geoff here. Is that Mrs Bradford-Brown?'

'Yes, yes. I'm . . . I'm rather worried. Mr Bradford-Brown went out earlier this evening. I . . . I think he was hoping to come across those poachers. Anyway, he was intending to join Farmers Hobson and Ryebank and Major Murray at the major's place to see what was to be done. I . . . I phoned the major a little while ago and he said that my husband hadn't put in an appearance. They imagined he had another engagement . . . I must admit to being worried. Would you mind telling your father . . . asking him if he would come and do a round in case my . . . my husband has been attacked or met with some accident?'

'Of course, Mrs Bradford-Brown. I'll do that right away; and I'll come along with him; I haven't been to bed yet.'

'Thank you. Thank you.'

He put the phone down and stood looking at it for a second, then hurried up the stairs, opened his father's door without ceremony, went to the bedside and shook him by the shoulder, saying, 'Dad! Dad!'

'Yes? What is it?' John turned slowly on to his back.

'Mrs Bradford-Brown has just phoned; the boss seems to be missing.'

'Missing? What d'you mean, missing?'

'He went out earlier tonight, apparently trying to locate the poachers, and he hasn't turned up. He was to go to Major Murray's, but he didn't put in an appearance there either. She asked if you will go around. I said you would, and that I'd go with you.'

'He could have gone into Durham to his club.'

'She didn't seem to think so. Anyway—' Geoff was moving down the room now as he said, 'if he went out after the poachers, he would likely take his gun. Are you coming?'

'Aye, yes; I'm coming.'

Ten minutes later they were both in the yard, their shoulders hunched against the cold night.

'Wild-goose chase,' John said. 'She's started some in her life, she has, but this is the silliest. If the truth was known, he's tight; he's got tight, as he's been doing lately, and he's sleeping it off in one of the rooms that she's never thought of looking in.'

'Yes, could be,' said Geoff. 'Could be. But we'd better look around anyway.'

So they looked around.

6

The blood-stained body of Ernest Bradford-
Brown was discovered by his estate manager,
John Fulton, and the manager's son Geoff at
half-past one on the morning of 1 April 1944.
Police investigation has revealed that while out
searching for salmon-poachers the deceased had
tripped and fallen, and in doing so had accidentally discharged his shotgun. Foul play is not
suspected. Mr Bradford-Brown leaves a wife and
daughter.

This short report in the local newspaper seemed to
cause little interest in or speculation about the death
of Ernest Bradford-Brown. There was a war on and
there was other news to report, not all of it good.
Bomber Command had just lost 94 planes of the 795
that had taken part in the raid on Nuremberg. Nor,
later, did his funeral attract much attention, for he
had not been a favourite local landowner; much the
reverse. He might have been envied for his money,
but he was despised for his lack of quality . . . county
quality. Even his wife's connections hadn't been able
to grease the locks on all the doors in the county to
allow him in. And then there had been his daughter's
divorce. That had been a nasty business. People still
had the smell of it in their nostrils. No woman worth

her salt would walk out on a man just because he had been disfigured. And so it had really not been expected that county representation at the funeral would have been other than thin on the ground. But when representation of local businesses was also lacking at the funeral, it was surmised that although Mrs Bradford-Brown was known as a very gentle and quiet lady, she was also known as a very proud one and, being so, she would take the slight badly . . .

Alicia *had* taken the slight badly. It had aroused her anger and settled in her mind an indecision that had been wavering there long before her husband had died. And now, she was relating her decision to her daughter.

Janis was sitting in the drawing-room, her face pale, and her dark dress made it appear ashen-hued. She sat silent, staring at her mother sitting opposite as she folded and refolded a cambric handkerchief and said, 'It is your own fault that he's cut you off completely. But he didn't do it just recently; it was after the divorce. That really upset him. He could have stood anything but that. You shamed him. You knew how much he thought of our good name. Your father had had a very hard life, a struggle to make his . . .'

Now Janis pulled herself forward in the chair and, bending towards her mother, she said quietly, 'Why are you so sanctimonious now about Father and his hard struggle? You never cared for him. You despised him, and you let him see it. You had the name and the position. You took him because he had money and was making more. You took him to clear Grandfather's debts and keep you in this house.

Say what you like, but don't talk to me as if you are mourning him, because you're not.'

'Who said I am mourning him? I was merely stating a fact. If you had let me go on, I would have proved that to you by saying he was a climber. He wanted to be thought well of. He wanted a position in the county; he wanted to be looked up to. The payment for that was his money. He knew it and I knew it. So, I'm not being a hypocrite or sentimental about him. In fact, at the present moment I'm feeling a great release. I'm sorry he died as he did, and there's one thing troubles me about his death. I've asked myself again and again why he was at that end of the grounds, when he was supposed to be with Major Murray discussing what they were going to do about the poachers. I spoke to him just before he went out. He looked angry. I suppose it was because we had lost so many birds of late, although not from that end of the grounds.'

Janis had her eyes closed and her head was bent forward, her chin resting in her hand, her elbow pressed tight into the arm of the chair, when her mother's voice came to her, saying, 'I'm surprised that you have taken his going so badly, because you had been at loggerheads for some time. It was only because I insisted that you were allowed to come for weekends. I will tell you something else you didn't know. He knew you were seeing that Fulton individual again.'

Janis's eyes were wide, her mouth open, and when her mother nodded at her, saying, 'Yes, that surprises you, because you have, haven't you?' All she could do was to gulp and say, 'Yes; he comes into the canteen.'

'Is that all?'

'No; he has been for a drink to the flat once or twice.'

Alicia Bradford-Brown pulled herself up to her feet and her lip curled and her whole expression was one of disdain as she looked down on her daughter, saying, 'How much lower can you get? All right, yes, yes, he was commissioned, but he still remains what he was before he went into the army. Well, as you have informed me more than once, it is your life and you are going to lead it in whichever way you wish. Well, in return I'm going to tell you that I too am going to lead my life in whatever way I wish. So therefore, perhaps it is as well that you've got him to fall back on. However, I will give you a choice: I am selling the estate. It has already been put on the market: Mr Gist is to manage the businesses and I am going to join my cousin in Cornwall. She is living on her own in that big, gaunt place and is pleased at my decision. Now, here is something for you to decide. As your father hasn't left you a penny and I don't intend to make you an allowance, you are welcome to come with me until after the war, when I intend to move to Switzerland. It is up to you to choose. I'll leave you to think about it.'

Janis watched her mother walk down the room and out of the door, and as she stared after her, she murmured, 'Oh, dear God!' She had fully expected her father to leave her something, because his income from the businesses, which included six estate offices, scattered along the Tyne, as well as the value of this house and land must have made him a millionaire. But he hadn't left her a farthing. What he had said was, 'Any remuneration that might come to her would be at the discretion of her mother.' And what had her mother said? Accompany her down to her cousin Beattie's mausoleum of a house in the bleakest part of Cornwall. Then after the war, to Switzerland. Tagging along dependent on this ageing woman who seemed to have shed her years and become young again, imagining a new life before her. And what would happen when *she* died? She'd likely leave the whole lot to some distant relative, just for spite, and all because she, Janis, was breaking the social code.

When she got to her feet her knees felt weak: she could think of nothing but that she'd have to see Geoff and talk to him, ask him . . . But ask him what?

'You really mean to go, Meg?'

'Yes, lass. It's better that I should. Anyway, I've burned me boats. As I told you, I got Bill McGurk to take me bits and pieces down to the new place yesterday. The neighbour next door had kindly scrubbed it out for me. She seems a very canny lass. She's got three bairns, but they're all safely away in the country, this way I think, and her man's at sea, and she's on nights at the factory, and the days are long, she said. So she did it out for me. We'll get on like a house on fire. She said I reminded her of her mother. I said, not her granny? and she laughed and said, no, her granny was still alive! her mother killed herself looking after her. Aw, lass.' She put her hand on Lizzie's arm, saying, 'Don't look so down in the mouth. It isn't all that distance to Shields. And look, there's three rooms; you can come and stay with me, as I said afore. On the other hand, I'll be sorry to leave you, lass. But things are not right here, are they? Do you mind if I open me mouth a bit wider?'

'No, Meg, as wide as you like.'

'Well, Lizzie, I think there should be some plain speakin' atween you and Geoff. And the sooner the better.'

'What do you mean by that, Meg?'

'Just what I say, lass. You're not daft or blind. He's a changed man these last few months. Well, since the turn of the year, and there's a reason for it.'

'And do you know the reason, Meg?'

Meg now turned and went towards the fireplace and, lifting up the kettle, brought it to the table and mashed the tea, then took it back to the hob, before returning to the table and putting the cosy on the teapot. 'I'm not opening me mouth any further,' she said, 'I'm just goin' to say to you, have some plain speakin', because you've got your own life to think about and that of the bairn, and it might need sorting out. Now that's all I'm goin' to say, really, so you needn't ask. I may be wrong in opening me mouth so far. Anyway, look, it's a lovely fine day and you're on your way out to give her an airin'. Have this cup of tea afore you go. Just wait a minute till it draws. By! she's bonny.' She was looking through the window to where the child was in the pram outside in the yard. 'And she's gettin' on like a house on fire. I've never believed in bottle feeds, but she's thriving on 'em all right . . . There you are.'

She now handed Lizzie a cup of tea, adding, 'One thing I'm sorry for, lass, is that you'll have it all to do yourself in future, and this is a big house.'

'When are you actually going, Meg?'

'Well, I said I would be takin' over from next Monday; that's when the rent begins, like.'

Lizzie sipped at her tea; then, suddenly putting the cup down on the table, she rose from the chair, pulled her felt hat firmly about her ears, and buttoned up her coat as she went out of the door. And Meg did not stop her with any more chatter.

As she pushed the pram through the gates on to the country road, her mind was nodding at her, saying, 'Meg's right. She's right. I've got to have this out. I should have spoken up weeks ago.' At the time, she had thought it couldn't be another woman, because when would he see her? He was at home most of the day, except when he went for his constitutional; and because of his leg, he had been to the hospital three times during the past few weeks and had had to stay overnight because of the tests he was undergoing. Could it be there was something wrong with him physically and he didn't want to tell her? She stopped pushing the pram. That could be it.

In a way, for some weeks now, they had lost what she described as personal contact. Before Christmas it had been nothing for him to put his arm around her shoulders or around her waist and give her a hug. And often in the evening he had sat holding her hand while they talked, especially after his father had gone upstairs and Meg had retired to bed. And more than once he had put his hand on the mound of her stomach to feel the baby kick. But such actions had ceased since the New Year.

In spite of having the child, she had felt very alone these past weeks and time and again she had felt inclined to phone Richard, but had considered it unfair to do so. It was almost a fortnight now since she had heard from him or his mother. Mrs Boneford

297

had rung up a number of times during the first week after the baby was born, and even Mr Boneford had spoken to her on the phone, his voice so loud that he almost drowned his own words.

Then there was Geoff's father. Strange, but less and less was she thinking of him as 'Dad'. Since his outburst when he had first seen the baby, he had hardly spoken to her. When she had mentioned to Geoff that his father's attitude was upsetting her, he had said, 'Don't worry. He'll come around. He's still missing Mother. Unfortunately, he's a one-woman man.'

She walked on steadily now, pushing the pram and every now and again bending over the handlebars and talking to the child, who lay, blinking its round blue eyes, in the shadow of the canopy.

She was about to turn about and make for home when she decided to take the pram down onto the river walk. There was a gentle slope from the road further along. It was beyond the boundary of the estate, but once on the river bank, there was no barrier. And anyone ignorant of the boundary, which was defined by an almost obliterated railing that sloped at right angles down to the path, could be forgiven for not recognising that they were walking on private land.

A week or more ago, Lizzie would never have dreamt of walking into the grounds. But now that Mr Bradford-Brown had gone, there seemed to be a lighter feeling all round. So within minutes she was walking along by the river.

It was strange that she had never been so close to the river since the night she ploughed into it in an effort to save Richard. She told herself it was a lovely walk; the path was quite even and so it was no bother to push the pram. She must do this more often. She noted that the path was well worn, so some people must use it. Likely John, on his twice-daily rounds. But she doubted if Geoff would take this way in his daily constitutional because it would mean coming down that slope which, she thought, would test his leg too much.

Her thoughts back on him again, she asked herself a question; did she really care for him? And while she searched for the answer she pulled the pram to a standstill and gazed across the river, the surface of which was glinting like myriads of stars. The answer came; who else was there to care for? Or who was there to care for her and the child? She liked him. She could live with him, and the house was her home and his home. What other future was there for her? Judging by the expression on her face it was an unsatisfactory answer, and she pushed the pram on again. And then, there ahead, she saw the old barn. She hadn't been around this way for years. She had once been inside and seen the relics of past torture on the walls, and her visit had given her an idea for a school composition entitled 'Old Farm Implements'.

She was about fifteen yards from the barn when she heard the murmur of voices. And the wheels of the pram had turned full circle twice before she pulled it to a stop, as she watched two figures emerging through the open doorway. And when they stopped and their arms went around each other, the embrace was as passionate as the lingering kiss suggested. She felt her whole face stretching, while at the same time there seemed to be a roaring inside her head, and within seconds it seemed to have filled her whole body. She could even see its colour: it was almost black, a dark reddy black. It seemed to scorch her eyes.

Lizzie imagined that she must have been standing for minutes before their bodies moved apart. It was the woman who saw her first, and as she slowly pulled herself away from the man she pointed at her; and then the man turned, and she heard his reaction: 'Lizzie. Oh God!'

Geoff made no move towards her as she swung the pram round to push it almost at a run along the path. Then she was in the open at last, well away from the scene . . .

'Now don't worry,' he said as he put his arms around Janis again. 'And you're quite sure in your own mind? You won't miss the highlights?'

'What highlights?'

'Aye, what highlights? But there'll be some pretty lows for you. I might be a lieutenant but I'm still John Fulton's son, and he's just a grade above a farm worker; that alone will shut the remaining doors in your face.'

'Geoff. Geoff. If you're willing to take a chance, I am. The only obstacle, as I see it, is your father, and what his reception of me might be. As for . . . well, the girl: will she be able to stand it, me coming into the house?'

'She'll just have to take it or leave it. If she doesn't take it I'll make her the offer, as I said before, of fitting up your place for her. Anyway, dear, everything's going to be all right now. Just go on back and tell your mother what she can do with Cornwall and Switzerland.' He smiled a tight smile as he added, 'And brace her for the shock that you're going to marry that Fulton fellow, and when she sniffs I'll hear it in the house, for sniff she will.

It's bad enough having me on the side, but marriage? She'll fly to Cornwall now. Go on, dear. Go on.'

She did not move but, putting her arms around his neck, she slowly kissed him on the lips, saying, 'It won't be an easy passage, but . . . but I'll try to make it as smooth as I can.'

'I'll see that you do.'

'Yes, yes,' she nodded at him slowly, 'I've no doubt about that.'

As she went to walk away he caught at her arm, saying quietly, 'If you should come across Ted – he's made himself scarce lately – make a point of thanking him, because he's been a good friend to you.'

She nodded once, saying, 'Yes; yes, I will; but you don't think he'll hold it . . . I mean, hang it over my head?'

'Not Ted. He carries a lot of secrets, does Ted.'

She was some distance from him when she turned and said, 'When . . . when will I see you again?'

'Later on tonight, at your place in town. It won't take me all that long to find out what line Lizzie's going to take.'

'Look, Lizzie,' – he was bawling at her now – 'come off your high horse and remember that marriage was never mentioned between us.'

'No, it mightn't have been in words, but you indicated it clearly enough.'

'Well, that's what you imagined; I was just trying to be decent and protective after you lost Andrew.'

'Oh, don't give me that. You wanted me, and if you had thought I was easy game and not the kind of girl your mother had brought up, except for my slip, as your father called it, you would have shown your hand in a different way. At times you had a job to keep up your brotherly attention. What do you take me for, a fool? Yet I must have been all these months. Your having to stay overnight in hospital! Funny that didn't happen last year. Then you were in and out within a couple of hours. And her, above all people; Richard's wife.'

'She used to be Richard's wife.'

'Yes, she *was* Richard's wife; but how many pseudo wives had she been before, and since? . . . *Don't you dare!* You lift your hand to me and I'll come back at you with the first thing I can lay mine on, and it'll be that.' And now thrusting out her arm, she picked up a twelve-inch bronze statue from the windowsill, then went on, 'And you've got the nerve to say you're going to bring her here as your wife; and you expect me to stay here! What as? House parlourmaid? Housekeeper? Skivvy? And the alternative: to go into her flat in town with its two rooms and a scullery!'

'You weren't brought up in anything any better. In fact you're . . .'

'No, I wasn't brought up in anything any better, but that wasn't my fault, and you did your Sir Galahad piece and rescued me from a life of sin into which you seemed to think I was in danger of falling. But you're mistaken, I fended for myself that night and I would have gone on doing so; and I emphasise again' – she now wagged the statue in her hand – 'that I would never become a Miss Janis Bradford-Brown, or yet forget that I was a Mrs Richard Boneford. And while I'm on, I'll tell you this; it isn't because of unrequited love, so to speak, that I'm blazing angry; it's because

302

I've been used. I was a sop to plug the hole that she made in your life. As you so charmingly admitted a while ago, she's always been in your life; she's always been the one. Well, now you're welcome to her. And lastly, I'll tell you this: I would rather take the child with me into the workhouse than stay here or take her flaming rooms, and I'll be gone as soon as possible and be glad to get out of your sight.'

As his hand came out to grab her, she cried, 'Don't you dare touch me! Don't come within yards of me! I'll tell you this: I wouldn't have minded, in fact, I would have understood, if you had come into the open straightaway, and you had told me you cared for her so much that you wanted to marry her and go off with her, but to tell me that you're bringing her here, giving me no option but to put up with her or take her leavings. By God! Geoff Fulton, I could . . . yes, I could strike you with this, this minute!' She flung the statuette down on to the couch, then stalked from the room, and almost knocked Meg over as she burst into the hall.

As Lizzie ran up the stairs, Meg followed more slowly, entering the bedroom as Lizzie was already pulling out drawers.

'It had to come out, lass.'

'Don't talk to me, Meg, not yet. Don't talk to me.'

'All right, but I can help you to put your things together. I've got my bits and pieces already packed, and there's some empty cases in the storeroom. I'll get them.'

When she next returned to the bedroom, the bed was strewn with underclothes and baby-wear. Opening one of the cases, she knelt down on the floor by it,

303

saying, 'Hand me what you want to go in here, lass.'
And Lizzie did so.

When two cases were full, she got up from her
knees saying, 'There's another one along there and
some boxes. I'll get them.'

'Oh, Meg!' Lizzie now flopped down on the side
of the bed and, bending forward, she covered her face
with her hands, her body shaking. But no tears came.
She was still fused with anger. Meg sat down beside
her, and put her arm around her waist and pulled her
head on to her shoulder, saying, 'What you goin' to
do, lass?'

'I . . . I haven't stopped to think, Meg.'

'I have. But . . . but what I think isn't goin' to do
much good, not for you, it isn't. There's my place,
but after living in this house you'd go round the bend
down there. It isn't the smallness of it, it's . . . well,
the locality. I'm used to it, in fact, I like it; at least
I did once. I don't know how I'm goin' to fit in
when I go back. But somehow you'd find it hard,
lass. Still, for what it's worth, in the meantime you're
welcome, more than welcome, and it would be lovely
to be with you for a bit longer.'

'Oh, Meg, to think it's come to this. At this moment,
I'm wishing I'd never been taken away from Minnie
Collier, as I always think of her. And you know, it
wasn't long after I left when I saw her again, and she
said to me, "One day you'll be sorry." It's . . . it's
as if her words have come true. There's Midge, my
sister. It must be three years since I saw her, and then
we had hardly anything to say to each other. She was
happy enough; in fact, I felt she was happier than I
was. It was her twenty-first birthday and I took her

304

a present. And there she was, her little house up to the eyes in dust and disorder, but she and her man and his people were having a right good time. I came away that day feeling strangely lonely, and apart from a Christmas card at the end of '41, I haven't heard from her since; nor have I troubled to write. And now, Meg, apart from you, there's nobody.'

'Don't be silly, lass. There's Mr Richard and his people.'

'Oh, Meg; Meg. I wouldn't dream of putting myself on them under these circumstances.'

'No, no, of course not. Well, I'll go and get the other boxes, lass, and then I'll slip out and down to the phone box and call up Miss Thirble. I'll go to the box because I don't want Geoff to hear what I'm saying. She'll still be in the office and I'll ask her if I can have the key the morrow instead of next Monday. So, come on, lass; keep your pecker up; things'll work out. Me mother used to always say, "As one door shuts another one bangs in your face." But I don't hold with that. No, I don't hold with that.'

She went out and into her own room and, pulling on her blue serge coat and flat felt hat, she picked up her bag from the chest of drawers and hurried out and down the stairs. At the telephone table she tore a piece of paper from the loose pad and copied a number from out of a book that lay to the side of the pad, then left the house.

In a few minutes she was in the telephone kiosk and when she heard the voice at the other end of the line, she shouted, 'Is that you, Mrs Boneford?' And the voice answered, 'No; but I'll get her. Who's speaking?'

'Me name is Mrs Price. I'm . . . I'm a friend of Lizzie's. Could I speak to Mr Boneford, please, Mr Richard Boneford?'

'Oh, I'm afraid he's away until tomorrow night, but I'll get Mrs Boneford for you.'

Meg stood with the receiver pressed tightly against her ear, thinking, Lizzie said the maids had a thick Scottish brogue, but that one didn't talk like that.

'Hello.'

'Oh, hello. Is that Mrs Boneford?'

'Yes. Yes this is she.'

'I'm Mrs Price; Meg; you know, Lizzie's friend.'

'Oh, yes, yes. Lizzie has talked a lot about you. How is she?'

'Not in a good way, Mrs Boneford.'

'She's not ill?'

'No, not that way, but . . . but she's in trouble.'

'What do you mean, in trouble?'

'It's . . . it's a long story. Just a minute, I've got to put some more coppers in the box.'

When she resumed the conversation she shouted, 'Are you there?' And the voice answered her, 'Yes, yes, Mrs Price, I'm here. You say Lizzie is in trouble. Can you tell me about it?'

'Well, kind of brief, like. It's Geoff, you know; the son of the house. Well, of a sudden he's . . . he's goin' to . . . he's sprung it that he's goin' to be married and . . . and he's givin' Lizzie the choice of stayin' there, or goin' livin' in this woman Bradford-Brown's house in Durham.'

'What did you say? What was the name?'

Meg looked up at the roof of the kiosk. She shouldn't have said any name. Well, she would find out in the

306

end. She now put her lips close to the mouthpiece again and shouted, 'I don't know how you'll take this, Mrs Boneford, but . . . well, it's Mr Richard's old wife; I mean, the one he divorced. She calls herself Miss Brown now.'

'Never! Never!'

'Aye. Aye. So you can see what Lizzie feels like, the predicament she's in.'

'Oh, my dear, something must be done.'

'Well, I had an idea, Mrs Boneford.'

'Yes? Yes, Mrs Price? Tell me what you think should be done?'

'Well, just afore I came out, I put it to her that she should get in touch with you, but she wouldn't have it. Takin' advantage, or somethin' like that, she said. So, if you could phone her in a little while and ask her to visit . . . well, I'm sure she would come. You see, I'm leavin' an' all, but I've only got a little house in Shields, and it isn't what Lizzie's been used to. She's as welcome as the flowers in May, but she'd be as miserable as sin there, I know.'

'Of course, of course, Mrs Price. Yes, I'll do that. Richard is away at present, but he would want her to come here immediately. I know he would.'

The pips went again and she had to put more coppers in the box and again she yelled, 'Are you there?' And the answer again was, 'Yes, yes, Mrs Price, I'm here.' The voice was calm, reassuring, and it went on, 'Now, I'll try and do my best to persuade her over the phone, and you must reassure her that she is more than welcome and that we are dying to see the baby. How long shall I wait before I phone the house? Say, half an hour?'

'Aye, yes, that would be fine. And thank you, thank you very much.'

'You will be coming with her?'

'Me? Oh no, no. I've got me own home, as I said.'

'You would be very welcome, Mrs Price, and she seemed very fond of you. Moreover, it's a long journey and I would feel happier if she had company.'

'You're very kind, missis, but . . . but . . .'

'Then I'll expect you too.'

'Wait a minute . . .'

'Goodbye, Mrs Price. We'll be seeing each other.'

The line went dead and Meg held the mouthpiece from her and stared at it as she said, 'Me go to Scotland? And into a place like that, with them kind of folk? No, no. I'll put her on the train; that's as far as I'll go.' . . .

When the phone rang Meg just happened to be in the sitting-room and she went out hastily and picked it up. It was Mrs Boneford politely enquiring if she could speak to Lizzie.

'Yes, yes, Mrs Boneford. I'll get her for you.'

Trotting across the hall, she mounted half-way up the stairs; then in a carrying voice she yelled, 'Lizzie! Lizzie! You're wanted on the phone!'

It was some seconds before Lizzie appeared at the top of the stairs and she was taking them slowly until Meg said, 'Put a move on, lass; it's Mrs Boneford.'

Still Lizzie didn't hurry, and when she picked up the phone, she said, 'Hello, Edith,' and the voice replied, 'Hello, Lizzie,' and then went quickly and quietly on saying, 'Listen to me, Lizzie. You are to get on the train tomorrow morning with Mrs Price and come straight here. Do you hear me? I am not going to discuss it with you. I am telling you what you must do. Just bring your light luggage with you; the rest can be picked up later.'

'I . . . I can't, Edith, no.'

'Listen to me. If you don't, then it only means that after Richard returns tomorrow night he will have to make the journey into South Shields to your friend's house, because that is where she says you are going. Now to save a lot of bother, my dear girl, do as I say. We are longing to see you. Get the same train as you did before and the trap will be waiting in the same place. Now I'm not going to argue. Whichever way you decide to come, whether it be on your own tomorrow or under escort from Richard, you are coming here.'

As Lizzie was about to speak again the phone clicked. She gave a gasp, put her hand to her throat as if she were choking, dropped the receiver on to the stand, then turned and ran across the hall, continued to run up the stairs and into the bedroom; and there, flinging herself on the bed, she gave way to a paroxysm of weeping.

Meg had followed her, and when she reached the bed she didn't touch her but sat on the foot and let her cry it out, and not until the sound of her sobbing subsided did she put her hands on Lizzie's shoulder, saying, 'There, it's out of you. Now to business. You can sort out the stuff that you need to take with you and have the rest sent on.'

Lizzie now turned and sat up, then rose from the bed and, going to the wash-hand stand, she took her towel from the rail and wiped her face before turning to Meg and saying, 'If I go there, you're going with me.'

'Oh, no, lass, no. Apart from everything else, I wouldn't fit in, not from what you told me. I hardly fitted in here and these are not gentry.'

'Meg, I can't do without you, at least for a time. I . . . I sort of . . . I'm lost. They're all wonderful at that end, really wonderful people, but . . . but I've lived with you for quite some time, even before Bertha died, and you're more like a mother to me than she was – she was always a teacher – and . . . and you know all about me, all about everything that's happened. I need you, Meg. If you don't come with me, I'll go with you down to Shields. So there you have it. Just . . . just for a time, until I get myself pulled together again.'

'Aw.' Meg wriggled her body like a dog throwing off water as she said, 'Well, since you put it like that, I suppose I'll have to. But they'll get a shock, mind; I'm not everybody's cup of tea.'

'You'll be theirs.'

'Let's hope you're right, but knowin' meself I doubt it, 'cos I'm too old to change an' put on manners; in fact, I wouldn't know how, 'cos I've never had any. Anyway, that's settled. Now what you've got to do, lass, is to see John and hear what he's got to say, and then we'll be off first thing in the morning.'

What John had to say was in keeping with his attitude towards Lizzie over the past months. He was sitting in his chair and didn't look towards her, but leaned towards the fire and knocked his pipe against the bars, and in answer to what she had just said, which was,

'Well, Dad, I suppose you've learned all about it,' he answered with, 'I hear you intend to leave us, just like that.'

'Not just like that, Dad. I've been given the option of having another woman come into this house or taking her place in Durham. What would you expect me to do?'

He now turned and looked at her and said harshly, 'Consider all that's been done for you over the past years, that's just what I would expect you to do, Lizzie. And if my son wants to marry someone, well, that's up to him. That's how I see it.'

'Even if the someone is who she is?'

'That's his business and hers. And after all, this is still my house, and you're still at liberty to stay here with your child, but you are not at liberty to say who else comes into it.'

Her voice rising now, she said, 'What would you have said if, before Christmas, your son had told you he wanted to marry me?'

'I would have said it wasn't a good thing. You're not brother and sister, no, but your natures are not fitted.'

She took in one long drawn breath before she said, 'No; you're right there, Mr Fulton.'

Hearing her refer to him by his surname he turned his head sharply towards her, his mouth in a slight gape, and she left him gaping further as she said, 'I had a child, but I'm not a whore, so therefore your son's nature and mine don't fit. He's certainly picked someone more like himself. I hope you'll enjoy living with your daughter-in-law.'

'Lizzie, how dare . . . !'

'Don't you say that! I'm speaking the truth and you know it. I'm going now. I'll be gone from this house in the morning and I should say thank you for the years of care, but when I think back, I worked for all I got. I was used as a maid for years. That's what I was engaged for, wasn't it? Even when I went to the typing school I had to do the chores when I returned. And when I began to earn, I tipped everything up, and she gave me pocket money; but I didn't mind, I was in a way repaying her for the music lessons, and those I've always been grateful for. Yet she'd always said she was saving for me and I would have a nice little bit when I married. But it's strange, isn't it, that when she died I was left her wrist-watch; no money, nothing else, and all because I had sinned. One thing I did learn from her: good people can be mean at heart.'

'Get out! I never thought to hear you say such things about my wife. You are an ungrateful individual. You have been harboured in this house for seven years, treated as a daughter. She even loved you . . .'

She took two paces back from him now and, her face grim, she said, 'She didn't, else she would have forgiven the so-called mistake I made. What your wife wanted from the beginning, I know now, was a pupil. Someone she could coach and dominate in her sweet, persistent way; but love, no. She loved one person and that wasn't even you; it was her son, and I hope, wherever she is, she will be happy in the daughter-in-law that's going to take her place in this house that was her pride.'

He was too angry for speech. She saw that his body was shivering – it was almost a repeat of Geoff's attitude – and that he would like to strike her. She turned and went out of the room and up the stairs and finished gathering together the rest of her belongings which, when all was packed, didn't amount to all that much.

7

'Eeh my! I thought all the kind folks lived in Shields, but haven't people been helpful?' They were sitting in the bus on the last lap of the journey. The conductor had taken two suitcases, a string bag and two carrier bags and placed them under the stairs, a man had got up and given Meg his seat, and a young boy had done the same for Lizzie and the baby. And when Meg shouted across the aisle to where Lizzie was sitting three seats further up on the opposite side, 'I like Scotland already,' the people within earshot laughed and some of them enquired, 'Where are you from?' And of course Meg was only too pleased to answer, 'Durham, County Durham. We've come all the way from there the day.'

'By! that's some way. Where are you going now?'

'Up in the hills, as far as I can gather, to a place called Beckside Hall.'

'Beckside!' There were glances exchanged among strangers, and one person said, 'Oh. Oh, aye, but that's some way out. Bus doesn't go anywhere near there.'

'No, I know; but we're being met.'

And so it went on until the bus had almost emptied, leaving them, apart from two other people, the only passengers. And then they alighted and the bus conductor hopped off the bus and put their cases and the packages on the roadside and waved to them as the bus moved away . . .

Lizzie looked about her, and there, further up the road at the entrance to the lane, was the trap. Standing beside it was a woman, a youngish woman.

Before she was half-way to them the young woman was calling, 'Hello! there. Right on time. And I've just got here.' She was now looking at Lizzie and saying, 'I'm Jean McKenzie. Matty's got the rheumatics bad and . . . and I think Edith told you, Richard won't be back until this evening.'

She was holding out her hand, and Lizzie, hugging the child to her, took it, and with a weary smile she said, 'Well, I'm Lizzie, and this is Jane.' She nodded down towards the child, and the young woman said, 'Oh, isn't she lovely!' Then turning to Meg, she said, 'And you are Meg?' and Meg answered, 'Aye, I'm Meg.'

'Let me take those cases.' Jean McKenzie bent down and effortlessly lifted the two suitcases, saying, 'What was the journey like? I hope you didn't have to stand. It's terrible these days. When I came up from Portsmouth I had to stand all the way.'

Even before Lizzie was settled in the trap she had realised that this Jean McKenzie appeared to be a very capable young woman, though not so young as she had at first imagined. She must be thirty or thereabouts. She was tall with a very slim figure, an abundance of fair hair and, below it, an attractive face with big, round, brown eyes. She talked most of the time, hardly waiting for either of them to answer.

They were bowling along the road when she turned her head and, glancing at Lizzie, she said, 'Richard

315

will be pleased to see you. He's told me a lot about you. Richard and I were brought up together, you know. Well, I say brought up together' – she laughed now – 'until I was seven and he was nine, when he went to boarding school, and I was packed off shortly after that. Then it was mostly during the holidays that we met up and romped together.'

Meg, who was sitting on the opposite side of the trap and next to the young woman, who had her back half-turned towards her, exchanged a glance with Lizzie, and Lizzie, turning her gaze away from what Meg's message might contain, said, 'How is Richard these days?'

'Oh, he's splendid. He's had another trip to hospital and they're doing a marvellous job on him. We are all so relieved. We went shopping in the town last weekend, and . . . and, you know, he wasn't a bit embarrassed, as he used to be. Oh, it was wonderful to see the change in him.'

Again Meg caught Lizzie's eye, and held her gaze now, and there was a similar thought in both their minds: was she jumping from the frying pan into the fire?

She had hardly slept a wink last night. As hour after hour passed she had become more aware that she was relieved how things had turned out, and she had realised where her true feelings lay. She recalled that Richard had said he would never ask her to marry him, but that didn't mean that he didn't care for her. Well, given time, she would do the asking. And now, here was this girl . . . no, this woman, speaking of her closeness with Richard, breaking the ice, sort of. Oh, yes, she was definitely breaking the ice to let her

316

know how things stood. She was the kind of person who wouldn't have waited for Richard to propose; in her breezy forthright way, she would have put the question and settled the business once and for all. It was a kind of sardonic joke, wasn't it? That she was walking into a situation similar to the one from which she had flown just a few hours ago.

And that word 'joke'. Mr Honeysett had mentioned it.

A half-hour before the bus was due she had taken the case along to the bus stop and Meg had carried the bags, and she had left her there to return for the child and odd bits and pieces. Geoff had not put in an appearance and his father must have gone to work some time earlier, for she saw no-one, and when she left the house for the last time she did not even stop to look around the kitchen; she wanted to get away and as quickly as possible. At the gate she had run into Ted Honeysett. He was pushing his barrow and, without any greeting, he had said, 'Going for the bus?' And she had answered, 'Yes, Mr Honeysett.'

'Well, put your bundles on me cart,' he said; and this she had done, then walked by his side in silence until they came within sight of Meg sitting on her case, when he had remarked, 'Takin' a holiday?'

'No, Mr Honeysett; we're leaving.'

He had shown no surprise but said, 'Oh aye?' then had added casually, ''Cos of her?'

She had glanced at him, and he returned her look, nodding and saying, 'Oh, I get about, Lizzie, I get about,' which had brought to mind John's summing-up of Ted Honeysett, that he knew more than was good for him. And she had realised that he must always have

317

been aware of the situation. And so when, as if seeking further enlightenment, he had added, 'He was always a bit of a joker, you know, even as a young lad. Could always cap anything you said, turn it funny, like. But then there are things that go beyond a joke. I don't dislike him, you know, so I hope this joke will keep him laughin' for a time, anyway. What d'you say, lass?' she had gone along with him and said, 'Yes, Mr Honeysett, I hope this joke will keep him laughing.'

'There you are then.' And he had taken the bundles from the cart and placed them at the side of Meg, saying, 'You off an' all on your holidays?'

'Yes, Mr Honeysett, I'm off an' all on me holidays.'

'And where are you bound for?'

'Germany, to see Mr Hitler.'

He had grinned as he remarked, 'Ask a straight question and you get a silly answer.' Then turning to look down on Meg again, he added quietly, 'When you see him, ask him to deal kindly with our Billie, will you? He's had him a prisoner for the last two years.'

Meg had pulled herself up off the top of the case, and, her tone altering, had said, 'I'm sorry; I didn't know.'

'No; well, there's no reason why you should, or that my second lad is in minesweepers, and Katie and Carol are in the WAAFS, and my young Fred's a mechanic in the Air Force, and Nancy, me youngest, she's with a concert party somewhere, making the lads laugh. She could make a corpse laugh, that one. Well,' – he had turned back to address Lizzie again – 'wherever you're goin' I wish you luck, lass,' and she said softly, 'Thank you, Mr Honeysett, and . . . and for your kindness one way and another over the years.'

'Aw, lass, whatever I've done for you has been nowt compared with what I've done and am doin' for others and likely get a kick up the backside for me pains in the end. Anyway, good luck to you, and to you, Mrs Meg.'

'Thank you, Mr Honeysett. I'm sorry I was sharp. I feel sharp this mornin', upset, like.'

'Aye, I understand. May I ask now if you're bound for Shields?'

'No, no; we're not.'

'Oh, well then.' He had looked fully at Lizzie, saying, 'In that case, give Mr Richard my regards. A nice fellow, Mr Richard. No trace of the joker there. Good luck to you both.' Then taking up the handles of his flat cart, he pushed it away, leaving them both staring after him.

Meg said, 'How could he know where we are goin'?'

Lizzie had hitched the child from one arm to the other before she answered, 'He's cleverer than people make him out to be, in fact he's cleverer than most around here.'

'Funny, but I never liked him.' Meg had pursed her lips. 'I thought he was sly, but the way he just put me in me place, givin' me the list of his family, I feel I've sort of misjudged him. He was likely brought up to pinch and scrape. It's second nature to him. But' – she turned and looked at Lizzie – 'what did he mean about Mr Richard not being a joker?'

Yes. What did he mean by that? But if he turned out to be one in this case, he would be an unconscious one.

She had the desire to cry . . . not burst into tears, but just to cry quietly.

319

The woman's voice broke in on her thoughts again, saying, 'We were thinking of having a little celebration this weekend; a party, with a few friends in. I'm glad you've come. You'll enjoy it, I'm sure.'

As Lizzie looked at the woman's profile she saw that behind all her chatter she was tense. Did she sense her as a rival? Well, she needn't. No, she needn't. She would stay for a few days and then she would go back to Shields with Meg. She recalled that she had left the pram and three cardboard boxes of bits and pieces in the outhouse. She had got in touch with the Bramleys last night and asked them to pick them up whenever they would be coming this way, which could be next week or next month, or weeks ahead; it all depended. Anyway, she could phone and re-direct them. That's all there was to be done.

'Aunt Edith and Uncle James are so excited about your coming; they are dying to see the baby.'

So it was Aunt Edith and Uncle James. Of course she would have to give them those titles, she supposed, having known them since she was a child.

She again looked at her profile. The head was held high, the shoulders pressed back. She could see her tramping the moors, climbing the mountains, riding to hounds. Oh yes, she would fit in at The Hall. She was born for it. Oh dear God! She wished she hadn't come. She again thought of Ted and his reference to the joker. But the joke seemed to be on her, and it was painful, more than she had imagined possible.

She had loved Andrew and her love for him was still very deep within her. But she had never imagined her liking, her deep liking, for Richard could harbour the seeds of another love, but overnight they seemed to have sprouted. Yet, not really overnight. How often over the months had she contrasted his ways with Geoff's? How often had she hoped he would get on the phone so that she could hear his voice and talk with him for a few moments? And why, when she visualised him and saw him as he really was, instead of being put off, did she want to go on looking at him? She should have recognised the signs with Geoff, for she was supposed to be such a sensible girl, but she recognised the signs here all right. This woman driving the trap was in love, deeply so, so much so that she was afraid. Well, she needn't be.

When at last they bowled up the drive and to the front of the house, there, as if they hadn't moved since the last time she saw them, were James and Edith. And the first thing Edith did was to take the child from her arms and cradle it, cooing over it, between exclaiming, 'Oh! how nice to see you again, Lizzie. And . . . and this is Meg. May I call you Meg?'

'You may, ma'am.'

It was a long time since Meg had ever called anyone 'ma'am', but she recognised a lady when she saw one. And when James took hold of her hand and shook it as if he were going to take her arm off, the while saying, 'Had a good trip?' she answered between gasps, 'Fine. Fine, sir . . .'

'Come along then; get yourselves inside.'

As they all made their way into the house, Jean McKenzie called from the drive, 'I'll just settle the horse and give him a feed.'

Inside the hall, there stood Phyllis, and she greeted Lizzie with, 'I'm so glad to see you again; I am that, I am that.'

'Thank you, Phyllis. I'm glad to be here.'

'Cook's done a special batch of bannocks for you.'

'Oh, that's nice. Thank her. Anyway, I'll see her shortly.'

'Come on, come in. Get your things off, and sit down. And what about that tea?' James had now turned to Phyllis. 'Stop gaping at the child; you'll frighten it with your mouth open like lock gates. Fetch in the tea.'

Meg had stopped in the act of unpinning her hat while this exchange was going on. And when Phyllis nodded at her, muttering, 'That's him, showing off,' she let out a high laugh that brought them all looking at her. Then they were all laughing, and Edith said, 'Oh, Meg; you'll get used to these two before very long. We have our own private war going on here, you know. There's never been an armistice; no let-up in hostilities. Come along in.'

Now divested of hat and coat, Meg stood in the drawing-room doorway and gaped, and only went forward after a slight nudge from Lizzie, and during the next ten minutes of cross-talk, she never opened her mouth. All she did was let her eyes roam as far around the room as they would without her turning her head too much, because, as she understood it, it was very ill-mannered to look about you in another person's house. But this place was something she had never even imagined. She had seen nothing at the pictures to compare with it. And those two folks chatting away to Lizzie, they seemed so ordinary. They

322

could be like anybody next door, except for the tone of their voices, which was different.

When the door opened and the young woman put her head in, shouting, 'I'm going to clean up. He was in a tear for something or other, so he kicked the mash over. He's missing Matty, I suppose . . . Was there a phone call?'

'No. No, nothing yet, dear.'

When there was a quick exchange of glances between the two elderly people opposite, Lizzie detected a touch of anxiety there, and she wanted to say, it's all right. It's all right, and I understand. The woman, she thought, was likely expecting Richard to phone to tell her what time to meet him as she had earlier met them.

Edith was saying now, 'We've sorted out the rooms at short notice: we've put Meg next to you for tonight, but perhaps later on she may like to be near Phyllis and Mary. There's a nice little annexe there; it only wants airing. Still, we'll go into that later.' She was nodding at Meg now; then as the door opened she said, 'Ah, here's the tea. Help Phyllis, James, will you?'

'Don't see why I should. Don't see why I should.'

As James lumbered to his feet, Lizzie looked at Meg. Her face was bright with astonishment at the situation. She could imagine how she would fit in here. She would love the sparring and would join in, but with diffidence, for she was obviously still overawed, not only by the house, but by James and Edith. Meg's word for them would have been gentry. And that's what they were: gentry. And only a few hours ago, she had imagined spending her life with them and learning, for she knew she was ignorant of so many

323

things. Again she had the feeling she wanted to cry quietly.

And this feeling persisted during tea; and when, later, she was settled in her room and Edith knocked gently on the door and came in for a quiet chat, the moisture came into her eyes as she told Edith briefly about the situation she had left behind.

When Edith said, 'But I understood Mr Fulton had asked *you* to marry him; Richard said as much,' she shook her head and answered, 'But not in words, Edith, not in words. He gave me to understand that that is what he intended. Anyway, you see I couldn't have stayed there, could I?'

'No, my dear, no. Never. Never.' The voice and words were emphatic. 'An impossible situation. And that person! She is, and always was, a hot-headed, impetuous, loose individual.'

Lizzie smiled weakly as she said, 'One of the first things Geoff stated and with emphasis was that she was no longer any of those things, and that I would get on with her.'

'Never! Never!'

'That's what I said, never! never! Anyway, Meg's got a nice little house in Shields and . . .'

'Now, we'll discuss that later. Let's get Richard back and then we can have a talk. I'm going to leave you now to have a little rest. Dinner will be in an hour. You lie down and rest with the baby. Was her bottle all right?'

'Yes. Yes, thank you.'

'Oh, Cook was delighted to think that there was a baby in the house. It makes a great difference when there's a baby in the house. Now do as I say, my dear, and have a good rest. We'll see you at dinner and do some more talking later.'

More talking later. Talking would be futile. Even if that young woman turned out to be an angel, she still couldn't see herself staying in this house with her married to Richard.

When Meg knew she was expected to sit down to dinner with the host and hostess, she quietly put it to Lizzie that she would be far happier in the kitchen with them two. Could she arrange it without upsetting them in there? Her thumb had pointed over her shoulder. And so, Lizzie arranged it. And now dinner was half over and Lizzie, sitting opposite Jean, wished she would stop chattering for a moment, because she was jumping from one topic to another. Then, of a sudden, she became still as the sound of the telephone could be heard ringing distantly in the hall.

Glancing from one to the other, Jean said, 'Will you excuse me?'

'Yes, yes, my dear. Go on.'

Lizzie watched her actually run down the room, and when the door had closed on her she saw Edith sigh as if she were tired. And she thought, Jean's wearing her out already. What would it be like if she lived here with her? But then Edith loved her son and she would put up with anything to make him happy.

The conversation lagged and they continued eating for some minutes in silence. And then the door burst open, and there she stood, this tall, good-looking girl, her expression transformed, and the look of delight on her face brought pain to Lizzie's heart, so ecstatic and full of love did she appear. She did not speak, but moved up to the table. And she stood there, her hands gripping the back of the chair, her head bowed for a moment, then she brought her laughing face up as the tears spilled from her eyes. James, raising himself up from the chair, went to her and placed his arm about her and said, 'I told you. I told you. Nobody could sink George.'

Lizzie watched Jean press her face into James's shoulder for a moment before she looked at Edith and said, 'I . . . I actually spoke to him. They . . . they haven't lost a ship, nor one man. They were strafed, but took no casualties. Wonderful! Wonderful! And he'll make it here for the weekend. Just think, he'll make it, Aunt Edith.' Impulsively, she kissed Edith on the cheek, and Edith put up her arms and held her face in her hands for a moment, saying, 'We're as relieved as you, my dear. I know we kept saying that no news is good news, but it's proved to be right.'

Jean now turned to Lizzie and said, 'You must think I'm some giddy goat. I've not stopped talking since you arrived. You see, George, my husband, has been away for months and I've not had a word from him, and . . . and although there was no report of a sinking, still . . . well, you understand. I'm sorry I've jabbered, but . . . but we got word two days ago that they might be in. A friend slipped us the tip, but I've not been able to stop talking since.'

'Sit down, sit down, and finish your meal,' James said. 'All this excitement about a mere captain. Now if he was an admiral, or Churchill's aide, or Eisenhower's second-in-command, but what does anybody want to bother about a mere captain for? And with a name like George.'

This should have caused at least a tinkle of laughter, but instead the others at the table looked at Lizzie with concern, because, her head bowed, her face held in her hands, she was crying, not quietly as she had wanted to do for days now, but loudly, sobbing openly, and howling uninhibitedly.

When they helped her from the table and into an easy chair, Edith said sharply, 'Get some brandy, James,' while Jean was saying, 'Have I caused this with my histrionics?'

'No, no. It's just reaction. She's been through a great deal, and . . . and you know the baby is only a few weeks old. And she had a bad time, with it, I understand. She's . . . she's worn out. Let's get her to bed.'

'No, no.' Lizzie aimed to get control of herself as, gasping, she said, 'I'm . . . I'm sorry.' Then through her tear-stained eyes, she looked up at Jean, saying, 'It . . . it is because your husband is safe.'

But, of course, it was not only because Jean's husband was safe, but that she *had* a husband and that it wasn't Richard.

'I'll be all right. I'm . . . I'm terribly sorry.'

'Nothing to be sorry for, girl. Drink that.' The glass was thrust under her nose. And when she sipped at the brandy, she coughed and spluttered, and James remarked, 'It hurts me, that: women always splutter over brandy, wasting half of it. Too good for women I say, brandy is.'

'Shut up! James.'

'All right, my dear, all right. Just trying to . . . to . . .' He moved away. And now Lizzie, lying back

327

in the chair, wanted to laugh. She wanted to laugh as loudly as she had earlier cried, except that she thought her laughter might become hysterical. She had to keep a grip on herself. So much had happened in such a short time. But Richard . . . well, Richard could still be hers. She only had to wait until he arrived.

It was a quarter-past eleven when Edith greeted her son at the front door. She had heard the truck rumbling on to the drive and she had left Lizzie in the drawing-room, saying, 'Don't go up yet, dear. That's Richard now. He'd love to see you.' And at that she'd hurried out of the room. And there she was now grasping her son's hand, while at the same time tapping her lips with her finger as she drew him across the hall and into the morning-room.

'What is it? What's the matter?' he asked her anxiously.

His voice was a whisper and she replied, 'Take off your coat.'

'Well, give me a chance to get in. What's the matter, dear?'

'Oh, lots of things are the matter. You've only been away thirty-six hours and the world's turned upside down.'

'Jean? She's heard that George . . . ?'

'Yes, she's heard, not "that George", but "from George". He's safe and sound in Portsmouth; he'll be up at the weekend.'

'Oh, good, good. Now she'll stop doing her Saint Vitus's dance every time the phone rings. So . . . what is it?'

'Lizzie's here.'

'Lizzie?' His eyelids blinked, the round one narrowing, and he repeated, 'Lizzie? Why?'

'Let me sit down a minute.' She pulled a chair from under the table and lowered herself into it, saying, 'All this excitement will give me a heart attack before the night's out. Well, now, I'll give it to you in brief; in her own good time she will likely give it to you in full. She's as good as been turned out of the house.'

'What!'

'Now, wait for it. Your former wife is intending to re-marry.'

'Well, that doesn't surprise me.'

'She is marrying the man you told me was planning to take on Lizzie and her child; the Fulton fellow.'

'Geoffrey Fulton? It can't be. He . . . he told me himself.'

'No matter what he told you, or what impression he gave you, as Lizzie has already told me, he was using her. Apparently, whether you knew it or not, he and Janis had an affair going from when she was at school, by all accounts. Her father threw him off the estate. That's why he joined the army. Anyway, he seems to have taken up where he left off, and it must have been going on for months. But from what I can gather and read between the lines, she is certainly not heartbroken over him; I mean, Lizzie isn't; but she looked upon the house as a home and she had a child to bring up, and she couldn't see any other way out. You see, Richard' – she now wagged her finger at him – 'nobody else has offered to marry her.'

'Now, Mother, Mother, that still stands. Don't get ideas into your head.'

'It's impossible for me to get any more ideas into my head, Richard, than there are already.'

'Mother. I'm not asking the girl to marry me, and that's flat. I'll be her friend; I'll do whatever I can. Don't you see, can't you see the position I'm in? And look at her, she's a beautiful girl, full of life. She deserves . . .'

'Yes, she deserves a good man, and a good home, and they're both here. Don't be stupid, Richard.'

He turned from her, saying, 'It's no use, dear. You must believe me when I say that I couldn't ask Lizzie, or for that matter, anyone else to marry me.'

'All right, ask her to live with you in sin, only don't let her go out of your life. I'm . . . I'm going to bed. I'm very, very tired. What with Jean and her understandable nerves these past few days, and now this, it is almost too much for me.'

'I'm sorry, dear.' He turned and took her by the shoulders and, bending forward, he kissed her on the cheek. And at this she put her hand up and touched his scarred face, saying, 'Oh, my dear, my dear, please be sensible for me, be sensible.' Then, shaking her head, she walked towards the door; but there she turned and said, 'She's in the drawing-room. Say good-night to her for me.'

He paused a long moment before he pushed open the drawing-room door, and there, seated between the glow of the table lamp and the flames of the bright wood fire, he saw her. His voice light, he hurried up the room, saying, 'Hello, Lizzie. This is a surprise; but a very, very pleasant one. My dear, I am pleased to see you.' He held out his hands to her.

She had risen from her chair, and she took them in hers and said quietly, 'Hello, Richard.' Then matter-of-factly, she asked, 'Have you had a nice trip? I . . . I understand you have been buying cattle.'

'Oh, that. I bought a few, but I was a little late in getting there, and the best had already gone. Anyway, how are you?'

'Fine now. Your mother has told you?'

He turned and looked towards the couch, then drew her to it, and they were seated side by side before he said, 'Given me the gist of it. I'm . . . I'm amazed. He told me he intended to marry you . . . well, that his intentions were that way. I cannot believe that he has been such a fool. And to take up with . . . with Janis again, after all that had transpired.' He shook his head. 'It must have come as a shock. Do you feel very hurt?'

'Not in the way you mean, Richard. Angry, yes. I . . . I almost hit him.' She smiled. And at this he said, 'You should have done, and with something hard.'

'It was hard enough. It was a bronze statuette.'

At this, his thin lips spread from his white teeth, and he laughed aloud as he said, 'I can't imagine you wielding a bronze statuette.'

'You'd be surprised.' Her face straight now and her tone quiet, she said, 'Can you understand why, in the first place, I was considering him? You see, it was the only home I knew. And then there was the child, and then there was someone else whom I cared for.'

'Someone else?'

'Yes,' she nodded, 'but . . . but he hadn't asked me.'

'Well, he was a fool, then.'

'Oh, I wouldn't say that.'

'Does he know of the predicament you're in?'

She nodded: 'Yes, yes, he knows,' she said.

'And he hasn't done anything about it?'

'No, no.' She shook her head, her eyes cast down now. 'You see, I overheard a conversation he once had with his mother, and I think she would have liked him to ask me to marry him, but he said he wouldn't.' She raised her eyes. 'He said he would never ask me.'

She watched him now close his eyes tightly and drag his teeth over his scarred lower lip, as she went on, 'So there's nothing for it but for me to say to him: will you marry me, Richard?'

He bowed his head but he didn't speak. And her voice soft and with a deep plea in it, she said, 'Please, please, Richard. I . . . I didn't know that I loved you so much until I was met at the station by Jean, and she talked about you all the way. I imagined you and she were going to be married. It was then I knew that this feeling I had for you was something strong, stronger than anything I'd felt before. I loved Andrew, but that was the young girl in me. There'll always be a love in me for Andrew because of his child, but the feeling I have for you, Richard, is that of a woman, an adult woman.'

'Oh, Lizzie.' She felt his whole body tremble as he fell against her and buried his face in her neck, and she held him tightly until he pressed her away from him and, his eyelid blinking rapidly, he stared at her and said, 'Take a close look, Lizzie, a very close look. I'm really never going to be much different from what I am now. Yes, they've straightened the eye and the mouth a bit, and they're now working on my ear, but the scars will remain, the drawn tightness will remain. I'll never be able to look at you with two eyes wide open. So, Lizzie, take a good look.'

'Oh, Richard, don't be silly. I've looked at you again and again right from the first moment I saw you, and I see the scars. I see them all. But I also see what's behind them. It's odd,' – she smiled faintly – 'but I can't imagine you looking other than you do, and it is as you are that I love you. I do, I do, Richard, I love you.'

'Oh, my dear, my dearest. Oh, Lizzie, Lizzie.' He was holding her tightly now, his head still buried on her shoulder.

When she pushed it away from her and now held his face between her hands, she looked into his eyes for a moment before slowly placing her mouth on his and, as if being injected with an electric charge, he responded, so fiercely that for a moment she felt she would choke for want of breath.

When the kiss ended he leaned back on the couch, his arms slack and resting on his thighs, his head drooped forward, and now he muttered, 'Forgive me, I'm like a bull at a gap. It's . . . it's been so long, and . . . and I've thought of you so much. I'll try and not act the wild man again.'

She now moved nearer to him and laid her cheek against his and, his arms going round her, he held her gently now, saying, 'I can't believe this, you know, I can't believe it. I'll wake up in a moment and know it was another dream. I have dreams at the opposite ends of the poles; I'm either making love to a beautiful woman,' he pressed her to him now, 'or I'm screaming blue murder as I roll about in the bed, clutching my head, and my mother and father are trying to wake me up . . . Are you prepared for some sleepless nights? Because they'll likely still come, those dreams, but not the beautiful woman ones,' he smiled at her.

'Don't worry; I'll deal with them both. If it's a beautiful woman dream, I'll slap your face, but if it's the others, I'll keep a bucket of cold water by the side of the bed, because if you start yelling, you're sure to wake the baby.'

'Oh! the baby.' He sat bolt upright. 'I'd forgotten clean about the baby. What do you call her? You said you were going to call her after your mother, didn't you?'

'I call her Jane.'

'Has she been baptised yet?'

'No. So now I'll call her Jane Edith.'

'Yes, Jane Edith Boneford, because she'll be my daughter from now on. Andrew would have liked that.'

'Thank you, Richard.' Her voice was soft.

'Oh, never thank me for anything, my dear, because right to my dying day, I'll thank God for you. I've never been a praying man, but whatever God there be, I'll pay homage to Him, because you've made me feel a human being once more . . . oh, Lizzie. Lizzie.'

THE END

THE TINKER'S GIRL
by Catherine Cookson

Close to her fifteenth birthday, Jinnie Howlett, a reluctant inmate of a northern workhouse, is offered a position as a maid-of-all-work. Jinnie's employers were to be the Shalemans and her place of work Tollet's Ridge Farm, a bleakly isolated farm near the Cumbrian border.

Before long, however, she was to discover she had exchanged one kind of drudgery for another, for the Shalemans – Rose, invalid wife of Pug and mother to Bruce and Hal – demanded much of her and she decided that if it had not been for Bruce's willingness to defend her against the taunts and harassment of the brutish Pug and Hal, she would have gladly returned to the house, as she called it.

Then she became acquainted with Richard Baxton-Powell, who owed his life to Bruce, but eventually his over-familiarity made her realize that despite everything her future would owe more to the Shalemans than any outside influence.

0 552 14038 4

A SELECTION OF OTHER CATHERINE COOKSON TITLES AVAILABLE FROM CORGI BOOKS

☐ 14624 2	BILL BAILEY OMNIBUS	£7 99
☐ 14609 9	THE BLIND YEARS	£5.99
☐ 14533 5	THE BONDAGE OF LOVE	£5.99
☐ 14531 9	THE BONNY DAWN	£5.99
☐ 14348 0	THE BRANDED MAN	£5.99
☐ 14156 9	THE DESERT CROP	£5.99
☐ 14705 2	THE GARMENT & SLINKY JANE	£6.99
☐ 13685 9	THE GOLDEN STRAW	£6.99
☐ 14703 6	THE HAMILTON TRILOGY	£6.99
☐ 14704 4	HANNAH MASSEY & THE FIFTEEN STREETS	£5.99
☐ 13300 0	THE HARROGATE SECRET	£5.99
☐ 1470i X	HERITAGE OF FOLLY & THE FEN TIGER	£6.99
☐ 14610 2	A HOUSE DIVIDED	£5 99
☐ 13303 5	THE HOUSE OF WOMEN	£5.99
☐ 14700 1	THE IRON FAÇADE & HOUSE OF MEN	£5.99
☐ 13622 0	JUSTICE IS A WOMAN	£5.99
☐ 14702 8	KATE HANNIGAN & THE LONG CORRIDOR	£5.99
☐ 14581 5	KATE HANNIGAN'S GIRL	£5.99
☐ 14569 6	THE LADY ON MY LEFT	£5.99
☐ 14699 4	THE MALLEN TRILOGY	£7.99
☐ 13684 0	THE MALTESE ANGEL	£5.99
☐ 14157 7	THE OBSESSION	£5.99
☐ 14073 2	PURE AS THE LILY	£5.99
☐ 14155 0	RILEY	£5.99
☐ 14706 0	ROONEY & THE NICE BLOKE	£5.99
☐ 14712 5	ROSIE OF THE RIVER	£5.99
☐ 10541 4	THE SLOW AWAKENING	£5.99
☐ 14583 1	THE SOLACE OF SIN	£5.99
☐ 14683 8	TILLY TROTTER OMNIBUS	£6.99
☐ 14038 4	THE TINKER'S GIRL	£5.99
☐ 14037 6	THE UPSTART	£5.99
☐ 12368 4	THE WHIP	£5.99
☐ 13577 1	THE WINGLESS BIRD	£5.99
☐ 13247 0	THE YEAR OF THE VIRGINS	£5.99